# MG Hardie's

# THEM

MoorRey Publishing



ISBN-10: 0-9968296-3-6
ISBN-13: 978-0-9968296-3-2

The correct citation for this book is Them, United States, 2018.

www.mghardie.wixsite.com/moorrey-publishing

For Humanity
...to the end.

Rugged leather boots splashed, then trudged, through the reed torn, murky waters of the Florida swamp. He trudged through the firefly scattered darkness with Commotion closing in behind him. The undisturbed water that once reflected moonlight now revealed undulating troubles.

Now, barely panting and at full gallop, Devon Heathrow wondered how things could have gone so wrong so fast. How could a mistakenly delivered device lead to him being strapped down on an operating table in a remote, secret military base in Montana, and now running through a swamp that went God knows where with his clothes ripped and singed.

An electric buzz cracked nearby and snapped locomotive thought. His feet rapidly carried him over a row of logs, and then he leaped fifteen feet up into a pine tree. He hastily disappeared into the pines in a zig-zag pattern. The pricks from swaying branches and falling pine needles caused him to refocus his thoughts to overcome the feeling of the strange alloy inside his limbs.

No longer able to feel his heartbeat, he bit down on his lip to see if he still existed. He glided from tree to tree, lightly touching each branch—this kind of thing could go on forever. Thunder roared, and lightning lit up the night sky. He paused next to a sizeable black cypress tree to glance at the heavens and then the pattern continued…

He weaved in and out of the trees and jumped thirty feet into a distant white cedar without hesitation. The fate of the world hung on what happens next.

Life was simple before… Them.

# CHAPTER 1

Most people like to plan out their lives, school, career, marriage, children, and that big promotion. For Devon Heath row, life was simple until today. The day began like any other day.

While leaving the house for work, his 5'10" frame almost tripped over a small plain looking package that was under a shrub near his car. He casually inspected the unaddressed package.

He got into his black Chevy Camaro and opened the small box. Inside the box was a note that only read 'Nwhit' next to stylish glasses. Transparent graphene covered the lenses. He could tell by the sliders and buttons inside of the frame they were high tech.

The wearable computer optics was metallic blue and accented his brown eyes. They made his shoulders less narrow and his face more hansome. Devon had precise features, a lot of very soft black hair. He had a look of look of calmness which would change throughout the day. His smile had aroused feelings of warmth, and more, in many women.

There wasn't anything in the box to indicate where it came from or where it was going. He gently put the glasses back into the box, fired up his car, and started on his way to work. The weather is quiet and peaceful except for when the spring showers come.

Oaks, shrubs, Russell maples, and rusted twigs lined the well- kept gravel road that led to their driveway. Slender sapling rose in the shadow of trees. Along the road contorted branches thrust athwart and curved inward, creating a patched arched of leaves. Most days the sky threatened downpour, while lofty mountains loom in the distance.

In the mornings, the low hanging sun played a game of Hide and Seek along the fifteen-mile stretch of road. This game was always interrupted by dashboard lights and screens. The leaves on the road momentarily part as he sped past. In truth, he paid no attention to the trees, to nature or to the way his tires chewed up the gravel and spat it back out.

Devon kept his windows up and air conditioner on, this insulated him. He uttered a command and his entertainment system turned the volume up but still couldn't down out nature. Devon preferred the sounds of radio stations, jackhammers and honking horns to those of nature. He drove the same way to work and the same way back home.

On that brief stretch of road, his fuel hungry Camaro couldn't communicate with other cars. The drive to work was the part of his day he disliked the most. Before getting in the elevator, he always stopped at the downstairs coffee shop to get his usual double shot Frappuccino.

The smell of the hot beverage made him smile; the caffeine did nothing for him; he was immune to it. Devon wore fashion glasses that he didn't need, to fake intelligence he didn't have. He used the arm of eyewear to point decisively; he waved it like a magic wand.

The drive to work was like any other day a quick ten-minute trek through the country down a winding road lined with trees. Here there was little traffic and no flashing lights; it was peaceful. Three years ago, they got married and moved to the outskirts of the suburban sprawl. Sarah, his wife, welcomed the spring showers,

"Spring showers are cool and inviting," Sarah said. "Fall storms wash dirt and film off of everything, including minds." Sarah was the 5'4", light brown eyed love of his life. She was smart, funny and passionate. Sarah felt that raising a child in a natural setting preserves innocence and spurs the imagination.

The rhythmic and constant tapping raindrops provided summertime with sounds other than crickets and frogs. Often at night, a light veil of mist surrounded the Heathrow's home. Their small house was simple and uncluttered. It brought the couple solace, even with Devon's bouts of buyer's remorse, second-guessing and overactive thoughts.

He used to wear tight shirts to show off his muscles, but now what was left of those muscles needed to be hidden. He wore light-colored suits that subtly beckoned a person to be looked at.

His mind was comforted by the concrete, metal, and glass erections that protruded into the heavens. It was the buses and trains that crisscrossed the city that drew his imagination. He only wanted a promotion because he was tired of competing for parking spaces.

For Devon traffic jams and long lines were all about him, it was just that people by no fault of their own seemed to be in his way.

"I didn't want to mothball my video game collection. I wanted a condo, but Sarah has a way of making you see her point. I ran out of ideas to convince her otherwise," Devon told his therapist. That wasn't the whole truth. He still managed to smirk through three weeks of renovations.

Sarah was weary of cities that try to be everything to everyone. She railed against the taller buildings that housed shorter tempers and the ever-widening freeways that drove narrow viewpoints. Sarah had a particular dislike for elected officials that always seem to overspend. For her, too many people desire huge homes but never take note of the smaller families that reside in them.

She had her fill of sprawling metropolises, mass transit lines, and eight-lane highways. She was done with twenty-first-century cities that push the affluence inward and immigrants outward.

In those cities, if you look close enough, you could see the unshielded poor. They could not hide from the supreme influence of the advertiser. Even in the wealthy suburbs, there are far too many people willing to become walking ads.

In those cities, throngs of people wait in line for the latest product intended to add more convenience to their lives, but somehow the result was a loss of time.

"How is it that people spent countless time earning more degrees, but gaining less sense? How could we build schools that promoted more knowledge, but less judgment? How can we live in times where people write more but learn less, where people learn to rush, and not to wait?" Sarah said last night as they lay in bed.

Sarah noticed that institutions of higher learning produce more experts but somehow managed to create more problems. Sarah would fluff out a pillow and mutter "I didn't take a hiatus from the N.W.F. so our daughter could be raised in a place where people have conquered the atom, but not their prejudices," and of course she was right as usual.

Moving to the outskirts was entirely her doing. This was her part to "balance out the equation" as she put it.

Her mother, Ann Dunnigan, was once a member of one-hit wonder singing group. Mrs. Dunnigan was beautiful, she liked Devon, and she was always smiling. John, her father, was a well-educated man and pretty good with a sidearm, at least that's what he told Devon. He was a big menacing looking fellow; well, he looked menacingly at Devon. He was a prickly man with pointed dislikes.

A retired aerospace engineer, he fixed problems. Beyond his densely packed way of speaking and the gold plated pens he carried, he was a man out of place in time. Devon had never seen him smile.

During commercials of sports games, her father would blurt out things like, "I don't know how we've managed to clean up the air and pollute at the same time."

It was no secret that Mr. Dunnigan didn't like Devon. Whenever the two were alone, he would show Devon his custom gun collection. Mr. Dunnigan would cock the revolver and say, "A mind is a terrible thing to waste."

"Here are the copies you wanted." Jennifer, the senior office secretary, said to Devon, handing him a stack of paper. Jennifer's overpowered perfume snapped him out of his daze; a daze he quickly fell back into. Jennifer always wore candy apple red heels and she always offered him coffee when he already had one.

Jennifer had been there for ten years, she was paid enough to care, but she didn't. Correcting her would only shatter his typical day, and it was best that she went back to gossiping. Each floor had a different smell to it.

He was in his cubicle before the clatter of noise enveloped the floor. In his cubicle, Devon would lose himself in the floating stock ticker stream. He was good at what he did, even though it was monotonous. Not everyone could manage these portfolios, show a profit, and somehow keep everyone happy.

In the cubicle next to him was James Hatwick. Devon rarely spoke to James. James tried hard not to work, he barely made his quote. Devon heard James complain to Jennifer about a different ailment every day. Today his muscles are aching, so he's telling her he has Lupus.

On Devon's desk were hundreds of papers with numbers and large lettering arranged in a grid. Devon didn't have the sharpest memory, so he consistently went over reports. Dozens of balled up paper surrounded the metal waste paper bin, with the basketball hoop over it.

Devon's cubicle was on the fourth floor, the last one in the fourth row on the left. It was one of sixteen cubicles, but the nearest to the window. He almost had a view of the city; a wall obstructed eighty percent of his view. The two photos on his desk were the only way you could tell it was his space. One was his wedding photo, and the other was of his smiling daughter, Brianna.

His desk was oversized; on each side were two undersized chairs that were situated to provide an unobstructed view of his broker of the month awards. A shiny computer sat on the mahogany desk. A small red teddy bear faced the corner as if it was on punishment.

At his desk, he eagerly touched screens as he read endless reports. His cubicle was the size of two small closets. Adding one more thing to this space would have cluttered it. No windows, no mini bar, no extras, and no new shiny title. Last month the boss met with all of the company's rising stars. The boss sipped on bourbon and told them that the Department Head position was up for grabs.

The boss didn't flash his practiced designer smile at Devon. Devon wasn't one of his favorite employees. Devon had a family, and it would be a few more years before he could jaunt off to bars after work and kiss ass like everybody else. He always arrived at least half an hour before the market opened. Once he sat down at his desk, it was go-go until lunch.

He made money; his team was always number one. Devon generally went home feeling good about his job. He made sure he got more work done than anyone else before he is pushing back from his desk. He frequently looked in the trash bin next to him because that where is career lay with the discarded papers. He should have had an office by now.

The weekly shoulder pat from department heads was no longer enough to sustain his dreams of advancement. Kisses from Sarah made him forget that his boss had excluded him from high-level client meetings. If he had any backbone, he would have taken the elevator ride up two floors, marched into the executive offices and demanded the promotion that was rightly his. His backbone, his strength was at home potty training.

Today his routine would be different; finding the package had made it so. Devon sat at his desk and appeared to be working. His mind was not on the ringing phone or thousands of trades that sat on the desk; possibilities dominated his thoughts. The glasses came with no manual and his mind brimming with possibilities, would it have a Head-Up Display, voice recognition, electro-optical presentations, motion control?

Sarah always made him a healthy lunch, which he supplemented with heaps of salt, sugar, and, of course, bacon. In the town square, the sky was clear as Devon checked his geo-synchronized watch. He sat down at a small café and ordered a latte. Removed the device from his jacket pocket, and after some fumbling, he managed to turn it on.

# CHAPTER 2

The device fit snugly on his face. It was sleek and cool to the touch. It brimmed with speech-powered technology. It had a dynamic holoscreen, a camera that focused instantly, tracked objects and people and it auto adjusted to various lighting conditions.

The lenses activated, and Devon looked around the courtyard, the floating heads-up readout flashed "Not Them." Devon managed to turn off the readout, and he smiled as he surfed the web with his eyes. He was so busy gesturing, stroking floating keys, playing music, watching cat videos that he didn't notice the newly blowing wind or the darkening sky.

"Call Sweetheart..." Devon said and the device called Sarah.

"Hello, how is work?" Sarah said.

"The same as always." "You seem distance."

"What's Bri-Bri doing?"

"She's taking a nap, waiting for her daddy to come home..." "Do you have on those black spandex pants that I like?"

"I do. How did you know?"

As Devon spoke to Sarah, the lens produced a three-dimensional image of her sitting in the lotus position. The subtle sweet fruitiness of her jasmine scent surrounded him. Devon slowly cocked his head to the side as he did whenever he thought about her.

Devon fancied himself with the latest gadgets. His guilt about opening the box disappeared as he used it. He was sure that no one else had a device like this.

"Why aren't you in your office?"

This caused Devon to spilled coffee on his shirt. "Damn it!"

He finished the conversation with his wife. He pressed the floating end button and simultaneously, two large, grainy, shadowy men who were in the courtyard faded from view in a visual ripple. This was worthy of a double-take.

Devon hurried back to his cubicle. He didn't eat lunch, but he refused to be late for face-to-face client meetings. The rest of the day dragged by slowly.

Later that evening while driving home, Devon put the device on and called his wife again.

"Call Sweetheart," he said. Immediately after he said this, the landscape slowly began to change, the sky darkened. Shrubs whipped around the road, Devon's eyes tightened as he and his wife spoke.

"I have something special for you this evening…" Sarah said. "Is that right…"

The tall trees began to sway, and from those trees, two dark, tall, well-dressed men descended into his path. Devon swerved into the adjacent lane, barely missing the two gentlemen. He swiveled his head back to yell, "Lunatics!"

"…is everything all right?"

"Yea…the weather is getting weird…"

Two miles down the same road, two men emerged from funnel clouds into his path. This time, Devon pressed down hard on the brakes, the car screeched to a halt. With the motor still purring, the two men approached Devon. At lunchtime, in the courtyard, he didn't notice the faint halo around them, this time he did.

Devon couldn't make out the red symbols that moved along their clothing. The device's facial recognition gave him nothing.

"Devon…Devon…are you there?" Sarah's voice queried.

Devon quickly pressed "End call," and the men faded away in a visual ripple. The running engine kept pace with his heart. He removed the device and stared off into the distance. He was confident that this incident and what occurred in the square were somehow related. Devon exhaled hard and checked his head to see if he were running a fever.

He placed the device in the backseat, gripped the steering wheel, pressed down hard on the accelerator and continued home. Once home, he hurried inside, leaving the device in his car.

"Baby, are you alright?" Sarah said.

"Yeah, there was just something strange on the road. I'm fine."

Sarah hugged him tightly; she could tell that he was troubled. As soon as Devon entered the house, Brianna stumbled over and hugged his knees, until he reached down and picked her up.

"Da-dees home…"

"Aww, baby girl…" Devon said, picking her up and kissing her on the cheek. Brianna was wearing a green dress. She was wearing a bib with "1st Birthday" printed on it in green lettering. She smelled like cinnamon and applesauce. Devon spun her around while she made flying noises. Sarah smiled at them from the kitchen.

"Bri… Bri… Did you miss daddy today?" "No," and she laughed

"You didn't…"

"No," followed by more laughter.

Her laughter stopped long enough for Devon to go to the bathroom. When he came out of the restroom, Brianna grabbed hold of his right leg, and she rode it into the living room. She ran to the couch, where she promptly fell and giggled.

"Where's the hat Nana made you?" "Nana…"

"You want to help daddy?"

Were it not for the fact that Brianna was Devon's daughter; he wouldn't have understood the saliva-producing, English laden babbling that passed for words that came from her mouth. Either way, he was pretty sure this is what she said.

Devon leaned over, and Brianna helped him undo his tie, then he lay on the floor, and Brianna crawled on his chest and patted him as she bounced, and bounced. Then she covered Devon's face with a pillow and then with all of her stuffed animals.

Sarah had made lasagna filled with ricotta, romano and mascarpone, a little basil, and parsley, topped with garlic bread crumbs. It was a bit burnt around the edges. This was her cure for any bad day.

After dinner, Brianna made gurgling sounds and played at his feet. He read nursery rhymes to her, and she fell asleep in his arms. He sat comfortably in his blue armchair, slightly cocked his head, and sighed as he studied perfection. His eyes trailed every nook and cranny of his wife.

"I'll put her in the crib," she said as she took Brianna into the nursery.

Sarah reentered the living room; wearing an almost see-through red nightgown. Devon slowly rose to hold her. 'Valentine's Fortnight' was his idea, 'Moan' day was hers. They kissed each other long, deep, and passionately.

Sarah went into the bedroom read a report and Devon, as usual, cleared the table and washed the dishes. He could have used the dishwasher, but he enjoyed washing the dishes, it was the least he could do. When he finished the dishes, he took out the garbage. Once he was outside, his mind filled with the day's occurrences.

There were times in his life where he was prone to fantasy; this wasn't one of those times. Night fell, and cold descended on the Heathrow's, secluded, three-bedroom house. Devon sat in his car, trying to make sense of these vivid hallucinations. The night was quiet.

Devon took the wrapper off a small pastry and lit an awful smelling cigar. The little confection wasn't authorized on his diet. "It must be vacation time," Devon sighed.

Just then, the device in the backseat started to hum. The sound froze Devon. He slowly looked into the rearview mirror. He saw the powerful green illumination on the device as it vibrated on the seat. Devon grabbed it, put it on, and said, "Hello…"

"Them are more than you'd imagine…" the voice said.

Devon pressed end and sank into his seat. He cupped his head with his left hand in frustration. The wind started to whip around his car. Caller ID on the device gave him locations from Guatemala to Siberia. He looked out the window of his car towards his house and noticed two large black crows perched on his stucco roof.

The hum of the device once again shattered the night's silence. Devon touched the device and yelled, "Who the hell is this!" "Them are more than you'd imagine."

"Them…who is them?" "Look up," the voice echoed.

Devon looked toward his house. His eyes panned up to the roof to where he saw the crows. He now saw two well-dressed men gazing down at him, their silver eyes glowing.

"Them…" the voice on the device cracked.

The men two stood up and dropped to the ground without so as much as a thud. Air vapor bellowed from their mouths as they approached.

"What, wa, wha, d, do, I do?"

"Press end and nothing will ever be the same."

Devon waved his hand over the floating end key; there was a subtle flash, and the large men vanished. Devon's heart felt as if it would escape the ribs that confined it. The device hummed again, and Devon nervously answered.

"Angels?" Devon asked. "No. Them!"

"The…Them… who are you?"

"That is of little importance… who you are, is all that matters." "I am Devon Heathrow from Greensboro."

"Are you not with the Whitman Foundation?"

"No. I live on Vermont Lane. What the hell is going on?" silence came from the device. Devon's chest erratically heaved up and down. He slowly filled his lungs with the poison from the burning cigar. He relaxed in his seat and said, "End call."

"You think you can end the call and everything is over? You have seen Them," the same voice from the device was now in the backseat of his car.

*How?* The thought was swallowed up in the middle of Devon's confusion.

Suddenly, his car doors unlocked, a large, cold hand reached in and firmly encircled his neck. Devon was pulled from the car and hurled into the side of his house. Devon's back slammed hard against the wall. The back of his head shattered the living room window. There was a snap, and from the agonizing pain, it was apparent that his leg wasn't the only thing broken.

The force of the impact and the pain shooting from his ribs indicated that he would not survive.

Devon's thoughts outran his screams of terror as he landed in the middle of the dirt driveway. Brianna was crying as the lights inside his home turned on. The smaller of the two creatures jumped over the house. Bleeding, Devon scrambled on his backside frantically in a futile attempt to get away.

"I am Him," said the figure, in the custom black bodysuit trench coat advancing toward him. Devon couldn't see the towering figure's face.

"Them placed addictive chemicals in your Swiss Roll," Him said, throwing the half-eaten pastry at Devon's face. "Them are everywhere, yet, nowhere…," Him said with his voice trailing off.

Him got closer; Devon saw his disfigured, almost ghoulish face. His eyes had a silver glow to them. His face was old, shriveled, yet he was grotesquely nondescript. Him wore a coat that had light symbols that move and stretch.

With one hand, he grabbed Devon by his throat and hoisted him ten feet into the air. The glasses urgently flashed a red 'THEM' across his eyes as life was choked from his body. Devon saw the muscles around Him's temples tighten, through his almost translucent skin.

Through excruciating pain, Devon squeezed out, "Are you one of Them?" With that question, Him tossed Devon thirty feet against the trunk of his car.

"Them are more than you'd imagine," he said as Devon's body came to rest crumpled underneath his car's exhaust pipe, his heart-rate slowed, and his body jerked as life left it. "All you have known has been done so as a sheep," Him said. The glasses fell from Devon's face as his eyes closed.

# CHAPTER 3

Devon's eyes snapped open. Water slowly dripped from a faucet unseen through the darkness. He squinted underneath the intensity of several operating lights. He tried to get up but he couldn't. He turned his head to shield his eyes from the brightness. Once the room stopped spinning, he lurched and tried to grab his throat. The suffocation, the icy choke was fresh in his mind.

Devon didn't know where he was. A steady obnoxious beep was heard in the darkness. In between monitor beeps Devon wondering if he was dead. He was on his back on an operating table, which was cold, hard and unforgiving to his backside, but there he was draped in a hospital gown…drip…drip… went the faucet.

"You think it was all a dream…" a towering figure in the darkness said. Devon flinched, but incisions made to side and legs made him wince. Nerve irritation caused his eyelids and facial muscles to twitch. His mind flashed back to the evening he spent underneath his tailpipe and the last thing he saw…was glowing eyes.

"I'm… not dead…" uttered Devon as nausea filled him.

"You were," said the shadowy figure. "I was able to get your heart beating and your lungs to fill with air. We are underground in Montana just north of Maelstrom Air Force Base. Yesterday a small cottage in Routt County, Colorado by Pearl Lake was engulfed by flames and Doctor Whitman is no more."

Devon's eyes adjusted to the darkness beyond the reach of the light; a wave of excruciating pain ran through him. It was apparent from his stiff and slow movements that some of his bones had been reset. There were strange black marks on his body, but the bruises on his thighs and forearms were hardly noticeable. His wounds were almost gone, but they still felt raw.

The room was stale, sterile, the blandness of the place suited Devon. He was just glad to be alive. It was the kind of place that, without trying to, made a person feel small, insignificant. Above the operating table was an empty viewing gallery; an operating theater where students were taught…another drip.

"Whitman microinjected me with his nexus serum during a training drill. The serum temporarily regulated my air intake and depleted my energy. Whitman's serum allowed me to dwell on this plane," said the figure.

"Nexus weakened me. I couldn't modulate my energy. I was visible and couldn't return. I was alone, scared, outcast. I was paralyzed by fear, and for the first time in my life, I had to think about where I was going to sleep, where my next meal would come from.

"That first night, I was exhausted, so I found a little plot of land to rest in. My first night on this plane was spent sleeping in a park. I stayed in a park filled with others who had no place to go. There, I was given a blanket and sustenance. It was barely what I required, but I witnessed kindness."

The shadowy figure wore a tattered jacket and worn pants and moved. He remained in the darkness; perhaps he was trying not to alarm Devon, but he failed because Devon was scared.

"In the daytime, I was shunned, so I remained hidden. The next night, I came out of the shadows and slept on the street, in front of a storefront. A disfigured outcast that could hardly speak, but I was given residence in a warm shelter. In this time, I have viewed passion, faith, and heartbreak.

"When humans aren't running around blaming others, they are quite special. There is something inside you, a gift of some sort. It has taken me almost a week to regain my strength. My time apart has allowed me to experience, to feel. I—I began to care, and then the waters came," the voice finished.

"The waters?" Devon said, clearing his throat, wondering what the power forward sized linebacker could be talking about.

"The waters came down my cheek and dropped warmly to the ground, and that's when I detected you." the voice said. As he spoke, Devon's eyes strained to look beyond the pale, military green walls On a large metal operating tray were all kinds of surgical instruments. Devon's white gold DNA wedding ring also sat on that tray, just out of the reach of his mind.

"My wife! My daughter! Where are they?" Devon said losing control of the volume of his voice as he struggled to get up, but he was a fly stuck like a spider's web.

"Lay back, relax." said the figure, pushing Devon back onto the table. The surgeon's touch was unusually firm.

"You were in my backseat," Devon weakly said feeling the tightness of the straps that held him in place.

"I was."

"Why didn't you help me? You could have warned me!"

Helping you would have revealed me. Your body was broken," He said, stepping forward. His hand held a syringe that moved with a green light. The needle and the unknown substance within it caused a new fear to strike Devon. Devon's eyes darted around the room, looking for a way to escape.

Looking into his surgeon's face, he couldn't tell if he was angry or not. His hands resembled long gnarled tree roots clutching the last piece of meat. Devon still struggled to free himself. The sizeable cold hand on the chest of the patient quieted these struggles.

The syringe was slid into Devon's right thigh and its contents injected. Devon felt something that could best be described as pain but was anything but. As the warmth moved throughout his body, the pain became a memory.

"Are you striking matches?" said Devon inhaling deeply.

"The process of coming to this plane turns our naturally sweet odor into a more distinct scent. Similar to what you call rotten eggs. Allow me to introduce myself; I am Ailden."

The surgeon's voice had a certain dispassion to it. Devon's eyes widened as his reaction teetered between terror and awe as his hand was split at the wrist without any blood dripping—.

"You are not with the Whitman foundation… do you even know who Doctor Whitman is?" "I…I…I've never met the man."

"At the risk of sounding nakedly self-serving, I have to start from the beginning then. Doctor Whitman was a brilliant scientist in the employ of the American government. Whitman was one of the few humans who of our existence. After his many creations, he was charged with creating an impervious metal. Whitman experimented with combining various alloys for years. He accidentally discovered a new substance—Hypernium.

"Hypernium stays a liquid as long as the temperature is kept at twelve hundred degrees Fahrenheit. Once that temperature is reduced, there is a ten-minute window, where the metal can be poured and molded. Once it cools, it can no longer be manipulated. On this plane, Hypernium occupies a spot on the periodic table that is yet to be determined. No crystallization and no observable molecular patterns.

"A single strand of Hypernium appears flexible; however, as you bend it, the stronger it feels. The more molecules there are, the stronger it becomes. Hypernium, in its solid state has proven to be almost impervious. Whitman discovered his research would be used in the building of killing machines, and he decided not to turn over Hypernium to the government."

While Ailden spoke, his eyes were full of tears. His behavior was subtly disarming as he spoke of governments and strange alloys, but Devon was bothered more by the constantly dripping faucet. Drip...drip... Devon could tell by the ever increasing tone that the drips had formed a little sink pond.

"This Whitman sounds like a smart guy," said Devon.

"The secret of creating Hypernium died with him, and there isn't much of it left. I am almost at full strength, while here I witnessed cruelty, violence, and apathy. I also bare witness of the transferable qualities of the human spirit.

"I'll tell you what I know. Energy surrounds us; it flows through us; it connects us. Your eyes have always lied to you; obviously, ten percent is too much. We will correct that," Ailden said, poking a long, cold index finger at Devon's face.

"Are you talking about the Illuminati, the Rosicrucians, the Skulls, shadow figures that run governments?" asked Devon, interrupting. Devon was slightly lightheaded from the smell of povidone-iodine. Ailden pressed down on Devon's abdomen, elevated a small laser scalpel, and began to cut. The lights above Devon seemed to intensify.

"Noooo," Ailden's disfigured face had an animated expression as he continues to speak of shadow organization and the multiverse.

Devon's mind remained on the drips that landed in the metal faucet basin. Each drip was a mortar shell exploding in his mind.

"Huh?" said Devon.

"Are you listening? We don't have much time."

Devon nodded his head in a half listening way. "You know the faucet is dripping..."

Ailden moved to turn the faucet off. "If this bothers you, the worlds are in more trouble than I thought."

"Well, I'm not following you. So, you are one of these beings and these beings are everywhere? What does the hell does that mean?"

Ailden came close to Devon's face and let out a subtle growl. Devon studied his pale, grotesque face. Ailden had large eyes that were sunk into their socket, an oblong shaped skull, and thin fingers. His movements seemed almost predetermined, deliberate. He was thin, and his abdomen had a slightly different skeletal structure. Ailden's breath was hot on Devon's skin.

"Haven't you, in all of your worthless life, ever wondered if only the wind was making automatic doors open?"

"I can't say that I have..." retorted Devon.

"Can I continue, or do you have any other questions?" "Ummm...what's with these strange names?" "Strange names..."

"He...Him... Violence..."

"To us they were known as Throne and Transition; you call them Isis and Hermes...how is that for strange?"

"Oh...continue"

"Dark matter does not have a gravitational or electromagnetic effect on light, so it can't be seen. My kind can only be seen with a sub-flux disturbance. This disturbance creates an opening in the fabric of ordinary space through which subspace protrudes. The device you received was a prototype created by Whitman. Here, your rules of physics don't apply to us. Here we can withstand extreme falls..."

"How about a nuclear blast?" Devon remarked sarcastically. "No, but that's not far off."

"All of this is just crazy. You're a psycho!"

"No, but I am a carrier," Ailden said, pulling out a clear piping tube and placing it into Devon's side.

"So, I guess guns are out of the question?" said Devon squirming.

Devon knew someone who had a lot of guns.

"Guns are old uncivilized relics from your plane; they have no effect on us." Ailden said.

"What planet are you from?" "Earth."

"Earth... but you're an alien," Devon said, shocked by the answer. Ailden quickly rotated the floating operating table.

"I wasn't always like this. I was normal once; all of my people were. Where I am from doesn't exist on any map, we have no military, no flag...We are Them."

As the electronic monitor beeped softly in the darkness, Devon watched dark lines spreading underneath his skin as if it were a cancer that had quickly metastasized throughout his body.

Devon heard the operating table read his vital sign as the surgeon shifted instruments around on the metal operating tray, the mix of sounds struck Devon with panic. Not the panic of fear, but the general kind of panic that is present when faced with uncertainty.

"Them…" was Devon's weary response.

"There have been rumors, stories, and myths created around the interactions between our two kinds. Your kind has pulled lore from our world into your own. Middle Earth does exist. Winged creatures that breathe fire do roam the plains; Leviathans lurk the depths as do many other things that bump in the night.

"Our cities are powered by fusion plants. Lasers strike a small fuel cell causing it to implode, to create fusion reactions. This powers the Dendrite panels that power our cities.

"Our streets and homes are made from Dendrite. Dendrite is a silver lined card, like your solar panels but far more efficient. Even with these minor adjustments, I am making to you, you wouldn't survive in my world, no human can." Ailden said.

He penetrated Devon's left thigh with a large, glowing object and the room filled with steam. Ailden finished the fluid transfer and removed the tubes from the patient. Devon felt feel the liquid making its way through his body; he felt heavy.

"We are all matter…"

"Wait…I know this one; matter takes up space or has mass – like an apple pie. I don't know what dark matter is."

"It's another type of matter."

"So, there are two types of matter…"

"It's all matter, most of it is dark! You humans exist in what's left over. There are fewer beings in dark matter. This causes those few beings to be different and more unique, while outmoded OMBs are weak and riddled with sameness."

"OMB's?"

"Other Matter Beings, such as humans. Whitman hurriedly sent out the package believing he was sending the device to another employee."

"How many of Them are there?" "Even I don't know that."

Devon closed his eyes and muttered under his breath. He hoped that this was all a terrible dream. When he opened his eyes, Ailden was silently staring at him with a stillness that was both friend and enemy.

"I guess that didn't work…" Ailden smugly said.

"An alien with a sense of humor, just what the Earth needs…umm yeah just stop! What do I have to do to make all of this go away?" "You are no threat!"

"Then, why tell me these things?" "Because you will be."

The operating table beeped out Devon's rising beta waves and el-elevated heart rate as Ailden continued to operate.

"Three percent of the human body, the brain, uses twenty percent of its energy. This energy creates heat; Hypernium will modify your frame. It will remove some of the temperature constraints which prevent humans from evolving.

"Enzyme and healing activities, neural transmitters, protein synthesis, all require energy. I am freeing you from environmental impediments by increasing your energy synthesis. Absent these you should become more intelligent; your focus should sharpen."

As a youth, Devon only had dreams of being either a connoisseur of fine junk foods or of being a competitive skipping champion; he wasn't prepared for this.

"Why me?"

"I can see that intelligence is needed sooner rather than later." "I just died, try being a little human."

Devon's body was being moved, prodded, and adjusted. He saw the steam and felt the heat, but couldn't see what was being done to him and that caused fear to emerge once again.

"What are you doing to me?" Devon asked coughing.

— Slice— Cut, Ailden continued to slowly pipe the bone-numbing liquid into each section of Devon's body.

"The same as a fly drowned in water brought back to life by salt. I'm giving you a chance. Your body was broken and in need of repair. I have transformed your body; it is up to you to reshape your mind. Your sense will naturally augment. You will feel disoriented, nauseated, but that will pass," Ailden added. "We do what we must."

Ailden put a small liquid crystal from himself into Devon's mouth and down his throat. The voice of the operating table simply said, "heart rate…not good."

Devon's neural scans resembled explosions in the sky. The lights once again intensified; Devon could only wrinkle his forehead. An exhausted Ailden leaned heavily against the operating table. Devon was unable to speak; in truth, Ailden preferred it that way.

Ailden applied soft cybernetic patches to stimulate the patient's muscles. The epidermal patches eavesdropped on the language of his internal systems and whispered brainwave data to the floating monitors that chirped in the darkness.

He lifted a multi-spectral imaging device and scanned Devon's body with it. The scan showed the bonding process was nearly complete. Devon could see and hear, but he couldn't move. Hypernium was versatile, elegant; Devon's cells didn't know they were bonding with an alloy. The scan made Ailden's lips form something that could pass for a smile.

"Hypernium molecules are bonding with your bones, but it appears that it is also bonding with the calcium molecules in your blood—interesting." As Ailden spoke, Devon's eyes could not hide his pain.

"Now, I can tell you that at this very moment, your wife and child are being buried. The job you loyally hurried to has been lost." He finished the scan and put the device on the table.

Devon closed his eyes, but the pain in his mind was increasing exponentially. Devon held his eyes closed, but could not force unconsciousness. Tears streamed down his face, and that was his only way of communicating. He placed his hand on Devon's side with the deftness of a surgical samurai and sliced open the patient's right leg, just above the femur.

# CHAPTER 4

Devon opened his eyes again; he was still strapped to the same operating table. His doctor was in the process of closing him and disposing of any leftover materials. His heartrate normalized as he wondered the why of it all.

This is the kind of thing that happens to people who blow off their studies in exchange for sex and drugs. This kind of thing that happens to a guy when his parents are murdered in front of him in a dark alley... not to someone like Devon. Whether or not Devon accepted what he was being told, Ailden felt it was necessary to fill his head with history.

"Throughout history, the Earth's pressure caused natural happenings such as volcanic eruptions large enough to create little riffs; these are bridges between our worlds. The Earth's core is a natural fusion reactor that produces significant volcanic eruptions such as Redoubt, Hikurangi plateau, Karoo-Ferrar, Krakatau; all were entry points for us.

Other ways of entry are naturally fluctuating magnetic fields, geomagnetic anomalies and the high frequencies seismic radiation produced by powerful earthquakes and massive asteroid impacts.

"Through these naturally occurring doorways my kind visited your spectrum—initially; we roamed among you only watching. As we travel between planes, we absorbed energy from these rifts.

"In the beginning, the light was separated from darkness. We were with you every day, yet unnoticed. The universe is a symphony, your world and mine are little more than the strings, keys, or notes on the page. Harmonious strings created the universe...all of this started by sound.

"Your dimension and mine overlap, conjoined if you will. We are sister worlds. Our worlds parallel, they mirror, and they share properties, such as gravity.

"There are entry points near large energy blooms. These are gateways for us to enter your world. The more people experiment with radiation, the more entry points we gain. Even on this plane, we are surrounded by radiation. It's everywhere from the three-day dose you receive from an x-ray to the three-year dose from an abdominal CT scan. Light itself is radiation; even intense light can damage the skin.

"Because of radiation, the cell phone towers were placed on mountains away from people, and now these towers are becoming more and more common in the suburbs. We use cell tower locations as entry points because of their abundance. Our bioelectric uniforms are the only thing to come through.

"The facial disfigurement you see is from my many times traveling through the divide between worlds. My kind hates your kind…"

Devon cleared his throat; he was once again able to speak. "My kind?" Devon asked.

"Yes, we have what your kind would call honor, but it's not just a word, a phrase you repeat to prove that you belong. What we share is more than a uniform emblazoned with lighted symbols. We are a brethren, each a comrade, each from a different affected city. Your kinds use and testing of high energy explosions affect life in my world."

"High energy explosions?" "Nuclear devices." "Nukes?"

"Yes, nukes. Humans test nukes underground to give the appearance that they are taking proper precautions; these tests create rifts in my world. These rifts rain radiation across my Earth. Your nuclear power plants have created sinkholes of radiation that appear in the black sand where our offspring play, in the fields where our food grows and on the streets where we live.

"This has caused disease and deformities to enter your world. The radiation we have absorbed causes the silver tint in our eyes. Some days our young cannot be outside unshielded, other days their eyes burn even while indoors.

"For years, decades, we didn't know that your kind was responsible for these rifts. Now, my mate curses humans every time our offspring's skin inflames, flakes, or peels. Human progress has forever altered our lives!

"I come from Madripoor, one of our largest cities. Elon 3, Ogacihc, Kroy Wen, Notcuoh, and Selegna Sol nearly all of our major cities have been affected. We come through the rift, but we must return before the gravity, the sounds you make, the air you breathe and your science infect us.

"We have watched magic turn into theorems, gyms replace arcades, and children become adults. We have witnessed the destruction, humans not only exacted on themselves but our kind as well. Our elders formed The Group, its mission clear, and now here you and I are, and the proverbial clock is ticking…"

Devon wiggled his toes, his fingers. For some reason that made Ailden smile. He unstrapped Devon and started to dress him the way a mother would do her child. He continued the bedtime story.

"Humans are creatures of habit, plodding along through time, eagerly looking forward to and trying to outrun the future, but rarely questioning the circumstances from the past which have set them on their present course. We have as many similarities as we do differences.

"I come from a place that is smaller, warmer—different. Our days are shorter, nights longer. Where I come from, we have two-trimester pregnancies. We live in harmony with nature and with each other.

"We have eliminated poverty and deprivation through fair distributing resources. We have abolished money. Our citizens only do work they enjoy and work that is for the common good. Most of the work allows us time to cultivate of arts and sciences. The tragedy is that we have done all of this only to have unfiltered radiation rain down upon us."

Devon's eyes began to glaze over. Not only did Devon not believe in any of this but to him, all of it sounded like complete gibberish. His knowledge of these things was based on movies and what he heard from Sarah while wolfing down his breakfast.

"All because of you!" "Not me…"

"You did this…"

"I didn't have anything to do with this."

"You have everything to do with it. All I have heard you say is me, me, me…You are just like all of the other miscellaneous yous. All you care about is how this affects you."

"Well, I'm not with them."

"You definitely are a part of the Yous." "How were we supposed to know?" "They knew!"

"I feel your pain," said Devon.

"How could you, human! I come from a place you could never understand. A place where education is government and politics was killed off many years ago. A place where there is still privacy. Where I am from, everyone is equal from birth, everyone is valued, and there is no discrimination.

"Every individual affects my world as a whole, the same as it does here. Only we are aware that one's actions effects society, in the same way, a splash ripples through a pond when a stone is thrown into it, with each splash pushing us closer or toward further imbalance. For us, justice isn't a byproduct of a system. Where I come from an individual's track record counts for something, and we do not waste fertilizer on weeds.

"My world is balanced, so natural occurrences are softer, less destructive. We rid ourselves of disease and crime. Once we rid our- selves of war, taxation was no longer necessary. We realized long ago that the more technology we garnered, the further away we got from knowledge, the more disconnected from one another we became.

"These realizations led us to choose simpler, obvious things, so our lifespans evolved. We don't have weapons in the way you think, and on this plan, we are the weapons. The actions we have undertaken have been done through a consensus and much consideration.

"We did not know that helping Ernest Rutherford would lead to this. Through the thoughtless actions of humans, generations of our offspring were deformed and mutated. We were unwarned and unprotected from the radioactive fallout.

"As a youth, I was inspired by simple things, the black grass, and the dark morning sky. I questioned everything; I was too young to conceive of this theatrical wrongdoing that occurs here in the netherworld. I was called to serve, like you, by accident" Ailden said as he adjusted Devon's vertebrate.

"Here is what you need to know to survive. We are only able to exist on this plane for short periods of time. Going through the doorway, we absorb energy. Once we spend our energies, we must return to our plane or cease to exist. Because of Whitman's serum…I presently hold the out of phase record. Dark matter doesn't come into contact with the normal matter…"

"But…wait, how did…" said Devon, rubbing his neck.

"Yes, you did feel him crushing your throat. We can use our abilities to manipulate elements; we can use air, fire, water, and the earth. There, now ocular scanners won't be able to identify you and you will no longer need a device to see Them," Ailden said continuing to adjust Devon.

"Our energy modulation makes us invisible to people. We absorb the energy required to complete our mission, as we breach the divide. You cannot detect these lower energies, but this signature is how we recognize our brethren. Our presence comes in two forms Males who utilize happenings while our counterparts Females who have a different gift.

"Happenings like landslides, tornados, floods, avalanches and freak downpours serve the purpose of our missions. The ensuing collateral damage from natural occurrences provides us with cover. When the moving ground reaches out and pulls someone in when the wind drops a roof on someone, when a wave drags someone under, when the earth opens up and swallows someone…there is no answer to the questions why.

"Carbon dioxide and burning fossil fuels warm the planet putting it out of balance. Natural events are the Earth's only mechanisms to maintain balance, we simply guide them."

"So now you cause hurricanes…?"

"Sometimes," Ailden laughed. "A slight temperature increase can cause calamity. These things occur naturally, and millions are affected by them, so our missions are never noticed.

"Females, our counterparts don't have enough energy to breach the divide in a destructive way, they can move things like keys, cause a cell phone to ring, lock and unlock doors or knock a book off a shelf; they whisper into minds. Females can guide, but can't control thoughts, but over time, they can change actions.

"Only fools think they are safe against the most incredible and destructive forces of nature, but people survive the suddenly moving earth, the raging fires, and the swirling air, but not many survive heartbreak. Any of these events can make a person stay on a particular path or change their path."

"And you make people commit crimes…" replied Devon.

"We are above that. The youngest of you are more in tune with nature and are thus easier to communicate with. A child that has visions of the future or death is not the kind of thing a parent is proud of.

"Those people are labeled kooks, conspiracy theorist, and charlatans. Their minds brimming with ideas that aren't their own. These actions torment the weak, empowering the strong.

"Too much manipulation and people become unable to discern between facts and conjecture. People think they wield power, they believe that they command it, they become arrogant, and as a result, we are often the fulfillment of that arrogance.

"Your decisions change every day on a whim or a sound, so our participation is unnoticed. Our tools appear as chance, fate, and random acts.

Some are small nudges, and others are large pushes. People are too busy, too self-absorbed to bother with the details.

"Humans don't notice how those among them take the minerals and leave behind a pile of paper, paper that is given an arbitrary value. This paper is the mortgage of wealth backed by guns, missiles, and bombs. To those in power, this paper is a legal check drawn on an account that is theirs to command.

"If people cannot see what is right in front of them, how can they even hope to understand Them?"

"So, while you are causing these 'happenings' do you ever feel remorse? What if someone has a family? What about the good a person might do?"

"At a moment's notice when no one is looking, people drop their morals, rules, and codes. In their last moments, they reveal themselves. The look in their eye at the exact moment when they know the twisting whirlwind means certain death isn't treachery—it's fear," He said, rotating the table and continuing to adjust Devon.

"Under Nixon, these systems flourished. It was the first time the media was extensively used to distract and create narratives for people to follow while we, in The Group, solidified our ranks.

"How old are you?"

"In terms of time, we can exist for hundreds of years. Let's just say that we aren't carbon-based. We are all nationalities, and we loathe coming to this netherworld. I wish that I could say that I will be here to help you, but Them will be sent after you as surely as a breeze does not miss a leaf. They will come fast, and they will be ruthless."

Ailden's voice started to echo. Devon squinted blinked as his storyteller flickered in and out of view.

"Devon, you must steel yourself, focus on my voice," Ailden said while hooking a device to the base of Devon's skull. "For me, there will be no salvation. Right now, in this world, the enemy must be defeated."

"Who is the enemy?"

"Them is! You will have to learn, see, and hear for yourself. My energy has almost returned fully." Ailden suddenly stopped talking and looked around as if he had heard something.

"I have done many wrongs; this I do today is the correction of those wrongs. Whitman was right; there is something special about the human spirit, something that is transferable. I have felt it..." Ailden finished.

"I don't know what you did, but you are no longer disappearing..."

"Quick adaptation—good. Them are everywhere, yet, nowhere…

They will find you as surely as you have been marked by School Lunch Programs. This is all the guidance I can give to you. You must go as I have done, as Whitman has done and find a way."

Devon sat up on the table and breathed out as if he was exhaling all of the week's occurrences.

"He'll be the best of us—" Ailden said as he stepped back into the shadows. There was a flash of light, a fading buzz, and then unconsciousness.

# CHAPTER 5

Angry bird chirps let him know that he was now awake. Devon found himself lying in a large barn, barely covered by hay. How he got there and how long he had been there was unknown.

What he did know was that any indications of any procedure to remove and reattached his limbs was not evident. He only felt some joint and muscle soreness in his ankles and chest. The incisions around his joints appeared as small scratches, the only thing remaining was a lingering headache.

The red barn had to be at least sixty years old, the farm it sat on was even older. The barn was well kept; no animals were inside, just old shoeing equipment, lots of seed, and fertilizer. Devon rubbed his eyes and examined his hands and arms for the dark lines. He looked for any trace of the procedure that bonded his bones with an alloy. He pressed down on his legs and examined his wrist, his abdomen, his face, his chest.

His worry extended beyond the cellular ink use to restore him; the visible spectrum was continually fluctuating. His vision was erratic, infrared, compressed ultraviolet, normal. He kept his eyes closed to offset the effects. He sat there until his head stopped spinning. Once his visual randomness subsided, he was able to stand.

Devon did not know where he was, or how he got there. He felt uneasy, and as he walked, he was unable to steady himself. He failed to keep his mind off his family, his friends, and his life. Overcome by grief, Devon loudly sobbed while he stumbled around the barn. He stared blankly at the floor. The sting of the operation had worn off.

*A hovering operating table…had to be a dream…*

The choking, the operation—all of it couldn't have been an accident, and why would some scientist he never met choose him? Would there ever be an answer to any of this?

Devon calmed himself. He picked up a small handful of straw pondering the quiet simplicity of being yellow like straw. As he did, he noticed that his hand slowly started to change color. Devon's nerves shot through him as if he were a bouncing knee. His hand had changed to a dull yellow hue.

The skin is the largest organ of the human body; this organ once functioned as natural camouflage. The skin's primary use is for heat regulation, and it is the body's first line of defense. The skin is a barrier against chemical, mechanical, and microbial would be invaders. It is the only body organ that is constantly influenced by internal and external factors at the same time.

A chemically inert pigment known as melanin exists within skin cells and is responsible for the skin's color and shade. Through a microscope, melanin appears as a polymorphic mosaic. Melanin can easily bear dark or light colors.

Both Charles Darwin and Aristotle before him noted the color changing abilities of reptiles, octopus, and certain fish, but what just happened to Devon would be considered radical by any standard. Devon's body had begun to translocate the pigment inside his cells.

This resulted in a temporary rudimentary change in color. Of course, this was purely accidental. The changes Devon's skin would manage would not be bright or vibrant. Humans have one class of pigment cell, but Devon's body had already developed another.

Devon slowly moved around the barn because he was having difficulty balancing. His muscles burned, and he felt heavy. Hypernium bonded with his bones, but the fact that his broken leg had not fully healed gave him an imperceptible limp. While falling, Devon reached out to grab a plank, and it crushed within his hand. He shook his head and then smiled.

*Perhaps, not a dream...*

As an only child, he learned to keep his thoughts to himself and make his expressions devoid of emotions, so that if he had a feeling, it couldn't be read. He never got into any real trouble beyond school horseplay. He wasn't bad unless you consider tipping over trash cans bad. His hands were average, he dropped stuff. He stumbled a lot, his legs were average. He had never been agile, particularly strong and he wasn't much of a thinker.

Devon smiled and did a flip, simple enough. He jumped eight feet into the air and rolled as he landed. The first time he scaled the wall, he became disoriented and fell ten feet to land with a thud on his back. After several minutes of practice, he was able to climb the walls to the rafters.

Devon's muscles seem to act by their own volition. He ran around the barn like a child with a new toy, feeling as if the flight was possible. From two hundred feet away, his senses focused on the farmer's morning egg breakfast, his frustrations with a broken tractor, and then his senses focused on the farmer's morning tryst with his wife.

He was mid-somersault when the buzzing began. Visions of disfigured faces entered his mind, and his stomach contracted with fear. It was the same buzzing noise he heard in the Montana base.

Devon quickly exited the barn and waited in the thick brush. The gale force wind delivered two dark figures. These figures looked as if there were cut out of the environment. They landed twenty feet away from where Devon hid, terrified.

The two searched the barn. In the brush, Devon felt the leaves, the earth and the air pressing on his skin. He closed his eyes; his skin changed to the same hue of the nearby foliage. If he didn't move, he would not be seen. He watched the two continue to search for him.

They fruitlessly ravaged the barn. Devon watched in silent horror as the farmer and his wife were broken for their curiosity. The wind whipped around, and the two were gone, as fast as they came.

Wood, blood, and body parts were everywhere. Devon was astonished by the carnage left behind. Devon wondeed what had become of his surgeon as he meandered along the windswept streets.

"Freak tornado strikes farm, husband and wife killed..." blared from the radio of a passing car.

Three miles down the road was an old payphone. His mind focused on his little girl and his wife as he rifled through his torn pants, looking for some change. His plan was to pick up the phone and call a familiar voice, any voice that could bring back reality for him.

As a child, whenever there were four or more people over, his father would start evangelizing. His father also suffered incurable bigotry; strangely, he was the most loved person in the family. He offended everyone equally with the truth. If Mr. Michael Heathrow answered the phone, he would say something like, 'You brought this on yourself,' or something about 'Revelations being at hand.'

Unable to find any coins in his pockets, Devon placed his head on the device in frustration. The receiver clicked with a resonating dial tone. Devon pressed the silver squares and waited. He froze when he heard his mother's warm voice; he heard her put the needlepoint down.

He smiled and listened to her breathe; she was all right. Devon stood there on the side of the road and thought about what he could possibly tell her. He hung up the phone without saying a word.

"I've been made into some kind of freak!" Devon shouted.

His hunger grew, he thought about going to the nearest chicken coop and stealing a few eggs. He had no idea how long it had been since his last meal. It was as if the lining of his stomach had started to devour itself. The spasms in his abdomen forced him to remove the payphone's coin box; in it, he found enough coins for a breakfast of scrambled egg, grilled chicken sausage, liver pudding, and hash over rice at a nearby diner.

He walked into the diner and sat down. He saw poetical vulgar words splashed across a scrren in a booth next to him. The smell of fresh bread was overwhelming. The pain in his belly was soothed by burnt toast with a heap of strawberry preserve spread corner to corner.

The truth about Sarah is that she burned most of the things she prepared, but Devon loved everything she made. No one is everything to you, but Sarah was everything to him. While the sweet taste of sausage caressed his lips, he sat at the table, looking out the window as more pleasant thoughts filled his head.

After his meal, Devon left the diner and began to run along rain gutters and rooftops. For the moment, fear left him, and the feeling of invincibility he had in the barn had returned. For three days he walked and hitchhiked, sore body and all to North Carolina.

Charlotte North Carolina is where Joshua Dougan's condo was. He and Joshua had been best friends since college. They had always been close, even in the worst of times.

Joshua Dougan was an unabashed bachelor. He had just started a software company, Softcom. He was twenty-seven and already head of the curve. Things between them had been different since college, especially since Devon had gotten married.

He and four other college friends still managed monthly poker and craps games at Joshua's condo. At these monthly games, they poked fun at their current situations and at each other's college awkwardness. This was not the time to rehash the last bad beat, but if there was anyone in the world Devon could trust, it was Joshua.

Metropolitan types rarely pay attention, so no one noticed Devon jumping from rooftop to rooftop and scrambling over fences. Devon avoided the questioning eyes of people by painstakingly scaling fourteen stories to reach Joshua's condo. He entered Joshua's condo through the always unlocked balcony.

Joshua was in his pajamas and brushing his teeth when he saw Devon standing by his bookshelf flipping through his books. Joshua's tooth-brush tumbled out of his mouth and bounced as it fell to the floor. Mozart #136 lightly played on the surround sound system as Joshua swallowed hard and wiped his face.

"D…Dev…last week I was at your funeral, your wife's, your child's. There were nothing, no remains, just empty coffins. Shredded clothes and broken toys, the tornadoes destroyed everything…" a rambling Joshua said.

"Brianna was just a child," Devon sobbed. "She was the little lump in our bed, hiding under the blankets. She was fascinated by butterflies. She had an electric laugh. She needed my protection, they needed my protection. Somehow I caused all of this…"

"Caused all of what?" Joshua said.

A wave of emotion caused Devon to stumble. He leaned up against the bar to gather himself. The metal bar dented from Devon's new strength and lack of discipline.

"Are you all right?" Joshua said, rushing to assist Devon.

"Tornadoes…" Devon said, walking over to where he knew Joshua kept his alcohol.

"They froze the money in your accounts. Your company is investigating you for securities fraud, and the police have been asking a lot of questions about you, but you look pretty good for a dead man," Joshua said, nervously joking. Devon produced a small smile.

"Man, it's good to see you."

"It's good to see you, too," Devon said as they hugged each other. "Have you been working out?" said Joshua, squeezing Devon's forearm.

"You could say that," said Devon weakly.

Joshua grabbed Devon, looked him in the eyes, and said, "Devon, what the hell is going on? You seem different."

"I am…different. Josh, let me show you something."

Devon quickly jumped to the top of the bookshelf, and then he flipped down to land beside Joshua. Joshua hypnotically sunk into the nearest chair. Devon poured Joshua a good glass of scotch. Joshua quickly gulped down the alcoholic pacifier; Devon could sense his friend's fear.

"Some people win, and some lose. I am afraid that luck has little to do with anything these days," Devon said.

Joshua's hand was shaking as he made a feeble smile. "Luck... right." He said feverishly drinking from his glass; his eyes were glued on Devon.

"It all started with this damn thing," Devon said as he handed Joshua the glasses and told him about the base in Montana, the operation, the barn, and Them. Joshua's opened wide, and he swallowed hard.

"We've been friends for a long time... I think I'm going to need another drink ... This is too deep for me," Joshua said, putting the glasses on.

"Too deep for you...My wife and daughter are dead! Dead! I can't go home; my life is over. They are after me..." said Devon.

Before Devon could stop him, Joshua stood up and ran his finger over the power button on the glasses.

"What's Not Them?" Joshua said, shaking his head.

Then, the buzzing began. Devon quickly spun and hopped on top Joshua's Victorian couch.

"Josh leave!" Devon ordered.

Seconds later, a powerful blast, followed by slow brilliant flames, unhinged Joshua's condo's door and shook the windows. The flames were followed by two giant beings.

Joshua fell to the floor, mumbling, "This is not happening... this can't be happening," He quickly crawled into the bedroom. The two beings seemed surprised that not only did Devon not react or run, but his eyes followed them as they moved. He could see them. People could be heard running the hallway.

"Your journey ends here," the taller of the two men said. "Ask, find the other one!"

Ask, the smaller of the two, began ransacking the condo. These beings had thin eyes, small pupils, a pronounced jawline and long bony fingers.

"Where is the other human?" said Ask.

"What other humans?" Devon said.

"Where is the device?"

"What device?"

"We will not play games with you—human," said the taller one. "Nice outfit. Do I know you?" responded Devon looking at the red moving lights on their trench coats.

"I am Me. How you managed to escape us for this long is unknown," Me said approaching Devon. Devon frowned as he jumped down from the couch.

"You are inferior," Me stated. Me's eyes turned silver as he began to harness elements. Devon lifted his eyes, and he began to bounce left to right as if he were a world champion boxer. Devon extended his right arm smiled, and said, "Ding, ding."

Me was on Devon as if he were lightning itself, Devon was hit with a tremendous blow. The blow was so hard that the windows of the condo blew out. Devon was and flung ten feet backward. He was barely able to breathe.

His skin ripped, and blood trickled from his mouth. The blow was much harder than he expected. Joshua's condo disintegrated as fires spread. Devon looked at what remained of his clothes. He scrambled to his feet and dusted himself off. Anger crept up his neck and into his face, this anger made his eyes faintly glow golden.

"I never got to say goodbye!" Devon said. Devon stood up, knowing that he should have run.

"Interesting," said Me.

Once again, Me went at Devon with a thunderous blow after thunderous blows. Silver light shot out everything they made contact. Devon hit Me with all he had. Me's body felt like punching cold flesh-covered steel. An unfazed Me picked up Devon threw him against the wall.

An explosion rocked the condo. That's when a stumbling Joshua Dougan made his escape and pulled the fire alarm on his way out. Devon's attacks were becoming more effective and small amounts of golden light radiated from his strikes. The silver in Me's eyes began to fade.

Without a hint, Ask busted through the bedroom wall and jumped on Devon. A blow meant for Devon's jaw whizzed by in a blur of gnarled knuckles. Devon saw his opponent's other arm begin a forward movement. He ducked this, but his hair was ruffled by the force of it. Ask hit Devon with a series of blows, and then Me landed a kick that sent Devon back against the counter.

"Who else have you told, human?" Ask probed.

The egg white paint of the condo swelled as a wall of flame went up to the bookshelf. The floor shook from the awkward ballet of violence. Flames surrounded them. The building's sprinkler system failed to engage.

The two being moved the fire with their fists. Devon felt the heat from a glancing blow graze his face. He felt the heat in his abdomen, where a roundhouse kick landed. Devon ducked a blow from Me that made steel chunks of wall explode like shrapnel. Ask hit Devon so hard that he was pushed to the edge of what was left of the condo.

"Don't flatter yourself, human. You will fall!" said Me.

Devon wanted to close his eye and curl into a fetal position. Fear ran through him as he remembered his job, his family, and his life. His wife's scent began to fill his mind, and he could taste the sweet wine of Sarah's lips. Trembling, he put his fingers to his lips, his arm and legs were no longer dense. He stood up. He gathered himself and channeled his rage.

"I have already fallen," he said, and then he leaped on the two.

Devon was more precise with his strikes as he battled the two. As he blocked their attacks, his eyes beamed a golden light. Upon hearing sirens in the distance, Me and Ask turned quickly and disappeared. Smoke swirled around Devon as he ran through the pulsating fire.

"Where are you? Come back here!" yelled a bleeding, disoriented, and still swinging Devon. Covered with reddish-orange embers, he roamed the destroyed condos, unable to find Joshua. There were five condos on the fourteenth floor; all of them were hollowed out by fire, only steel beams and girders remained. Fires still burned on the other levels.

Devon fell to his knees as he looked over the city and screamed, "I didn't ask for this. I didn't ask for any of this!" He looked down at his bleeding, burnt and bruised hands.

"That choke ended the last normal day of my life. Devon is no more; I AM (After Man)."

His anguish dominated his thoughts as he climbed down and jumped from rooftop to rooftop.

# CHAPTER 6

Three broken ribs, burns, gashes and both of his eyes were blackened, but he had to keep moving. He wore sunglasses for a week as he slowly recovered from his confrontation with these otherworlders. It was reported that seven people had been seriously injured and that building had to be demolished.

The buzzing dogged him as he roamed from city to city. Daily a different part of his body ached. He was sleeping longer hours as non-human silhouettes caused him to spend nights twitching like he was in withdrawal.

He was scared to close his eyes, afraid to open them. In his dreams, he could see Sarah, he could touch her, but she wasn't there. He would slightly cock his head to the side, and her scent would be with him. At the end of every dream, she would squeeze his hand, softly say "goodbye," then her face twisted in a woeful grimace as a fiery whirlwind carried her away.

"Them are more than you'd imagine." His surgeon's words rattled inside Devon's head as he walked the streets watching vehicles whizzing quickly by, their occupants oblivious to the real world. He couldn't stand the image looking back at him from the mirror. He had failed as a husband, as a father, and as a protector.

How would he redeem himself? He tried to stop a bank robbery.

"Stop right there!" Devon said.

"Who the hell is this guy!" replied the startled bank robber.

Devon tried to be like those guys in the films his wife loved to watch so much. The problem was that those movies never showed the effect of a bullet graze. Devon's neural impulse interpreted these grazes as pain. His intervening brought SWAT, the media, and the buzzing The tornado that followed the bank robbery left two dead and six hurt. Devon almost didn't get out of there in time.

Devon had to get away; he filled a backpack, scavenged what he could and bought a ticket on a train heading to California. The sound of the horn, the rumble of the tracks told Devon he was on his way. There was a hiss of steam; a WOOoooOOH came from the front of the blue and silver train as it pulled away from the station. Night fell as conductors patrolled the cars asking for tickets. An automated overhead voice was repeating station stops over the clickety-clack of the wheels.

Devon looked out of the train window. The cities the train passed were dirty but full of life, and that life gave way to ever unfolding rural scenery. On the train people sat at various tables, reading, writing, and using devices. The movement of the train was like the gentle rocking to sleep of a child by their mother. This soothed Devon's throbbing headache.

He was uncomfortable, but the trip was going better than he had hoped. The train sped past schools, highways, refineries, offices, alleys, and empty pastures. Trains have a certain rhythm as they roll along. They have a specific sound to them. Cows… horses …fences … brake hiss…stop.

Out of the large window, he saw the effect of the wind, but couldn't feel it. The train insulates like a car does, except the vehicle is a more solitary way of travel. The vehicle provides protection from the troublemakers of the world. On the train, troublemakers are insulated right along with you.

"Do you mind if I sit here?" asked a rather large man.

Before the change, Devon would have definitely minded, but not now. He shook his head anyway. This interruption served him right for not being in a private compartment. The train was filled with noises, and smells that made noses tingle, so what difference did one more offense make.

At each station the train came to a stop, the doors slide open, slide close, and then the train would move along again. He heard the automatic compartment door close behind him as people moved from railcar to railcar. Everyone was just a preoccupied as he was, a couple kissing, a woman looking out of the window, a child whining. An elderly woman sat across from him. A plainly dressed man in the corner of the compartment stared at him.

Was he one of Them? No, he's just staring.

When Devon was in the dinner car, the rain started to fall. There was a faint buzzing but no disfigured faces. Devon thought he saw something large quickly move outside the train.

*I'm I being paranoid?* Devon thought to himself as he went down the narrow corridors to the thin-walled railcar to eat an overstuffed roasted turkey whole wheat sandwich. Rain dropped quickly and glided diagonally down the large windows. Devon thought of the window as a high-definition screen that instantly displayed images and erased them.

The train was halfway across the bridge when it alarmingly jerked, the idle chatter stopped. The air brakes squealed as the train pivoted on the track. In front of the train, a section of the bridge had collapsed into the cold river.

The conductor quickly applied the emergency brakes, clanking couplings signaled danger. It was too late, derailing was inevitable. Devon grabbed the elderly lady and used every ounce of strength he had to steady both of them as five passenger cars hit the side of the bridge and skidded into the river. The rest of the train came to a sudden, forceful stop.

Everyone that was holding on to an overhead strap was thrown to the floor, or out of a window. The screams and moans were too numerous to count. The side of the train split as if it was aluminum foil. The cab, caboose, baggage car, and five passenger cars fell forty feet into the frigid river. The remaining railcars were hung up on the bridge's steel trusses.

Several passenger cars were teetering between falling into the river and being stuck. A smoking railcar fell on a group of passengers swimming towards the river bank. Devon pried a door open and jumped down with the unconscious Lady, she'll be alright.

What was left of his railcar was still on the bridge. He jumped into the water and swam to the river bank. He repeated this several times, carrying several people from the train to the river bank. The rain became more intense, and the waters of the river rose.

Searchlights were everywhere as people stood on the muddy river bank shivering and crying. Devon looked helplessly at the smoldering wreckage. When helicopters appeared on the scene a cold, wet Devon made his way six miles to the nearest town, changing clothes from his backpack as he went.

He sat in the hotel lobby, looking at the images of the wreckage on television. He overheard a man and a woman at the bar, talking about the incident.

"The authorities said the cleanup is going to last for days; the investigation is going to be even longer. The swollen river must have loosened the bridge's foundation," said the man.

"...all those poor people," said the woman.

"It could have been worse. When a river swells up like that, you never know what's going to happen. The train probably hit a weak spot on the bridge."

The couple continued talking about the accident for forty-six more seconds and then asked for the TV channel to be changed.

Of the two hundred and fifty passengers that bought a ticket, fifty fell into the river. Devon knew this was no accident. Seeing the Earth move as if it were looking for him scared the living daylights out of him. He needed information, and he had to get away any way he could.

Devon stowed away on an Oasis-Class cruise ship. There were no tracks to get hung up on, no bridges to fall off of and no rivers to fall into. He got rid of his shoes, his watch, and any device that could be tracked.

For three days, he exchanged pleasantries and head nods. He engaged in all manner of ship's activities surfing, dining, ice skating, mini golf, and zip lining and his mind needed the distraction. The third night, during the magic show, the ship began to sway back and forth, and the lights started to flicker.

"Remain calm; we are working on an electrical problem..." the ship's loudspeakers announced. Devon knew better because the buzzing had started. When the magician and the band quickly exited the stage, everyone knew it was time to panic. Waves began to lift the ship.

Tsunamis are unnoticed by passengers on ships on the open seas. In open water, a tsunami's energy is distributed across a large area. The ships at port and the people on the land have to worry as a tsunami moves into shallow water.

Tsunamis stack waves. This is why they have such devastating power. Cruise ships are designed to withstand storms and forty-foot waves, but this wasn't a tsunami; it was a series of rogue waves.

When the lights went out, everyone started running and scream- ing. The slow-moving waves increased in height from twenty-five to eighty feet. Each wave picked up the two hundred and twenty thousand ton ship and dropped it back into the water as it were a toy. The stern thruster was offline. The righting arms limits had been exceeded, and the vessel started leaning on its side.

"We hit something that wasn't on the chart," someone said over the shouts.

Cold ocean water rapidly flooded the staircases. People made ropes from bed sheets and climbed decks to escape the advancing water. People were struck by flying tables, chairs, and anything that wasn't bolted down—killing some, injuring most. Flashlight beams cut through the corridors. Flickering lights, flash fires, and electrical sparks were all dominated by the water.

Devon jumped easily from deck to deck. Those who were on lower floors were trapped. In the distance bangs from explosions could be heard. As the ship filled with water, Devon went to the other side to see who he could save. Devon opened the door to help an elderly couple get out.

The two had been married for fifty years; this was their golden anniversary trip. They declined Devon's offer and decided to stay in their cabins, resigned to their fate.

An hour later, the ship had tilted fifty-five degrees on its left side. Multiple blasts from the horn signaled everyone to the lifeboats. People were pushing each other out of the way; some were jumping into the sea. People were running, and those that fell were trampled. Because the ship was leaning on its side, the other lifeboats were impossible to get to.

"Women and children first," someone kept shouting as families were separated.

The lifeboats had long lines in front of them. Water rushed down several corridors as the engine room was flooded. Devon slid over blood-soaked panels as the ship was thrown around. And just as quickly as the waves came, they stopped.

And underwater explosion bent the deck upward in grotesque configurations. A terrific fire had started; bloody, bodies were bent in ways they should not have been. The ship was ablaze from stem to stern as the flames spread.

Everyone was shouting in multiple languages, and all of them meant, "Help me!" The ship started to crack in half, and Devon made his way to higher decks. He helped as many people as he could get to the boats, but there were so many, too many.

People were bruised, crying, and bleeding. They desperately clung to vertical stairways, hoping to be rescued. Emergency strobe lights flashed down every corridor. The ship split and violently shifted, everyone, including Devon, slid across the cold, wet, top deck.

"Jump, jump, jump!" everyone shouted.

The cracks in the ship's hull caused it to sink faster than the lifeboats filled. The lifeboats were so full of people that some of them broke as they were lowered into the water, spilling people into the ocean.

Swimming in the open sea is not as easy. The water was twenty-five degrees, and the temperature was dropping by the minute. The sun had gone down, and the shore was three miles away. Those in authority shouted contradicting instructions, and Devon handed out as many life vests as he could.

"I can't swim," a lady tearfully screamed.

Hundreds of people furiously paddled away from the ship. The dark sea was dotted with flashing lights that moved up and down.

"We're all going to die!" said a lady huddled with a makeshift family. Loud cracks could be heard as the water found its way to the top deck. Hands clawed at Devon, forcing him to jump into the icy water.

In the water, his body became cold, his movements slowed, his eyes heavy. Thoughts of his daughter's laugh, his mother's hugs, and his wife's warmth flooded his mind.

Above the frosty liquid, shouts were followed by screams, and screams were followed by cries. For a moment, the voices were close, and then there was silence. There was nothing but darkness as he bobbed up and down in the freezing water.

Devon had been so busy handing out life vest that he didn't get one. He could fell the hands underneath him, clutching at his feet. A few hours ago, music filled the ship, and every deck was brightly lit. A few hours ago, people were laughing and playing games. All that remained was the sound of breaking of wood, clasping metal and the occasional up and down movement of lights.

It took Devon forty minute to swim the three miles to shore. He dragged his lacerated and bruised body out of the water. Exhausted, he lay on the beach cryin, wondering why he just didn't allow himself to sink to the bottom of the ocean. Sarah wouldn't have approved of him giving up; she never let him give up.

Just before the waves hit the ship, the buzzing occurred. He had to be better at recognizing the warning signs. Currently, his abilities were unpredictable. On the boat, he helped as many as he could, but it wasn't enough.

Devon always pictured himself with the best parking spot, running the company, sipping cognac while laughing with the board of directors. Those things were now vaguely remembered notions. He was becoming numb inside; this was the only way he could go on.

The cruise ship had five thousand registered passengers, at least one hundred and fifty people were unaccounted for, and divers don't look for survivors after dusk. One thousand three hundred were injured and in hospitals. Evacuees were huddled together in hotel lobbies, schools, and churches on a nearby island. Devon was surely noticed and would probably be listed as dead. Were it not for the changes, he would have been.

Desperation caused him to board the train and fool hearty notions that made him stowaway on that cruise ship. The lens through which he viewed the world was changing. He couldn't stop thinking about how and why he lost his family as the waves lapped against the shore.

Devon lay on that beach crying for an hour before sorrow forced him to sleep.

# CHAPTER 7

Devon traveled by boat, the smallest ones he could find. He was a strong swimmer, and he was comfortable in the water. The amount of worldwide nuclear detonations made his take daunting. The safest place he could be was on the ocean. There hadn't been as many high energy explosions in the sea as there were on land and he didn't want anyone else to be harmed because of him.

For two days, Devon cried as the terrifying realization that he had lost everything he held dear and the world had become too big. He sailed the ocean on ketches, schooners, and catamarans. Blood flukes, tapeworms, blastocysts, and things beyond description were expelled from his body.

On the open water, his body violently rejected the toxins he spent two decades putting into it. The briny smell assisted him in forgetting his boss, but he remembered every crease his suit had. He remembered his mother's needlepoint and his dad's way of obsessing over the smallest screw.

Devon's Earth had the lion's share of water. Perhaps these beings couldn't swim, or they weight too much to deal with him on the ocean. He drifted the sea with fishing lines, binoculars, a wetsuit, translucent fins, food, and water. After he conquered the instinct that caused his fingertips to prune, his main objective was survival.

On the open water darkness extends forever, he had to navigate by stars to sail from place to place. When he slept, he often found himself wondering what life was like through the void.

His surgeon's tale of rifts and dark matter fueled his speculation. Devon was just getting used to this universe, and now there was another verse that shared elements. Devon was afraid, but more than anything else, he wanted to understand.

Had this other side conquered their world as humans had? Were their zoos were filled with amoebas, viruses, and things that humans considered microscopic? Was dark energy is the missing part of the equation of every equation.

Whatever the missing part of the equation was it gave beings abilities on this plane. They were all around us, yet unseen. Like two cities that exist side by side, both unaware of the other's existence. These other world beings exist in something that is only sensed as a mathematical calculation, yet they have homes, places of worship, schools, and cities.

He didn't know what they are going to do. He didn't know what they want. There were no friendly reliable faces, no one to trust; just uncomfortable loneliness. All Devon knew is that someone was sending these beings.

Their world didn't sound all that different from his, but was. The thought of such a dark matter place wasn't pleasant to Devon, but it would still better than thinking about the vague, gauzily vision of his present terror. The Earths mirrored, and exist as primordial Siamese twins, separated only by a dark matter veil.

On the ocean, there are no bucket seats, no windshields, no heaters, and no brakes…just the water lapping against the boat and the occasional splash. Floating in this cold salty liquid, Devon quickly learned that cold is merely the absence of heat energy. Yet cold is needed for heat to be usable. The flow of energy from the body to the environment is constant.

Devon's heightened senses allowed him to feel changes in temperature and pressure. As he shopped for supplies, he could hear the heartbeat of the people around him. His body was outgrowing his mind.

In school, Devon wasn't fond of puzzles, games, or word problems. He was an average student, and now he had no way to explain why the size and shape of countries were distorted from what he had been taught. Had he been miseducated, had we all? Maps, charts, and cryptographs had filled minds with myths and left people chasing dreams of nothing.

Nature had no feelings, remorse about killing, but to use nature for your own purposes is unfathomable. These beings were not like the ghouls who haunt Edgar Allen Poe; nor were they horror movie creatures. They are flesh and bone, fiber, and liquids. Devon had felt them. He had spoken to them, they possess a mind, yet they are invisible.

While governments profit from psychological deviations and compete for planetary market share, keys get lost, spacecraft go off mission, something inexplicable breaks, a vote unexpectedly turns, a cruise ship overturns, someone is swept away in a flood, a vehicle loses control, and all of it is just another mission accomplished for creatures.

Devon couldn't verify any of his speculations. However, there was one unavoidable fact: there was only one of him and many of them. His only advantage was that these beings needed to create natural phenomenon to harm him.

In these boats, his childhood memories came to him. His first steps, his first fall, his nervousness on the first day of preschool. How he felt inferior in the presence of many. His parent's frustration with 3rd-grade homework. His prolific bedwetting, awkward teen years and his mother's tears through all of it.

As he floated in the blackness, his mind went over every smiled greeting, every stolen glance that was an ode to depression. He recalled the eagerness of other students, like him that would jump at the slightest chance to love.

The salty ocean spray interrupted his thoughts. A tidal wave is a budge in the planet. The tide isn't coming, individuals are moving towards the tide. After a week at sea and the lapping waves became lullabies. It's hard not to fall in love with the simplicity of the ocean, the white sails slowly waving in the wind, the warm sun on your back.

In the water, Devon was alone with his thoughts; it was here that he could close the world out. Beneath the surface he was subjected to the human frailties of water pressure and oxygen toxicity, the more he practiced, the less those frailties mattered.

In the sunless depths, he dove deeper with minimal strain on his lungs. In the undulating nothingness, trying to modulate his skin pigment was pointless because the creatures that live in the water were aware of his presence. They felt his body electricity or heard the rhythmic beat of his heart.

The curved surface of the human eye accounts for two-thirds of the eye's refractive power; this is lost when air is replaced by water as a person submerges underwater. The eye is not focused underwater, and small objects remain vague because water changes the direction of light the same way the cornea does.

The more he used his eyes, the better his underwater sight became. His vision improved, and he no longer needed a face mask. He could also hold his breath for prolonged periods of time, and this made exploration and seafood more enjoyable.

He slowed his heart rate, and this caused his blood to conserve oxygen. He was soon able to hold his breath underwater longer than he could on land. The Hypernium allowed him to evolved in never before imagined ways.

The calm of not panicking about being eaten or drowning brought with it the ability to find underwater currents. These liquid breezes moved faster near the surface. The shape of the shore and water temperature changed the speed and direction of these water subways.

Devon could swim four meters per second; with his bodysuit and fins on, he could swim even faster. He spent most days being pushed along for miles in these currents, there is only one word for it—amazing.

Some fish see ultraviolet light, and some are sensitive to polarized light. When light enters the water, the intensity decreases, and the color changes. Light scatters due to particles and other small objects suspended in water. The more particles that are in the water, the higher scatter effect. The clearer the water, the more light penetrates.

The colorful creatures near the surface vanish as Devon dove deeper. They were still there, but they just appear black. Most sea creatures are black or reddish. At ninety meters a redfish looks black and is invisible. Once Devon's eyes adjusted to different light wavelengths, no creature was invisible to him.

Devon was in the water so long that dolphins would whistle good morning to him as he nursed teeth punctures from sea snakes and jellyfish stings. Large seafaring vessels would approach his boat, its crew believing that he was adrift, or in need of aid.

'Nesecitas ayuda?" they would yell down. "Esta Bien," Devon would smile back.

Or they would say, "Help yuh a do?"

"Yeah everything, cool man." Devon would nonchalantly say as he deboned fish, even pirates left him alone.

Daily he was awakened by the smell of salt, the call of seabirds and the rhythmic clapping of waves. Sound travels faster in water than it does in the air. When he was beneath the glassy surface, he had to use vibrations to hear.

The ocean was full of sounds; he was immersed in it, the natural kind, and the human-made kind. The human sound came from the mechanically repetitive nature of shipping freighters, naval ships, and submarines. Devon was surprised by how many submarines and underwater vessels travel off the coast of every nation.

Oil rigs, drilling, mining, and sonar all made changes to the underwater soundscape. Those noises actually change marine behavior. Some marine life survives only by using sound. These noises, over time, have produced different behaviors in underwater life. Devon saw these uncharacteristic behaviors as a psychosis.

Huge seafaring ships emit aerosols, tiny particles, in their exhaust. Water vapor in the air condenses around those particles, forming small spheres of water like cloud droplets. If you look hard enough, you could see the cloud formations that followed the path of a vessel; even the ships and their engines stopped normal underwater feeding patterns.

When it rained, each drop made little thumps as it hit the ocean surface. Downpours sounded like music when the thumps mixed in with percussive thunder. No two songs sounded alike, and they never last long as the winds moved the bands along. Most fish don't like this rain music, and they dive deeper during storms, an instinct to protect them from surface lightning strikes.

Devon was on the coast of Venezuela as a lightning storm moved in from the sea. Lightning struck the water's surface, the current zipped around in every direction. The color of the current changed the further it moved away from the initial strike point ...red ...yellow ...blue ...green.

Devon had three hundred and sixty degrees of view of the lightning strike. From cloud to the surface, it was the most fantastic thing Devon had ever seen. For a fraction of a second, the ocean was illuminated by half a billion volts of electricity. Witnessing this first hand was impossible to do on land—and survive.

Lightning striking water sounds like a raindrop hitting a window pane. The surf sounds like rushing wind, only softer. Cracking ice was the loudest; it was the most jarring thing he heard. The sound of cracking ice scattered fish for miles. It scattered Devon as well; he thought it was Them.

Devon would briefly surface to intake fresh air and then submerge. In the ocean, he was surrounded by whale pods, schools of angelfish, blue tangs, big-eyed squid, damselfish, groupers, sea urchins, and phosphorescent fish that glow. The sheer size of some of these gentle creatures was humbling. The ocean floor was dotted with wrecked ships, tires, cans, shipping containers, plastic bags, and other discarded things.

Next, to the sunken ships, brightly colored sea sponges popped out of the coral. Small fish seemed to have full lives. They play hide and seek all day. A massive ball of small fish, from a distance, looks and behaves like a much larger one.

The ocean was a dangerous place; a little fish could get lost easily. Some fish had strange tactics to capture food, like laying-in-wait for hours, motionless, waiting for the right time to strike. Other larger fish would just seek out and destroy their prey.

Sharks never bothered Devon; he was just passing through. Nothing came close to doing him any real harm. From all the news reports and movies he had watched, he thought he wouldn't last an hour. Most sea creatures aren't suited to star in horror films. Ocean creatures were as curious about him as he was about them.

What is the two-legged intruder doing here?

The ocean was more active at night than during the day. It is comparable to a large city where certain people go out in the day, and different brands of people come out at night. At night, he tried not to shine his flashlight in the eyes of this nightlife. He needed the truth, he needed answers, and staying on the ocean would provide him with neither.

# CHAPTER 8

Devon roamed Panama, Honduras, Nicaragua and Columbia's El Mirador jungle; he was closely followed by dark world overlords. His stay at bars adorned with images of Christ was brief.

There was no time to view the caves turned homes or enjoy the leisurely Jamaican or Gypsy Moon songs. He borrowed laundry and ran through cornfields. He was just another fugitive that ran through these nations.

South America was full of radical volumetric heat changes, granite cliffs, and updrafts. In the ground, there were six-meter high termite towers that glow blue and green from beetle larvae, wolves. Devon had to be careful of the rhea, tapirs, and jaguars that also roam here.

The heat of the countryside was made worse by ash explosions, and lava flows from the Avenue of the Volcanoes. While on a ridge Devon slipped and lost his bag that contained his money and supplies down a watery gorge. It took him two days of scavenging before he could recover his supplies.

In Baños de Agua Santa, a city in central Ecuador, also known as 'Gateway to the Amazon,' the smell of beans roasting in the sun filled the air. In each city, Devon visited the cuisine was exquisite. On the small cobblestone streets, he bought freshly fried plantain chips before zip-lining through the cloud forest.

To the people here he was an unchecked box, another stranger, who struggled with the language. He would show up, and then he was gone. Devon made sure to use 'please,' 'thank you,' 'ma'am' and 'sir' as he spoke. He frequently began conversations with the phrase 'excuse me.'

*I was just getting comfortable when everything started rattling. The walls jerked toward me. The balcony windows shattered. Light poles and power lines shook violently. Things were thrown off the shelves, hurled in my direction.*

*Then the passage lights went off, and everyone panicked. People ran along narrow passages and down the staircase, and I ran with them. People pushed and tumbled over each other to get out of the buildings.*

*As I sprinted, walls crashed down around me. The noise was ear-splitting. I spun to avoid the heaving pavement, and then everything was still. People were moaning, cars were overturned, buildings had collapsed. The building I was in was now in ruins.*

Thousands of people aimlessly wander the streets screaming, and then the first aftershock hit, knocking Devon down in the middle of the broken street. The earthquake lasted less than two minutes, but it seemed like an hour. The earthquake busted out windows, displaced people and lives. The sun was setting; the air was thick with dust as fires raged throughout the city.

Ecuador is nine thousand feet above sea level. Each of its dirt roads led to breathtaking vistas and waterfalls. Ecuador's uniqueness caused him to slow down, if only for a moment. Some of the cities are sparsely populated; others are filled with redwood trees

Indigenous women in colorful clothing with babies slung on their backs ran the markets. In the market square, he saw two ladies laughing with each other.

"Hello… Can I have two of these and one of those…" he said.

"Sure Guapo…" Martha said.

"Thank you."

Devon bought two tacos and a spicy burrito from Martha's cart. She smiled and was pleased when she spoke to him. Maria, her twin sister, was dressed like a Hollywood socialite. Maria looked at Devon in disgust through her sunglasses. These two made him curious.

The next day he watched the two sisters prepare for their day. Maria lived in a sizeable well secured house. She put on her tailored business suit, jumped into her maroon Nissan 370Z, and stopped by the church to pray. Devon followed her.

From there Maria quickly made her way to five drug houses on the outskirt of town. Before the day was over, Maria, put a gun into the mouth of one of her workers and threatened to kill his whole family, if he came up short again. She didn't kill him, but she rendered him unconscious by hitting him with the gun. Maria went home alone. She hid money in her safe and drank until she fell asleep.

On the other side of town, Martha gathered tomatoes, lettuce, tortillas, and her satchel of sauces. Martha and her three children set up a little stand in the market square, where she made burritos and tacos. The children spread out selling pastries and sodas. Devon bought corn, red onions, cilantro, limo chilies and twenty-five black cockles from Maria's children.

*It was two dollars for the ceviche mix, but I gave each of her children two dollars. After all, these kids were the ones dealing with the maze-like roots of the mangroves, snake, and sulfurous sucking black mud to get the cockles... I'm just buying and them.*

Martha spent the day in the square until she was out of tortillas. Before nightfall, Martha wiped her brow, and she and children went home to a small, gray two bedroom apartment. As the children bathed, she cooked. They prayed, ate, and happily slept.

How did these two sisters end up so very different? The drug trade, like the pray trade, ran through everything and everyone here. participation in either was through victimization, volition, or voluntary. Fear, disappointment, uncertainty, and hope infuse life here.

Devon ran pass the quarries, the mines, the abused prisoners, and the night drug laboratories. The grass crushed underneath his feet as he ran past the slowly turning windmill, near the children jumping rope. Out here, one life ran into another, often without note or consequence. Devon slowed down but kept moving through colorful unnamed streets. A month ago, he didn't know places like this existed.

He made torches out of coconut husks like he had seen others do. These torches gave out low-level light but produced a lot of smoke. The smoke from one torch lasted for hours and kept mosquitoes black flies away.

He tiptoed by white sand beaches, and tiny tucked away harbors as he made his way through the forest cathedral they call The Amazon. He didn't stay in Brazil long because there were too many cameras for him to remain unnoticed.

The male otherworlders adjudicated life and death, while the female otherworlders ruled hearts and minds. The females were everywhere as alarms went off; people were locked out of their rooms, and some missed their flights because of them. They didn't bother him, but he wondered how these things and killings benefitted their mission.

Crossing the Atlantic, he thought about his wedding. Sarah wore a tulle and satin back dupioni mermaid gown with colored trim and flower sash. Devon didn't know what any of that was. He just knew she looked so beautiful.

Sarah wasn't complicated; she did ask for a titanium white and yellow gold DNA wedding ring. There were only twenty people at the wedding, that's how she wanted it. He could see the nervousness in her face as she walked down the aisle, her father held her hand tight.

When her father finally let her hand go, he looked at Devon and said "This better not be a mistake," and then he patted the left side of his tuxedo, where his pistol was inevitably housed. Devon just nodded and took Sarah's hand.

*She could have married anyone; she chose me. I don't know why, I was hilariously conceited, with average athleticism and average rhythm. I loved watching romantic films, and she liked science fiction films and comedies, go figure. I ate fruit off her back, and she'd sex me back to sleep. When I was sleeping, she'd go into her basement lab.*

*In college, it was hard to wow me but was wowed by her. She had an unbelievable skill set. On tough days, she was just a call away. Every morning she walked me to the front door. We kissed; she'd smile and say, "Create hope."*

*And I'm talking about her like she's right here...*

Devon was continually moving through town, country, and continent. Devon was running as fast as he could from these beings, but he was also learning. These invaders could enter a home even if all the doors were locked. They registered as a breeze and were unrecognized by security systems.

People were lucky they didn't have to run from the howling wind or from the petals of purple trees that swirled like a swarm of locust over Devon's head. Devon observed zebras, wildebeest, olive baboons, and red tail monkeys, spotted hyenas, lions, bush elephants, and Soda Lake flamingos as they all gathered at the same watering hole.

Devon also watched the plants. Plants react to chemicals, light, infections, temperature, oxygen and carbon dioxide concentrations, parasite infestations, disease, and physical disruption... sound.

Plants can remember stresses and events, and they have the ability to respond to the environmental. They can sense gravity, the presence of water, or even feel that an obstruction is in the way of its roots and they do all of this without a brain.

Devon became the unwelcome voice of reason at uprisings. Slightly altering his skin tone allowed him to be any nationality. He was able to elude paper checkers as he entered or left a country. Disappearing into crowds and into the night became his specialties.

Devon started balancing rocks, one on top of the other. This balancing grew from small rocks to boulders. He used the center of gravity in an object to balance it. In the heart of the jungle, there would be rocks strangely balancing on top of each other.

The blemishes on his face and skin cleared up, and his hair grew slower. He didn't need to shave daily, but he found that a beard made for a suitable disguise. The little tire around his midsection that caused him to join a gym was gone. He looked fit with a slightly muscular build.

He lived in the wilderness and cooked food like a veteran boy scout. He ate live foods, herbs, berries; he hunted small animals and sampled everything. He ate meat, but he mostly ate greens. He ate more vegetables in one month than he had his entire life. His body processed everything faster and performed better on things that weren't artificial.

Artificial sweeteners and flavorings lingered on his tongue. He could taste the additives. Devon listened to his body—even alcohol didn't have the same effect. He felt every bit of the Earth's 23-degree tilt. Devon's right-handedness gave way to awkwardness with both hands. There was a two day period where all he could do was run, his hands were useless

Every new moment revealed by new abilities was followed by the pain of being alone. The changes to his body made his skin stronger. Devon was stronger than he was yesterday, and he was faster by a hundred of a second.

Devon had never worked with his hands, yet he found himself in the middle of water projects in Mambilla, railway projects in Chad, building projects in Nairobi, and construction projects in Cape Town.

In response to the 'How are you?' by coworkers, Devon responded, "I'm not well, yet I've never felt better."

Here the frameless way the light pierced the sky, the sweet water that quenched his thirst, the gentle breeze, all of it… different. Everything was different, the water on his face, the rush of wind going by him. The urge to put food into his mouth decreased. His body increased in conjunction with increased brain activity.

His mother's needlepoint lessons came in handy as he created a fire-resistant jacket that could be transformed into a sleeping bag. When dealing with people became of too much for him, he wandered the jungles.

Despite the rain, despite the damp conditions and despite the jungle teaming with life, it was a solitary place. Most of the rain didn't even hit the ground. Rainwater stayed on the leaves of trees, some of which reached heights of one hundred and fifty feet. The jungle was a murky depth of shadows.

The jungle floor was moving with life. He marveled at the insects that squirt honeydew and the night blooming flowers. The shade from the overhanging leaves darkened the floor bed. The moss covering the trees added to the natural ground cover.

The ground was a carpet of browning leaves. To avoid using his machete to hack up plants, he chose to walk along the eucalyptus covered riverbanks. The small plants had oversized leaves to capture sunlight and any rain the trees missed.

The bright green trees had oval shaped leaves, which funneled water into the tree trunk. The animals that resided in the inner forest were brightly colored toucans, lizards, and tree frogs; he even saw a few panthers. Devon could see the life flowing through plant leaves, the nutrients filtering through stems.

At night, the Jungle was dark, wet, and very cold. Devon never knew how much he needed light until he didn't have it. Being rendered sightless was more frightening in the jungle than it was when he was on the ocean. The night ocean is black, but he was insulated by the boat. In a few hours, his sight was useless, and then the whole world was dark.

Tents, sleeping bags, fires, and warm clothing were no protection from the cold. In the darkness, glowing eyes and primal screams kept him company. Devon built fires when he was in small caves to stay warm, but the light often attracted more attention than he wanted. The pain was still a factor, this made traveling at night slower.

He was now able to see in the dark. At night, everything had a particular sheen; there was an array of colors and color combinations he had not seen before. He was surprised by the number of insects and creatures that emitted light.

Battling blindness and the elements kept him awake for seventy-seven straight hours. Every noise was louder in the dark. When the sun peaked over the mountains, he, like most creatures slowly poked his head out into the morning warmth as if he were being born. Sunrise, as far as most beings are concerned is the universe's greatest creation.

He emerged at dawn to be engulfed by Monarch Butterflies too numerous to count. He stayed close to the water and away from bee colonies.

He hosted newly ousted leaders that drove bullet riddled busses towards the asylum.

In the daylight, he dealt with monkeys, pythons, anacondas and numerous leeches that needed to be picked from his skin each morning. At night, his perception aligned with boa constrictors, bats, caves, rivers, constant insect sound, and warm fires.

Here there were hundreds of bird and dozens of mammal species.

The jungle was filled with an abundance of plant life. Every now and then he sat along the river's edge, watching water dragons run on the water's surface. The feats of these lizards inspired him to do the same, he didn't fare as well.

Twenty miles into this journey, it happened. He was too close to the trees along the river's bank. It happened so fast that he didn't notice it until after the emerald green mamba recoiled. He had been bitten. A burning pain shot through him. His body's reaction was almost immediate. His forearm began to swell.

He had no anti venom. He poured all of the water from his canteens on the wound and furiously washed the wound with soap. He wrapped an elastic bandage around the wound to create pressure. He almost panicked, but panicking would increase his heart rate and speed the blood flow, allowing the toxins a faster way through his circulatory system.

The venom was slowly making its way through his body. He couldn't swallow. He stumbled as his vision blurred. His muscles began to stiffen, and he fell against a large red cedar tree. He struggled to catch his breath as the trees filled with animals. The audience chattered the news of his approaching death. His skin blacked as it began to die.

Nausea had set in, and his throat constricted. Sweat streamed down his forehead and neck. He remembered all of the times he felt Brianna move inside of Sarah.

*Brianna was better than any alarm clock. She was so tiny when she was born. She was so warm and the look in her eyes. I looked at her, and a fantastic sensation ran through me. I kissed Sarah lightly on the cheek and squeezed her hand. And all the kicks and punches I felt through my wife's belly were put in context.*

*Sarah was a genius, but neither of us could remedy for the crying in-between sleep cycles, or find a way to make teething more pleasant. She spit up on my best suits. I loved bath time; Bri-bri would splash water all over me.*

*It was a month before I returned to work and two weeks before that Sarah and Brianna were tired of me. I was worried about everything.*

*Brianna loved being outside, she was fascinated by the wind dancing on the leaves. She loved music; daily she'd bang out tunes on her toy piano. After a week, we regretted buying that thing, but it made Brianna smile.*

*Brianna dominated the floor of any room she was in. She was mommy's little assistant. She even had a little white lab coat. We bought it for Halloween and it kind of stuck. Brianna wasn't in the nursery full time...*

It was then that his body began to push the toxins out of through the very holes that delivered it. Devon's body had created an anti-serum.

The pain from the snake bite was nothing compared to the sting of the Palestine Yellow he received two days before. In terms of pain nothing compared to the sting from the Bullet Ants, a nest he fell into last week, he still had welts from that. It took his body ten minutes to reject the venom from the green mamba bite.

With subsequent bites, his body needed less time to recover from them. Break time was over, and Devon slowly refilled his water canteens, he needed to be more mindful. To prevent further unpleasant incidents, Devon scaled trees as a quicker way of traveling through the jungle.

Tugging on a thick liana vine wouldn't allow a person to swing as they did in the movies, it did, however, cause hundreds of insect to rain down on you. The 'liana sway' is similar to what children do on playground monkey bars. Swaying from vine to vine was slow and tedious, and the hordes of biting insects sent Devon falling to the ground.

After he had hit the ground the fifth time, he realized another way of getting through the tropics had to be found. He practiced balancing on branches, then walking on the branches, running on them, and then jumping from one branch to another. He jumped almost fifteen feet from one tree to the next. He could drop twenty feet from one limb to swing on another for a quick descent.

Even when he was in a city, everything was new to him again, the sights, smells, and foods. Anything higher than the fifteenth floor gave him a good view of landscapes, and the warm sunshine hits your face first.

City nights are different, muted. During lunch breaks, workers smoke cigarettes together. Devon metabolism worked faster, and it was more efficient. When he did eat, he ate alone. He made efforts to sit in the coolest place; occasionally, a coworker would come and talk to him about the project they were working on.

"We are working on the twentieth floor today," "The foreman is so lazy, I could do his job." they would say to him. Devon would just nod his head.

At random points between the constant hammering, whirling machinery and huge earthmovers, people would engage him in idle talk, and he'd pretended to not understand them. Devon saw the linguistic references beyond their time and space. There was no metaphysical primacy to one language, over the many.

"How much is this one?" Devon said. "Three US dollars," said the woman.

Devon was speaking Amharic without knowing it. He adapted to a language's quirks and structure. This allowed him to converse fluently in a language a day after being immersed in it.

There was a vowel change here and there, but the constants remained the same. Devon emphasized tones and spoke the languages, he didn't adopt them. He didn't have the mannerism and vocal affectation of native speakers. If you looked at him long enough, you could see a loss in his soft brown eyes. If you spoke to him long enough, you could hear that loss in his voice.

Coworkers talked about their family, their friends, their dates, and their interests. What would Devon say if he could talk about his day:

"Do you want to climb the tallest building in the city tonight?"

"Do you want to explore the sewers with me?"

"Let me be clear, these beings are out there. They don't have a political party or a religion. And they absolutely will not stop—ever, until their mission is complete. I had a wife, a child, a job, a home, and I lost them. All of it was taken away by beings from another Earth."

And then he'd jump over a house or two just for show. "Them, who is Them?" people would most likely say with the missed remains of their lunch still on their face.

To which Devon could respond by grabbing the nearest boulder and crushing it in his hand. Then he could furl his brow look at them and say, "The anger is still growing…"

Devon could do that, he could make himself the enemy; he could have humans after him too, but why. When night fell, rising music in the distance mixed with happy voices, when he added his subtle laughter, it was clear that he didn't fit in. Before the change, all he wanted to do was fit in, and now he didn't know how.

"I must remain hidden," he said while watching them shoot weapons at each other.

Being alone was okay because his body was always in some state of shock. He wore long sleeve shirts and pants so his injuries and body discolorations during the healing process wouldn't alarm anyone. He hadn't been sick, not even a sniffle. His allergies were on vacation.

He had new feelings, new sensations, in some ways, he didn't hate these things. Muscles growth was no longer sacrificed for increased brain power. He was performing physical feats in less than the time it took to describe them. Forward rolls followed landings showed he was besting gravity.

He endured all of the bumps, bruises, and cuts to climb on top of structures. He took pains to lift his body with two fingers. He scaled rooftops, buildings, and construction machinery. He haunted bus stations, backyards, subways, and three-hour towns.

Bengali is communicated in long, rich, contextualized sentences which take on different meanings in relation to body language. Many business deals have been lost due to the tapping of feet. The beings showed up, while he taught English in Bangladesh.

*Landslide appeared far above me, and he split his energies into two paths. A ram ran across the first and then the second slide with no incident. I followed the ram and found myself stuck in between two landslides.*

*Landslide looked at me, his eyes glowing, energy flowed from his body. I stood there, watching the ground fall away beneath me. Fear gripped me, everything within me told me to run, but my knees were too weak to move my body. It was too late to run anyway.*

*I ran and jumped as far as I could to the far side, and I grabbed onto a tuft of strong grass and pulled myself out of Landslide's path, but he grabbed my legs and pulled me in. I was pinned under a half a ton of mud and debris. The crush of dirt, rock, and wood fell on me.*

*The slide stopped moving, and I caught my breath. By the time I clawed through the dark cinnamon colored mud, rescue workers in orange and red uniforms were using machines to hoist debris away from the scene.*

*The rescue workers were surprised that I was still alive; they said I had been buried for ten hours. Fifteen buildings had been swallowed up by the landslides. It's best that I keep running.*

"With the first, the cut penetrates into the timber; then make a wedge and then split a chip of wood out. Logging looks simple, but it's very mathematical, repetition, always the same repetition. If you don't bring the edge of the ax down at the proper angle, you create a glancing blow, and that could take out a limb." Devon explained to a new worker.

The sound of his ax striking a tree had the effect of scattering birds for acres. A felling axe is a cold, brutal lump of steel on the end of a stick, with a razor sharp edge. When he wasn't cutting down trees, he sharpened his axes with a two-faced diamond stone with two grits. That was the only time he was alone with his thoughts.

Whenever anyone was around, Devon would temper his swings so he wouldn't be too far ahead of the daily quota. A fell tree brought a moment of silence, and then the chopping would begin again. In routine fashion, Devon finished his share of the work early and spent the rest of the morning gazing at the clouds.

He chopped to make way for more highways, more vehicles, and more people. He chopped trees so others could extract every piece of paper, every board, every article of furniture, every structure no matter how ugly or superfluous from them, but any fool can destroy trees.

People didn't want the trees broken by time, wind, and earth. They wanted the unbroken ones. A tree cannot run away, and if it could, people would find it and destroy it. The chance to pull a dollar or two out of its branches was far too tempting.

Very few people who cut down trees ever plant replacement ones, even if they did it could never replace the eradicated magnificent forests that took thousands of years to create. For centuries those trees stood in beauty and strength, and a few swings ended that history. Nature created, cared for, and saved them from droughts, diseases, avalanches, storms, and floods, but they could not be protected from whims of fools.

Electrocutions, smoke inhalations, and numerous cuts were the results of Devon's newness to manual labor. He was severely burned, putting out an oil rig fire in Namibia. Being injured was how he discovered his recuperative ability.

Devon developed a much broader binocular vision and spectral range; which made his late night practices easier. His speed and strength grew due to the development of more long and short twitch muscle fibers.

He healed quickly but sometimes even after an injury healed he still felt phantom pain for days. Devon would also injure himself just to see how long it would take to mend.

His agility afforded him the control to perform backflips, ma- caquinhos, and butterfly twists in succession. Not only was he able to do full splits, but he was also able to do them quickly. He had almost photographic reflexes. He could see something done once and he could duplicate the same skill.

Through old films, he saw what it was like to have a family, what it was to be loved. Besides new films move the camera jarringly to hide the lack of fighting techniques, and they always pair the hero with a little girl as they were entirely produced metaphors for future social engineering projects.

He moved at speeds that would injure the average person; he had to restrain him from maintaining pedestrian human speeds. His vertical jump was almost seven feet. He jumped building to building, climbed twenty-foot walls, and he hardly bent a knee when dropping from a roof.

Devon had learned to grasp and to dig his fingertips ever so slightly into stone and metal. This allowed him to scale taller structures. He could leap onto the small buildings. The larger ones he had to climb, he stopped at the top to regain the sensation in his fingers.

He picked up the martial art of Lathi Khela from Bangladesh, Ten- shin Sho-Kai from Australia, Kali from the Philippines, and Hapkido from Korea. He used Judo for tossing and immobilizing, Aikido allowed him to back opponents off without injuring them.

The bow and arrow, nunchaku, throwing stars, daggers, the staff, and the sword were all mastered. The katana, with its long grip, squared guard, and the curved blade was his favorite tool. He liked the feel of a double edged sword, so he always had a layered, hand polished blade forged with Damascus steel on him, for meditation purposes only.

In the same time it took him to paint the nursery green, he mastered the sniper rifle, the shotgun, the assault rifle, and the handgun. He could switch hands; flip and pull the trigger with his eyes closed and still hit the bullseye.

His skill with any firearm was such that a standard such as "expert" was a novice level effort. Tactical reloads, tension grip, center axis relock; he was passed the point where stance and balance mattered.

Carrying a firearm transformed everyone into a potential target. The gun was cold, forged steel, and his least favorite weapon to use because it was the least personal. This weapon provided the least amount of thought time between action and consequence.

He could quickly overwhelm, disarm, and injure. In physical encounters with humans, he implored anything from pressure points and small joint manipulation to crushing rib cages. There were no schools of thought, no skill sets only move, fight, survive.

In physical battles with humans as one human will unavoidably be at odds with another. The chance of conflict increases when a stranger to the town dances the Kizomba with a warlord's girlfriend.

He fought through slurred speech masses that may have been pushed into fighting by these beings but more often than not, they were full of eighty proof liquid excuses. In these few months, he had more fights than during his adolescence.

Forethought allowed him to avoid nasty entanglements with weapons. He was a whirling tornado of movement, too fast for the eye to follow. Most of the time, he let gravity humble his opponents. The fights, when done right, took seconds.

On the other hand, the otherworld beings aren't above stomping on shins and knees. They also aren't opposed to snapping necks, collarbones or pushing a fist through a chest to rip out a spinal column. Devon would need more before engaging with them.

Devon could sense the coming rain. His attention to detail was astonishing, and his observations were unrivaled. His knowledge of human ability, limitations, and movements only made these encounters more predictable.

He randomly spun a ka-bar blade in his hand like a magician turns a coin. Devon talked his way out of most conflicts before they started. And when that didn't work, he incapacitated any would-be opponent until the next morning

To people he was unknown, and they were comfortable not knowing him. People ate lunch at the same time, and they talked about all the things Devon didn't want to think about. The morning skies could darken above him at any moment; his life was far from average.

# CHAPTER 9

Devon was northeast now. He existed outside of agendas, platforms, and labels. He was no longer moved by a television network schedule, a work schedule, or a timepiece… He was only driven by the world, and he had detailed notes.

Water fell from Devon's lips and evaporated before hitting the sand. In the Sahara desert, Devon was comforted more by the hisses of burrowing creatures, than meaningless conversations. Eroded rock faces provided temporary shelter from the sun; sand storms reduced his visibility to zero. These storms carried dust a hundred feet into the sky. Stinging sand swirled and piled up into mile long sand dunes.

Devon traveled the ever-changing windswept dunes. Out here clouds filled the sky to deceive because rain rarely falls. The darkness was similar to being on the ocean, except the ground didn't bob up and down.

Between mountain ranges, sand was interspersed with stone and rock. The unpolluted sky allowed light to reveal the heavens. The galaxy has all the characteristic of something alive, a living organism. Stars are different colors and brightness; they change form, have layers, have cycles of birth, life, and death, each one is singular.

Nuclear reactions within stars are the neurons that connect the brain. They communicate by light, heat, and electromagnetism. They breathe and exhale solar wind, and when they explode, they evolve into pure energy. Is a star is life-form that is beyond human understanding? People are stardust, but perhaps people are all stars.

Devon haunted beautiful places like El Tag, Kufra Oasis, Guzara Palace, and other castles. When he couldn't make it through the lung-clogging sand storms. He frequented towns that rested on the edge of the world. There was beauty in the people and the land. These people are not the barbarians they have been reported to be. Here, things were simple; it was like their own little slice of heaven.

The privileged don't have to worry about hunting, tracking, or cooking food. They don't worry about shelter and safety. They use clothing to draw attention. The privileged don't have to prepare, to structure, to organize, to defend their existence every single hour. Devon was still struggling with the concepts of first world nations and privilege.

He had rescued families before their homes were engulfed in flames, he moved someone out of the way of a falling crane. He was a more capable Jeff Jeffries, yet every night he was horrified by dreams. He was terrified by the rage inside of him. He wanted to know where his fear came from, but his main problem was keeping his feet warm.

The actions of the female otherworlders were seen as an untimely breeze that passed through a room to scatter papers about. They'd randomly knocked a book from a table, cut off the television or caused a faucet to leak. These beings were smaller but similar to their male counterparts. They had the same odd shaped head and silver glowing eyes, but they were thinner, smaller, and not as grotesque.

They wore lighter colors and seem to engage mostly when a person was asleep. They glowed when they were locked in on a subject. The target couldn't speak, wake up, or move a muscle. Their arms and legs acted as if gravity has been multiplied a hundred times.

When their target woke, they felt as if an intruder was in the room, and for a fraction of a second, they saw what appeared to be a creature that looked like something out of a horror movie standing beside their bed. They heard voices in their head.

They seemed to appear in a room or an area, they also seemed to appear and disappear at will. Devon could see how these beings could be mistaken for angels or aliens.

These smaller beings were everywhere; they dotted the landscape. Devon could now overlook them as if they were out of place sign spinners. Devon started drawing. Drawing made him see things clearer. He drew the rocks, the river, and all the animals.

Devon was particularly fond of using soft charcoals because they blended well, made deeper darker lines that were easy to smudge. Charcoal drawings have their own light, their own density. Charcoal applies to the canvas with little pressure. He smudged with his fingers here to shade and used his kneaded eraser there to remove small sections.

*These charcoals race across the page, as if the drawing were the proof of another presence as if someone else had taken up residence in my body. As I create, another part of my brain was busy inspecting the curves of the branches, the placement of mountains, shapes, contours, and the composition as a whole. My mind was the tip of my charcoal.*

Devon's drawings captured magnetic smiles, kindest hands, and eyes that are gloomy without showing the faintest academic tendency. He would occasionally leave a drawing at the base of his rock monuments, to give it an audience.

*I thought this place was just a jungle, full of savages. Most of Africa is not a jungle. This place is not war torn. These people are not savages.*

*My privileged educated caused me to feel sorry for the people even before I had seen them, but here there were white sandy beaches, pink lakes, and university campuses.*

*There were the bloated stomachs of malnutrition set against a backdrop of intrastate warfare; there was no Tarzan here. This soil I hold in my hand is where all of the humanity originated; the land here is so precious. The ruins are not only sexy; they are goldmines of opportunity.*

*The people were the friendliest people I had ever met. They lived off of what they grew. Most were interested in brotherhood, camaraderie not capitalism. Their business plan was simple… happiness.*

*If they could keep this business plan in the face of economic invaders, these places would be utopian. Unfortunately, economic invaders had already sent destabilizers into these regions bringing their morals, vices, and weapons with them.*

Devon felt that he had traveled further than Bodhidharma. He had to keep moving, and he needed information. None of the places he went were how he had been taught they were. He had little time to wonder about this educational malpractice. He had never questioned the tilt, rotation, spherical nature, or the perfect placement of the Earth, but now everything is in question.

Old men played sitars and sang old songs as he walked by. The world was filled with music, the long drawn out sentence keys of birds, the phrased pitch of cats, the deft rhythm in dog syllables, the melody of insects, the instrumentation of dolphins, the harmony of whales and beat of the human heart…without form, it's just noise.

Devon explored Reunion Island where ethnic origins define the Islanders, yet they are one people, they are colorless. He dived hundreds of feet down in the Marianas Trench. The seven-mile deep trench is the deepest part of the world's oceans.

He could only imagine a descent that deep. The deeper he dived, the more different the marine life was. It was sights like these that caused him to forget those parts of the ocean that were littered with waste.

The loudness of the world prompted Devon to visit small quiet towns where mornings smelled like fresh jasmine. He would sit just on the outskirts of villages and just breathe. He could see for miles because atmospheric pollutants did not cover these places.

There were fewer otherworlders among the inhabitants of less industrialized places. Perhaps the sun rays bouncing off of white lotus flowers kept them at bay. These places were only poor if you are an outsider.

Devon quickly hiked through the maze of islands, tidal flats, and mangroves. A Bengal Tiger and her two cubs disappeared into the hilly forests covered by mist. Here dolphins and saltwater crocodiles mingled in the slow moving river.

He was in a place on no map, in a village with no name. This village was filled with timber and straw shack houses that were painted sun bleached shades of green, pink, and yellow. This village was ten kilometers from Temburong.

Devon drank from coconuts and watched the children playing with rocks, sticks, and torn pieces of cloth— life should be simple. When these children weren't in school, they laugh and happily roll in the dirt. Devon sat on a large rock and fed a small black dog with bread from his backpack. The dog happily wagged its tail as it eagerly waited for the next piece of bread.

Heaven is whatever one wants it to be, like a dream. In the afterlife, everything one is able to imagine is possible. Heaven within humans exist in a state of flux, and its inhabitants assume whatever identity that pleases them. Heaven is becoming who you want to be and, of course, where you want to be.

Heaven is big enough for everyone to have their own private universe, and heaven is what they had right here on the edge of this jungle.

Watching people be thankful for every morsel on their plate, for every drop of brown water, for the clothes that barely covered their backs; made Devon smile. They were thankful for their narrow doorways, small windows, and dirt floors. They were not craving electronic devices, hurting one another or themselves, they were simply happy to be alive.

Devon heard the buzzing, and his expression changed. This sound was different; it was a sustained hum. People in the town stopped what they were doing and looked up. He wasn't the only one that heard the sound. The sound got closer and then from the clouds came two missiles.

There was a moment of silence, a loud noise followed by a rising cloud of flame, rock and dust rose up from the ground. The machine dropped down from the clouds, first a crackle of a jet engine and then a deafening sound as its metallic body preyed upon the people.

Metallic rocks filled with explosive payloads shot from this unmanned flying machine, shattering the quiet of the town, the calm of so many towns. The machine darted back into the clouds, came around and launched another volley of missiles into the village. One missile landed two hundred feet away from Devon, the explosion knocked him to the ground.

His ears rung, and his lungs refilled as five seconds of chaotic silence passed. Bodies were torn in half; arms and legs pieces were flying. There were unmoving bodies lying in the red mud as the earth hugged tightly those that had fallen.

Men were running, women were screaming, families separated, children dead, homes are gone, their world was burning. Their place of worship was in flames. This was not some dictator they could oppose or a rebellion that had come home to roost. There would be no one to blame, no one to be held accountable for this.

The sky turned white, followed by a tremendous roar as another missile struck. Bright orange fireballs rose up from the village as the hum drifted away from the hoarse screams, leaving behind only anger and fear. The goal of this metal predator was fear sanctioned, money approved slaughter.

Years before, suit and tie, fist pounding politicians spoke of abstract values within the controlled architecture of intelligent systems. They spoke of these machines in terms of saving lives and essential benefits. They commissioned these machines to be created with a top-down moral philosophy.

Today, right here, molten copper landed on those that were not hit by initial blasts. In the distance, cutting a swath through the jungle was a rhinoceros size robotic moral agent; this machine was also a representative of those political discussions.

This was a weapon of the insane. It was solar powered, eco- friendly, and capable of firing a half a million terrifying rounds per minute. This armored machine used its appendages to trampled bushes and pulverized trees. The machine's Advanced Countermeasure Defense (ACiD) and Defensive laser shield did not recognize Devon's thermal signature.

A glowing eyed Devon was upon this machine as it stepped into the clearing. He disabled its Direct Energy Weapons before they could be used on the inhabitants. Devon removed the monstrosity's legs and rendered this hundred million dollar investment into nothing more than a broken remote controlled car.

Devon knew that could only be the beginning. He quickly commandeered a truck and filled it with as many wounded as he could find. He clenched his teeth and endured seven miles of crying, praying, and cursing as he drove the injured to the regional hospital, some of them babies, some pregnant women, all of them human.

Smoke billowed in the distance as the village burned. Devon's foot pressed down on the gas pedal. He kept his eyes forward; he could not bear to look into the truck bed; his eyes swelled with tears. Tears cut wide paths down the soot and debris covering his face. He could smell death upon them.

In less than an hour, this town was leveled. Were they militants? Of course, living where they lived, militancy is the only way you can survive. Their simple life is strange to first world people, and it is a crime to outsiders. These people were not guilty of anything; even the most militant among them didn't pose an imminent threat.

Before Devon was changed, he glanced over articles about an airstrike like this. He defended these actions, he thought these strikes were for a good reason, but it was all a lie, this lie. This is not how to get rid of militants; this is how you created them.

The mothers, fathers, nurses, doctors, even the local farmers were forced to the mountains. They cursed the country that would allow this to happen and the citizens of any nation that refused to see them as human beings. They were faceless, voiceless, and scared to death that at any moment they could be terrorized again. Without warning, without reason, they were all found guilty.

They lived in caves for protection. For these people, what was could not now be. They'll build structures in the mountains that cannot be seen from overhead. They'll prepare to defend themselves from an enemy they cannot strike. They'll gather weapons, make alliances, and became exactly what those with agendas said that they were. Life should be simple, but it wasn't.

Devon arrived at the hospital and helped the wounded onto gurneys. He could no longer stay near the defenseless corners of the world. He moved to the concrete jungles where he would work as a pipe fitter, bottler, and laborer just to keep his mind busy.

The faces of the killed, maimed, and missing haunted his dreams. He would awaken from nightmares of blood and bone to sweat soaked sheets and darkness. He put on a uniform of shadow with his muscles still twitching. He left the confines of his hotel room and strolled through town. The fear of nightmares kept him up. His nightly excursions were his only escape from them.

Devon seemed to be at his strongest at night. His energy surged during what he called "Red Moments," moments where the infrared light was at its peak, just before sunset. His body absorbed more energy during Red Moments. Here near the equator, UV rays are at their strongest.

He tried his best to stay out of the way of the enlisted. The uniformed are told that the enemy is an object to be eliminated. They are trained that the enemy will kill you if you don't kill them first. It's not murder; it's self defense in defense of others.

This is what they believe it until they are face to face with a real live human being, who they must hate and kill for political reasons. Poor, small town kids pummeled and traumatized by life, never quite understand how wrong it all is and they sign up first.

Devon saw the soldiers who were baptized in the war together and would lay down their lives for one another. Most soldiers were happy to get away from the safe space engineers, microaggression pushers, social media agendamongers and the striking, ironic celebrations of the excess of those back home.

Back home, the people around them argued about taxes, street lights, roads, and whether or not they are for the violent aggression the nation is currently engaging in. They do this while waiting on those highly marketable memes of war heroism to fill the erotic red-and-white-and-blue figment of the public's imagination.

To them, a soldier's life and death is proof of the nation's character. The public loves the idea of war, but they never love the actual battle, and the troops know it. This shared trauma is hard for most to let go. For most, this is the only thing they are good at, for some, this is all they know; they are soldiers.

In each country, on each continent, people who are unable to tell instinct from deviancy were engaged in a myriad of conflicts from the large to the small, from the preemptive to the reactive, to weapons sales operations. Devon was at border skirmishes where artillery rounds were fired every twelve minutes. He traveled in underground chambers where rebels loaded their gun magazines in the dark.

The reasons for such violent interactions were beyond Devon; he only knew that it was best to stay out of family disputes. He scaled K2 unassisted; K2 is the second highest mountain on Earth, after Mount Everest. It is called "The Savage Mountain" due to the high number of people that have died trying to scale it.

It had been snowing in the days preceding the ascent. Devon was near the summit when an uneasiness came over him. Devon's sweat turned into ice as he saw the entire top of the mountain come down. He dropped his gear as the seismic shift triggered something primal in his brain.

Turning his head back, he saw Avalanche grab one group of experienced climbers and pull them under his whiteness. Another group of mountaineers tried to spike ice picks into the ravine as an anchor, but Avalanche ripped the anchors out and covered the people with empty whiteness.

Devon was ahead of the slide. Avalanche closed in behind him. Devon moved sideways to escape, but Avalanche hit him in the side with a large rock, knocking him into the snow. Avalanche grabbed Devon's midsection and pulled him down.

Devon kicked loose and jumped to a higher ledge. Behind him, Avalanche directed the snowpack towards him. Avalanche rolled a slab of snow the size of a small apartment building towards him. This snow monster's destruction was breathtaking.

Devon did the only thing he could, which was to lock into his bindings and point his skis downhill. He buried the nose of his skis and kicked out the tail, sending up fluffy waves of white spray. He turned his femur to rotate the skis; this drop broke his bindings.

Devon was almost swallowed by white powder. He cornered with his body leaning in the opposite direction of his skis. This rapid descent was full of with survival turns, fields of high ice clumps and jagged ridgelines.

Devon skied faster than the speed of money. He slipped and slid down the long mountain face. After another drop, the clouds dissipated and the snowfall softened.

Avalanche's last bit of energy was used to cover a hotel, the cars in the parking lot and to toss Devon into a wall near the bottom of the mountain. Devon sat there bleeding while he looked at the wake of boots and hiking equipment that stuck out of the snow.

Devon skied two miles, three thousand feet downhill in ninety seconds on broken skis. His body was sore and limped for a few days. While he healed, he wondered if the illusion of time was on his side.

A person is bored when their interactions are primarily with other parts of the body and not so much with these time circuits, this reduces our mass-energy, so time seems to slow down. Too much interaction with the brain circuits has the opposite effect of speeding up.

Mount Kilimanjaro isn't at tall as K2, but from the top, you can see other nations, and if you look hard enough, you can see your whole life. Through deep meditation and silence, Devon experienced the present, remembering the past, and sensing the future at once.

The certainty of death gives meaning to time, it allows for each moment to hold its own significance. We can travel forward, backward, or stand still in time. As Devon explored Kilimanjaro's volcanic cones, he wondered if it were possible to go back in time.

He wanted to go back in time to prevent all of this from happening, but going back in time wouldn't change history. Going back in time would create a new history, only an alternative one.

Time is measured in seconds, minutes, hours, and years, but time doesn't flow at a constant rate. Just like water in a river rushes or slows depending on the size of the channel, time flows at different rates in different places. Everything is slowing down photonic light, matter…maybe even time and gravity…

*Today it is Tuesday, and I could very well be experiencing this day in the past… Perhaps, I am now living in the past, and everything that is happening has already happened, and I am somehow experiencing it as the now… I am living in the past, the method of how is beyond me.*

Devon had done things that no one had ever done before, but the smiles on the faces of children were the only thing that calmed him. The feelings of being out of place were leaving, but whenever he started feeling free—the buzzing would begin…

# CHAPTER 10

The further away he was from big cities the more beautiful everything became. Human encroachment moved like a virus entering a host. He watched people take pleasure in debating the merits of saving the planet, but everyone could see that the Earth was sick. But these people published papers and gave speeches to thunderous applause.

Devon used various names, identities, and costumes, but he would eventually be found. Around him, the earth moved and clawed out, and small creeks turned into the man killing rapids. These beings were proficient in destroyed homes, moving propane tanks, and giving the wind a mind of its own.

Out of a window, down a fire escape, over a rooftop, underwater or solely on foot, he ran. Devon ran after weighing the present net value of his welfare.

The nightmares were affecting him. Devon was lonely and now more than ever he wanted to go back to not caring, back to frappuccinos, back to his obstructed view of the city. He wanted to go back to when that noise was just is an old creaky door.

But he couldn't go back to the way he used to feel, the way he used to think. He had been reduced to t-shirts and hoodies, he had spent too many nights curled up in a fetal position to have sustained regular conversations. To him, the conversations he had with the average person barely registered over murmurs in a dark alley.

Sarah wouldn't approve, but he thought of killing himself a dozen times before, but today would be the day. He was welding on the seventh floor, contemplating his death. Down the beam across from him, Akbar lost his balance, hit his head, and fell. Akbar landed in a pile of rebar. Devon quickly descended the building.

The foreman and crew had already roped off the area; blood was everywhere. The last gasps of life left Akbar, and the foreman yelled: "Everyone back to work!" Devon slowly retreated as the emergency crew arrived. The lunch horn sounded, and Devon walked away, never to return. Akbar's screams had been added to Devon's nightmares.

*One hundred and fifty-five thousand people die each day...why does this one death matter? Akbar always said 'good morning' to me. People die. If I do nothing to prevent their death, am I letting them die...*

Devon had fallen several stories before with only the wind being knocked out of him. Now he wasn't sure that a fall would kill him. Before the change, he had cat-like reflexes—an old cat.

After deciding to leave school, Devon thought he would vault up the corporate ladder. In positions above him, he saw untalented people. Most of them were taking the other side of trades, betting against their clients. Speed is a company's advantage; it's how they rig the markets. With these algorithms, money moves faster than the speed of light.

Algorithms earned the company two cents per trade before even buying a share for their clients. Everyone wanted to be a trader. Part of his job was to find anything under the category of "bullshit" and use it to bring in clients, and he kept them. He worked tirelessly, but he was merely an instrument of his boss, a tool without brains or backbone. Buy low, sell high...everyone says that, but no one follows that advice.

*There is a lot of money is to be made in the market, especially in difficult times. Every trade has a position. I analyzed equities, derivatives, Forex commodities, spikes in short term holdings, and group patterns. Basically, I nodded my head and sat where I was supposed to sit.*

*All those connections I made and none of them can help me now. I would pitch a client ten different tangents; I would even pitch them tech companies that speculate in financial engineering. I went from "Hello, this is Devon," to "Sir...welcome aboard" faster than most did. It doesn't take a genius to trade stocks, although, most people think that it does.*

*"There is no use sitting on cash," I would say to them. Most people don't even know what debt is, so you say what you are taught to say. You engage people, you form a relationship, and you move on... always closing, always closing. You tell them how consistently you generate twenty percent returns or beat the market. A thousand different accounts, and each one is different, all started with a lie.*

*You could buy a million shares of a puff of smoke and change lives. I specialized in controllable fiction. Every one of my near-deaths beat the hell out of being stuck in a cubicle. It beat being stuck in a place where I only interacted with another person in a break room or hallways. In a way, being chased around the world was better than scarfing down antacids all day.*

*Pattern recognition and market algorithms were one thing, but right now, I feel my brain receptors waking up. I feel them turning on. I can see the lines, the strings; those unseen connections between people, things that cause a person to do what they do. I see the patterns, the patterns that were always there; they had always been there. Everyone was connected, except me.*

Devon helped build a carbon neutral city in Masdar City. He delivered steel piping to the underground city in Amsterdam. He helped shape the glass of the pyramid cities in Tokyo Bay and combated the rising water in the Maldives.

Devon couldn't wait in line or to fill out loan applications, so he paid a few visits to ATM machines, where he removed enough cash to accomplish whatever he needed.

A well dressed family had spent seven hours riding buses to the Centre for Ophthalmic Sciences in New Delhi. The Singhs were on their way home to Safipur. Safipur is a town and a Nagar Panchayat in Unnao district in the Indian state of Uttar Pradesh.

On the crowded bus, they held their ten-year-old daughter tightly. The little girl was lowly singing "Nini baba nini; Mackhan roti cheese, Nina baba so gaya; Mackhan roti hoa gia." After she had sung the song, she giggled. Her infectious laugh reminded Devon of Brianna. Sunita was her name.

Sunita wore a new yellow summer dress, white tap dance shoes, and a self colored yellow heart patch over her left eye. She wore thick glasses. She happily played with the second hand Legos that she strained to see.

The little girl smiled, but the pain was evident on her father's face. The Singhs had spent their life savings and six years on therapies and treatments for their daughter's eye. From the other side of the bus,

Devon read the girl's diagnosis…

i. "Amblyopia, Degenerative, progressive high myopia, and Anisometropia. This is a one in two hundred and fifty thousand cases of high anisometropia with pathologic myopia. Glasses, contact lenses piggyback indicates visual processing from right eye interrupted. Right eye visual acuity is five feet, which is blurry, beyond five feet nonexistent."

Sunita was lucky to get any care, because of India's caste system. The caste system gives better treatment, better goods, and services to high caste members. By nature of birth, the Singhs weren't a part of the caste system, but Sunita still may not have been given the best treatment.

Today the Singhs learned that any surgery would be costly and likely ineffective. They were told to prepare their daughter for disabled life. There were eye surgeons in the United States that could help Sunita, but the family's bills were mounting.

Sunita grabbed a Lego, held it close to her right eye, she moved her head up and down scanning it for shape and color, and then she would decide how to use it in her shipbuilding project. Sunita was quite skilled. She put this ship together as if it was something she had built in different ways a hundred times before.

Her mother smiled at her daughter's creation, and her father kissed her on the forehead. As Devon watched this red, blue, and brown ship slowly take shape, a single tear ran beneath his sunglasses.

Devon looked out the window. He was almost at the construction site. Two days later, the Singhs received a new Lego set that contained forty thousand dollars in an envelope that simply read, "For the Singhs' trip to America."

Devon had arranged a meeting for the Singhs with the U.S. Embassy physician, and U.S. visitor visas for the family were being processed. The surgeons at the U.C.L.A. Eye Institute were waiting to examine Sunita.

Devon's risk over return numbers got him noticed over those with advanced degrees. He rose quickly from the market floor, and that's high paced applied finance, in real time. In the cubicle, he bought, sold and managed hedge and pension funds. He saw volatility before his peers did, his position was better…equities, commodities, margin… He didn't have time to help anyone but himself.

In busy towns, he saw weaker connections between people. He saw a line going from one person to another, lines that they were unaware of it. These lines first appeared as static as people walked by him. Some of these lines were faded; others were, solid. These otherworlders had no connecting lines.

When Devon had his fill of Britain's ancient byways and rough-hewn granite cliffs, he made his way to London. The New Westerfield Shopping Mall is where he decided to touch one of these lines connecting people. A man and a woman sat on a bench on the second floor; lines of connections shot out in all directions. Devon moved slightly so he could touch a fading line from the man.

From this touch, he got fragments of people, places, and things. He touched a more robust line, and he could see a passionate embraced between the man and his mistress. Devon looked at the man's wedding ring and lies thick as any funnel cloud surround him. He heard the name calling, the hiding of money, and the cries. He quickly let go of the line as he was overwhelmed.

He looked at the man, and he loathed him. After loathing, the man for another minute, Devon turned to the smiling woman, and he touched one of her solid lines. This connection was to her garden, which she cultivated daily, there were no jasmines there. The woman smiled and went about her day; she managed a prominent hotel. This brought a smile to Devon's face.

Devon touched a fading line from the woman this connection showed that buried deep in the garden that she loved so much, was her mother. A mother she had poisoned over the course of a year until she died, leaving the house to her only daughter. She buried the body in the garden fifteen years ago. The line showed the guilt she couldn't erase.

He looked at the woman and almost vomited. In an effort to clear his head, he touched connections of people that were just passing by, and each time he removed his hand as if it had been resting in a fire. He touched another connector, and another nightmare was present.

Hearing 'no' only encouraged deviancy in people…they admire resistance. They get drunk and fall headlong into the laps of classmates in—forgettable, regrettable encounters in the restrooms, cars, hallways, and alleys. They throw back glass after glass of alcohol, not to have a good time, but to lessen their responsibility.

Having multiple relationships was their way of avoiding total intimacy with one person. Never being adequately represented in any one relationship makes them feel less vulnerable. They cling to people who they have grown apart from. They resent their dysfunctional codependent relationship mates for not calling them out.

They lose respect for them. They lose respect for anyone who ever chose to be with the likes of them… because long ago they lost respect for themselves. People are always outraged or offended by something or someone. They just conveniently overlook their own appalling deeds.

They have evolved in an atmosphere of fear; they have become counterproductive, degenerates, itching to hate. At any given time, they come into your life, destroy, and harass, and then they disappear.

People, these human cramps were preoccupied with profession and only acquainted with ambivalence. Their actions are motivated by the fear that they are unlovable. They hated who they were. Not one of them was honest…not one.

Devon wanted to turn all of them in. He detested all of them. Exhausted from touching these connectors, he had to get out of there. He left the mall, and that country with no with answers and more nightmares added to his own.

Devon should have forgotten his horrible imaginings. He should have come up with a marketing plan for Whitman's Glasses. He could make a fortune selling devices that allow people to look into a different world. Before he could think up a marketing plan, an explosion ripped through the Cairo neighborhood, bright red balls of flame lit up the night sky. It was things like that that prompted him to leave a city.

Twilight dew draped his neck, and he was over the hill before dawn. The provincial capital of Luang Namtha is the largest city in north-west Laos. It is a popular destination to hike from Laos to China. It is an excellent place to trek into the hills and visit tribes. Devon rented a scooter so he could travel to nearby villages and waterfalls.

No buildings stood over three stories to disrupt the skyline, and traditional melodies floated through the air, mixed in with repetitive car horns. Motor scooters dominated the streets under the low slung electrical wires. The brightly colored tents of the night market lined either side of the road. In some of these tents, meat sizzled on bamboo skewers. You could smell the vegetables, noodles, and peanut sauce.

At the counters of these markets, there was no corporate social engineering. Devon's eye was caught by a small stuffed white elephant; it reminded him of the red teddy bear he didn't have a chance to give Brianna. He purchased the elephant and attached it to his backpack. Here everyday people, assassins and weapons traffickers all mingled together. They were aware of their heritage of being one people for a time. What they felt for each other could be called hate except they each had a homeland, and were comfortable in their ethnic separations. They hated outsiders more than their differences.

Pop music fueled young kids in the day, while for some reason songs by 'The Police' were a significant fascination of local bar patrons at night. In these bars they did Bing Crosby imitations, prostitutes unruffled by mayhem and violence in their workplace, beautifully lied to patrons.

Days of punctuated equilibrium caused Devon to wander, to live off the land, to ride horses through open plains, and to bathe in streams. When his muscles to ached, he watched the breeze dance on leaves and cloud banks cover green mountain tops.

Those moments of healing were when he thought of his family the most. Those were the moments when being evasive with his answers didn't seem to satisfy the average person. He would respond to a question with a pause so long it clearly represented an internal debate on whether to respond at all.

He decided to keep his mouth shut, so people could think what they want. They'll make up their own answers. It can only end badly if he allowed someone to get too close.

Devon forgave his boss, his coworkers, and his cousin who always asked for money he never paid back. He forgave anyone who ever had an unwarranted, unkind word towards him.

He was no longer defined by his suit or his job. He no longer impatiently waited on his bonus. The memory of a murdered wife and child burned freshly within him.

In two years Devon went from late night parties and beer pong to marriage and being a father to at this very moment wondering about every danger imaginable. Devon's internal thoughts overflowed; he needed to share what he was learning.

He took jobs near learning intuitions; his brain needed an outlet, something he couldn't do in a monastery cleaning pots. While mopping the floor of a university, he wheeled his water bucket into the corner and wrote on the whiteboard.

**Ketosis**: the liver burns fat and exports ketones to the body. It shortens the carbon fragments. The body wants ketone fuels more than it wants glucose. Self contained beta-oxidation independent energy of glucose can reverse insulin dependence. This process affects how a brain works.

'*Change the mental disposition; change the impact on gene expression. The cumulative effects of nutritional deficiency from your parents can be reversed*' he scribbled.

Devon wrote random musings down and erased them, but some- times he would smile and let what he wrote remain.

"Humans are the only creatures that drink milk from another creature. Milk produces cataracts and eye problems. Industries mention calcium to sell it. Milk causes an inflammatory body response within humans. Most humans are allergic to milk," Devon explained to a department head. The way an idea lit up a face was a guarantee that his thinking would spread.

While he emptied garbage bins, he explained to the European Food Authority Board, that the food pyramid had always been upside down and that the great myth about natural medicines was that they were not scientific.

The multiple plaques on the walls called for board members to object, when he said, "plants don't want to be eaten, this is why they have built-in defense mechanisms. Twenty percent of plant function is devoted to self defense. This self defense is what makes fruits, such as chili peppers, hot."

Worldwide there were thousands of doorways for these beings to enter. Devon made sure that he stayed away from Nagasaki, Hiroshima, Fukushima, and Chernobyl.

In Turkey, he immersed himself in a white turquoise hot spa, which lay below the ruins of Hierapolis. The locals call it 'The Sacred Pool'. This seventeen tiered pool overlooks the city of Denizil. This spring was created by layers of cool calcium carbonate mixing into white limestone.

The water of this infinity pool was just over two hundred degrees. The sunset was more beautiful than any he had seen before. Devon sat in the liquid and cocked his head to the side, and he was at peace, a peace which lasted ten minutes.

A car exploded in the middle of the street. A few more explosions rocked the city. The main building's glass doors blew out spraying large shards of glass. A flaming pole crashed down, dragging its wires onto the pavement. Bodies were flying through the air.

Close to him, a man and a woman had smudged and scorched faces. Devon walked through the town as cries filled the air. Dust filled the air; people stumbled past him, moving away from the smoke... Devon looked away.

Explosions were a theme woven into the fabric of human lives, just like the funeral processions that moved through the streets following such blasts. It took three hours for Devon to pull the first body out of the rubble. She was alive but wasn't the last child to be dug out of the debris. This time, it wasn't otherworlders.

Explosions took place in Beirut, France, Germany and Japan, and Egypt. There was further human carnage at beachside hotels in Grand Bassam, Ivory

Coast, a mosque in Nigeria, a soccer stadium in Saudi Arabia, and a park in Lahore, Pakistan. An explosion left a Somali bus filled with burnt bodies.

An explosion ripped through a mosque and a shrine in Saudi Ara- bia while armed attackers assaulted a nightclub in Cameroon. Among the victims were Jews, Christians, Atheists, Hindus, and Buddhist, Americans, Chinese, Congolese, French, Germans, Israelis, Lebanese, Macedonians, Peruvians, Polish, Russians, Laotians.

Three hundred members of families were blown apart by bombs as they celebrated the end of Ramadan in Baghdad. Sixty-seven were dead at the Istanbul airport, fifty-three in Afghanistan, twenty-seven Italians, thirteen Japanese, five American students and one woman from Bangladesh.

There were two thousand surviving relatives: four hundred people who had lost a parent, one hundred twenty left with without a spouse. More than nine hundred victims, young and old, left behind parents, whose language of mourning translates across borders.

The victims were musicians, scholars, teachers, waitresses, police officers, farmers, students, airport workers, an owner of a textile factory, a tour guide, a blacksmith, a woman on horseback, a graduate in a cap and gown, a man strumming a guitar, a team lining up for soccer trophies, a family eating dinner, a seller of chickens, a bride and her groom, a mother was killed along with her son and two daughters, niece and nephew—all gone.

Unseen submersibles capsized two large rubber dinghy packed with immigrants, on its way to Italy. Five hundred were pulled to safety, one hundred fifty were not so lucky. This week long stream of death was becoming common.

For some reason, hate spread rapidly, like venom. It enters through the extremities and travels to the brain, closing the mind. Then it makes its way to the heart to blacken emotions. This dehumanizes the enemy, whereby the opponent is viewed as less than human and thus not deserving of moral consideration.

As Devon nursed his wounds, more bombs and bullets tore holes in homes and communities. Behind and in front of each tragedy, children tightly held books against their chest as if shields. Worldwide the edge, the terror of war had been lost due to its familiarity.

Devon's spirit was in tatters. He had little time to explore hand tunnels cut in the Swiss Alps. He roamed Hagia Sophia, Sagrada Família and Saint Basil's Cathedral. He hid his tears with Byzantine stained glass windows. The

Romanesque and Gothic style apocryphal medieval custom architecture sparked his mind further.

Devon meditated and did yoga, yet the nightmares remained. His subconscious held on to dreams of being choked, it held on to the pain. It was only when he kissed Sarah that the dream felt real, but every night he would wake drenched in sweat, soaked in fear with his daughter's voice echoing "Daddy…daddy…"

He missed his talks with Sarah; he missed the walks, but more than anything else, he missed her embrace. He liked to look at her when she wasn't looking. He imagined her voice as she hummed Brianna to sleep. In these dreams of the past, he was still socially awkward. The music played, and he and Sarah stepped on each other's toes and laughed.

The higher the frequency, the less human the stock market became. Most people trade in bulk; these companies see the orders before anyone else, buy low and sell them at a higher price. That's how companies play both sides of the public and private exchanges.

The Feds never come down too hard on these companies because buying and selling were always good for the economy, and it's all just too big to control. No penalty can outpace profit. Devon didn't aggressively turn over client accounts. He was personable over the phone, he wasn't a genius, but he could sell… boy, could he sell.

None of that mattered now as Devon hoped the pitch-black darkness of catacombs would provide him with protection and help him forget. Some caves were submerged in water. Some were so deep that diving to the bottom of them was impossible. Some provided a refuge for those who were religiously persecuted.

Water scorpions, salamanders, and cave fish without eyes lived in these acidic environments. Rope ladder and narrow stone stairways cut through ten-mile cave systems that were filled with sulfate breathing microorganisms and bacterial landscapes. These underground domains were filled with limestone formations.

Two meter cones frosted with gypsum hung from the ceiling. Erosion helped create this multi-level river system, waterfalls, and passages with alternating layers of limestone.

Most of these caves were filled with almost translucent creatures and high levels of carbon dioxide. The pools of warm water stunk of rotting eggs when you disturb it as hydrogen sulfide is given off. Cut off from the world, bats, rodents, snakes, giant insects, and troglodytes thrived.

One chamber had three meter long blue ice crystals that rose from the ground; they were surrounded by sulfuric acid streams. Some caves had ceremonial pyres filled with human bones, skull bits, legs, and arms bones; others had monograms still inscribed on the limestone walls.

Located in the remote Georgian mountain range was The Voronya. Centuries ago, large caves like this one were places of worship with levels that didn't go deeper than seventy feet. This cave was partially eroded from exposure.

Devon easily navigated narrow passages, low ceilings, and small crawlspaces. Before the change, he had a touch of claustrophobia, but now nothing of that condition remained.

Devon didn't mind the distance, the darkness, and the solace. He did mind crawling on his elbows and the water that trickled down the walls into his underwear. The marble that lined this cave made the slightest sound linger on its walls. Even with his thermoregulation, it was still cold.

People, in all of their glory, had created these underground networks. They created networks of simple dirt rooms next to rooms that were so large they had their own arches and art gallery. This cave had an intricate labyrinth that spanned for miles.

The high carvings and frescoes on the walls depicted scenes of deliverance. Other representations were banquet scenes that showed human perfection. Wall art often portrayed people as supernatural beings disguised by everyday existence.

Devon imagined the ceremonies that went on in this place. He explored all of it. The soft stone, rubble, intrigued him. His plan to listen to music to fill the time was foiled by the mildew and dampness that caused his music player to malfunction. He was left with only with a whistle, two pocket knives, a fire kit, a small mirror, braided rope gear and harness, a space blanket, a water filter, a compass, and extra batteries for flashlights.

He smoothly went down twenty meter shaft lines with ropes. He crawled through tiny limestone tunnels, with half the usual concentration of oxygen. He was careful not to disturb the ancient sanctuaries. After three days underground, the shaking earth woke Devon. He moved chamber to chamber and quickly climbed.

The walls of the cave were collapsing. The shaking ground shook him to one knee as jagged cracks cut up the wall like a snake. Devon went through a small opening as dust and rock fell from the ceiling. Devon crawled twenty yards in knee deep water.

Devon had crawled into a dead end. As water filled the room, Devon used his hands to frantically tunneling up through the dirt. He held his breath as he tunneled through fifteen feet of earth, to emerge from the muddy tomb. He gasped as he inhaled the night air.

He was barely out of the cave when it imploded, taking half of the forest forty feet down. All of the care Devon took not to disturb these environments, only to now have them destroyed. Devon pulled himself out of the mud and ran down a concealed path that wound through hundreds of trees. The trail led to an icy lake. Trees were still breaking in the distance.

He breathed heavily at the edge of the lake, pulling off leeches.

Was nowhere was safe?

# CHAPTER 11

It was dangerous for Devon during the day, but aside from the night obstacle course of burned-out ruins, unexploded bombshells, unlit trails, and metal drums with bodies inside of them.

Warlords drafted children, who could barely lift a rifle, for their makeshift army. They had armed forces which roamed the night, and they had no rules. Some went into villages to kill and kidnap people in the middle of the night. They beat people, set fires with no fire or police departments nearby, they were feared. He had to watch out for warlords.

Devon was cautious at night because a lot of families sleep on rooftops because of the heat. Below them, uniformed soldiers shot hungry dogs that tried to take pieces from their fallen squad members. On the other side of the city, dozens of marauders ride in the back of old pickup trucks to gather in the jungle, to set up training camps, to shoot rifles into the air.

The lawless make way when a Kunai knife, thrown from over a hundred feet away, whizzed by their ear. In places where all they have is faith, those people that are feared—fear ghost, omens, and bad signs. When those tactics didn't provide the necessary movement, there's always cognitive recalibration.

Devon was growing tired of staring at ceiling fans, counting molecules, and regularly seeing new faces and relationships that don't last. He had lost everything, and now nothing gave him peace. His moment of pity would, for the first time give way to the thought of going back to where it all began…

*Home. Back to all the things I hate.*

Devon was running from them, but he was enjoying his encounters with these otherworld beings. With these beings, he was able to express frustration, anger, and fear. He didn't have to pretend, hide, or hold back. Sometimes during these encounters, injuries to people were unavoidable.

As far as Devon was concerned, these beings could keep their glowing eyed birds, orange waterways, fire trees, flowers with petals of ethereal light. They could have their quad volcanoes that spewed ice, soft flats of black sand, white water dragons, and canines that burst into flame when angry. Humans won't resent their bio suits, airships, kinetic shields, and their disease free society.

And we, humans, will keep our wheeled vehicles, no-fly zones, government contractors, cyber treaties and separate but equal internet. We'll enjoy our fads, microbrews, bucket challenges, brontobytes, and genetically altered children. Humans will be utterly unhappy with our class stratified society, unequal distribution of resources, and smartphone filled slums.

Devon could have gone back North America aboard La Bestia, the beast, the immigration train. This was a ride so perilous that women dressed as men for safety. He refused to ride in trains for the safety of other passengers.

He could use the tunnels that ran underneath the border. These tunnels were used to move drugs, people, and weapons from place to place. Taking underground tunnels that might be filled with people and weapons was too much of a risk for him to impose on anyone.

He would go back home by Coyotaje. The small town was just beyond the farms of old men. He and eleven others would be smuggled across the western United States border under cover of the night in an old, refrigerated van driven by Juan and Guillermo.

Street vendors of all types lined the Mexican streets with their wood carvings, baskets, tortilla holders, hammocks, cowboy hats, sombreros, ponchos, and handmade wares. The border between the United States and Mexico was full of holes when enough money is involved.

Devon was eager to leave the aroma of leather and wicker. Most of the people in the back of the van slept for the journey. The Perez' did not sleep. To blend in Devon slightly changed his skin tone. He was unremarkable, but the Perez' had been watching him since the trip started.

The Perez' were undocumented, meaning that they were immigrating without paperwork. They sought to launch their dreams and give their child hope by arriving unseen in a new country. They were traveling to a country where they would live in constant fear; for a chance at second class citizenship.

In the back of this van, several countries were present. They spoke different languages, Devon understood all of them. A man lying on the floor said this was his third time crossing the Rio Grande into the United States.

The Perez' mouths smiled, but their body language and the sound of their empty bellies indicated the seriousness of their situation. Devon eased down next to a man who slept on the floor; Devon's face grew dark with anger because he hadn't foreseen the indignity of the dirty van.

The Perez' were so filled with hope that they spent their last dime to fund this trip. All they had left was each other. They huddled together in the back of that uncomfortable vehicle, where the heat rose by the minute.

Nations use war to impose second class citizenship; visa programs allowed them to raid countries for bright minds and able bodies. Faceless and voiceless, these people and their status would be the fodder of weekly televised debates.

"Mister, do you know what happens if we get caught?" asked Margarita, the mother asked Devon as the vehicle rolled through the valley.

"I'm afraid I don't know much about it. My guess is they'll send you back," Devon said. He was relieved that he wasn't talking for the sake of talking. He smiled and opened his backpack, reached in, and pulled out some bread.

"Mister, can I have some?" asked Fernando, their son. Fernando couldn't have been more than eight years old.

"Fernando...mejia, stop," his mother said.

"It's okay," said Devon, breaking the bread, and dispensing it to the family as they eagerly extended their hands.

"I am going to America to become a doctor...," Fernando said with his mouth full.

"Why are you in the back of this van? Isn't this your country?"
asked Fernando's father.

"It used to be."

"What is your name?"

"I used to be Devon Heathrow..."

The family ate and drank and shared their stories with Devon.

Devon smelled the burning PCP Juan had brought along for the trip. From the front cabin, he heard Juan and Guillermo taking over the Ranchera music. Juan and Guillermo planned to rob the passengers. When they were sure everyone was sleep, they would stop the van short of its intended destination. They brought a shotgun and a magnum to help them with this plan.

Guillermo and Juan took a particular interest in Devon because he paid his fare quickly and without haggling. They were sure he had more money. These two jackals planned to shoot everyone, they planned to shoot Fernando's father in the face.

Fernando's father was an authoritative speaking man. He talked them into giving him a discount for the trip.

"She's pretty but too old to be sold to an American," Guillermo remarked.

Instead, they would sell Margarita to a law abiding, corporate citizens who didn't quite have enough money to take international business trips to satisfy their deviancy.

"We'll train her," Guillermo said. "After we drug her." Juan laughed.

The two chuckled as they spoke of the sticks that would beat her with and the chains that they would use to hold her while she was groomed to go from bed to bed, to take cold showers, to use quickly use makeup and accept strangers.

Five men per night, ten, twenty— maybe Margarita would survive for a few years, perhaps she would kill herself. They laughed as they talked about turning her into an object of whatever the buyer's fantasy was.

"Your life or your son's…"

"We don't have to take the little brat with us, leave him here. If he gives us any trouble…shoot him.

"Si este gringo causa problemas, matelo," Guillermo said.

These are the things Devon overheard. He had to hide his emotion from the rest of the passengers.

"Mister, why are you going back? What are you searching for?" Margarita words brought Devon's mind back.

"I am searching for the truth."

"When you find the truth, what are you going to do with it?"

Devon did not know the answer to this question. He sat in silence for the rest of the trip and ate bread with the Perez'. Once the groans in their bellies calmed, the Perez' were able to sleep. All Devon could think about was how his actions had once again put people in danger. These people gave their trust and money to someone they did not know to bring them to the other side of an imaginary line on a map.

This family was desperate, but at the least, these parents gave a damn. Once they were out of the valley, the vehicle slowed and rolled to a stop.

Devon got up and quickly forced the cargo door open and quietly stepped out. Fernando sat up, wiped his eyes, and looked at Devon.

"Go back to sleep. I'm just stretching my legs," whispered Devon. Fernando laid his head back on his mother. Devon moved along the side of the van. Guillermo must have heard him because he grabbed the shotgun and opened the door. Devon quickly slammed the door closed. The cold hard steel of the double barrel shotgun struck Guillermo in the head. He fell over unconscious.

Devon opened the door and with one hand, threw Guillermo into a cactus. Juan lifted his pistol to fire, but Devon grabbed his hand. He squeezed Juan's trigger hand, breaking it. Guillermo recovered, and ran to the van. As he came to the door, Devon kicked it open, again striking Guillermo in the head; still, he was unconscious.

"Mister, please let me go," whined a bleeding Juan.

"You weren't going to let any of us go," Devon said and then he tossed Juan out of the van. Fear danced on their faces as Devon walked towards the men. It was the same look Devon had on his face when his back was broken. Tears flooded down their faces as Devon dragged the two men into the darkness.

He returned to grab the shovel and spent the next twenty minutes, digging a ten-foot-deep grave. Devon buried both men up to their necks in the desert. The passengers only heard a few thumps as the truck briefly rocked.

Devon drove the van the rest of the distance. In the light of dawn, Devon woke everyone up and announced that their drivers had abandoned them, but they had arrived at their destination. Everyone gathered their belongings and exited the van.

"Are we in America?" "Yes, mejia, we are."

Devon turned to Fernando and gave him the elephant that hung from his backpack.

"What is it, mister?" Fernando excitedly asked. "A White Elephant...for luck," replied Devon.

"Gracias, mister, gracias..." Fernando said clutching the stuffed animal.

"You will have better tomorrows," Devon said.

The family's tomorrow will be better. They had passed their stories to Devon, and he had passed a few thousand dollars into the father's bag. This was the money he relieved the drivers of. The rest of the way would be on foot, they all went their separate ways. Devon disappeared into the approaching morning; his destination was beyond borders.

He quickly made his way through America's midsection, and he immediately went to Pennsylvania so he could visit Sarah and Brian- na's grave. He walked through the cemetery, slowly crushing blades of grass under his feet. A weakness hit him when he saw the headstones of his mother and father. They had been killed in a car accident during a freak downpour.

Devon lied down in between the headstones and cried out. The winds whipped about his head as he knelt beside the graves. He placed lilies on the grave and a single pansy on Sarah's headstone. On Brianna's grave, he placed daisies and a small stuffed blue dolphin. He didn't speak because he couldn't. He kissed his wife's headstone and embraced the tombstone of his daughter.

Devon ran from that place. That night, the sky darkened. The night sky seemed to darken whenever Devon was at his saddest, which was quite often. Everything that mattered to him had been taken away, yet once again he was pushed into the heart of death and destruction. The dreams that infested his subconscious became worse.

Devon could now clearly see Them. It wasn't the same as when he had Whitman's glasses on. These beings hardly made a sound. When they were near, Devon still heard the buzzing, but it no longer disoriented him.

The otherworlders Mist, Aftershock, Explosion, and Sinkhole had become increasingly more involved in happenings. Devon wondered how many of these beings could there be. Devon hadn't been attacked since his return. Devon wasn't sure what he had done to stop the attacks and talking to Them was pointless.

"What are you doing here?" "What's your mission?" "How is your day going?"

Other than showing surprised that they could be seen, these otherworlders had an impressive array of growls followed by "Sapien." These overseers looked down on humans. Human cities are technological marvels; learned places of commerce and exchange, but to these otherworlders, people were more notorious than the people of Kamagasaki, Zhejiang Village or Kowloon Walled City.

Devon had learned the otherworlders, could manipulate elements on a molecular level. They controlled oxygen molecules to cause fires. They joined hydrogen and oxygen molecules and summoned rain. They controlled substances in the bedrock to create seismic jolts that triggered tectonic faults.

They are physically similar to humans, and they didn't always kill. The movement of the lighted patterns on their coats varied. The lights quickly changed from unrecognizable symbols to symbols of whirlwinds, fire, earth, waves all of these symbols glowed with a silvery luminescence. The lights increased intensity and frequency at various times during their missions.

They seemed to appear out of thin air. They would jump over a building and disappear. Devon saw more tornados created than anything else, probably because tornados are common in most countries.

Tornado, with his eyes glowing, carefully moved his hands as the funnel cloud was summoned down from Devon walked through the destruction as it happened, ducking flying vehicles, and items destined to be found somewhere in the woods. Homes were flattened, closets exploded, lifeless bodies were scattered on the ground.

Tornado's eyes lost their glow, and the funnel clouds dissipated. The winds settled and crying people walked through the broken town. They picked up their belongings among the shredded wood, careful to avoid the sparks from high tension wires. Devon felt lost as he looked over the destruction. He helped those he could; somehow, that made him feel better.

Natural disasters, symbolize the vast and indifferent power of the universe, a power that gives life and cruelly snatches it away.

Downpour grinned as he called down heavy rains that raised the river. Within an hour, the river crested and flooded three towns; water was high as a car roof. Downpour finished his mission and jumped into the sky.

Devon again ran into Tornado and his assistant as they completed another mission. They had created a series of funnel clouds that never touched the ground. These small twisters were harmless; they shook a few telephone poles. Then the two ran through a field and into a nearby neighborhood.

Devon followed them to a small, quiet street where instantly, the sky darkened as the light was pulled into the other plane. Tornado and his partner ran right passed a young girl and a boy riding bikes.

Time slowed down, or Devon began to move in slow motion. Either way, there was a slowness accompanied by the shaking of the street. There was a thunderous sound the street cavitated as molecules broke down as were torn apart.

A small bright orange, almost neon light radiated a few hundred yards away. The small hole expanded the way a metaphor expands within the conscious. Them ran into the void and were gone. On the other side of the void was a larger world full of dark fury, but the light distorted the view of anything beyond it.

The light disappeared as quickly as it had appeared, the sky brightened, and Devon felt the pull no more. Devon walked down the street, wondering why no homes were damaged. Not even a piece of litter had moved. The children playing on the sidewalk stopped riding their bikes and stared at him.

"Did you, did you just see…" said Devon.

"See what? Mister…mister…" said the little girl.

Devon was the only thing strange on the street. The entering of the rift had occurred within a matter of milliseconds. Devon saw them go through the gateway. If he had blinked, he would have missed it. Devon witnessed the doorway into this other world, a rift. The rift was still there, but it was not inviting to Devon.

Devon had been told that no human could survive the journey between Earths and that the travel between worlds was the reason for Them's disfigurement. Seeing the swirling rift up close extinguished the flames of Devon's curiosity. He looked for the sub-flux that made the entry point possible. As he walked, he heard a low hum.

The sound came from a large tree. He thought that it was the clatter of some insects, but as he walked closer to the tree, he could see that it wasn't a tree at all. It was a cell tower made to look like a tree. The perfect Trojan Horse.

# CHAPTER 12

In big cities, Devon avoided the drone patrolled sky and ubiquitous cameras disguised as gargoyles attached to buildings. He spent countless hours watching the untoned, relaxed fat bodies go in and out of fast food establishments.

Sounds, lights, and endless promotions bombarded storefronts that doubled as billboards. There is always a railway line that provided pristine views of dirty parking lots, day labors taking cigarette breaks, and metallic colored roofs dotted with air conditioners.

The thing about big cities is every time Devon hit refresh he was furiously bombarded by millions of mindscapes. He traveled above or underneath it all; pigeons were his only company.

Otherworlders went about their mission, with no fanfare and no high fives. They come out of a rift, complete their task, and return to the rift within hours. Devon had to always be ready to move, and he moved if a pin dropped, if the wind blew too hard, if the ground shook or if water dropped from a cloud.

Before he was changed, he had planned his drive to work, he timed the elevator ride to the fourth floor, but today he had absolutely no idea what he was supposed to be doing. He looked for clues, any connection between people and these otherworldly beings, and he did notice things.

He noticed how people slightly raise their voice in passive denial. He could tell the history of a person if he watched them long enough. Each time he arrived in a new city, he carried a smile and new hope. In every city, he walked precariously on ledges until the night air was filled with the smell of cheap drugs and alcohol.

Car lights probed the darkness on deserted streets, and this light gave birth to forms. Devon may have been in the shadows, but he wasn't the only one. Every nation had prowlers spying on citizens. From the shadows, he watched arch criminals disguised as humanitarians run corporations.

Agents of chaos were in every country, wearing business suits as they stroked the economics of conflict. Companies injected people, who marginally respected life enough not to kill on sight, into barley holding peace processes. And these agents weren't armed with words; they were armed with slogans, guns, and all the bullets they could carry. To them, good business is where you found it, and it was without morals.

Devon felt better walking the streets for long periods of time during in climate weather because rain and snow kept most people in their caves. When it rain, Sarah's favorite thing to do was make love. When it rained, he missed her even more.

Water gurgled downpipes and made large rooftop puddles for him to splash through.

*I am wet.*

The gently falling rain filled his mind with images of lit candles, chocolate drizzle on Sarah's mouth, and ice slowly dripping down her back. Devon jumped to a larger building as the rain washed the streets cleaner than any city program.

In this alley, the soon to be arrested, James Anderson, a known male supremacist, only stabbed because he was too obese to fight. Further down the street were a group of gloomy children, a stylish man wearing gold chains, and a miniskirt wearing Healthcare professional who spoke loudly on a gaudily decorated smartphone.

Could he just walk up to them and ask them about themselves? Even if he did, they would never tell the truth about anything that mattered. There is innocence in animals that is not found in people.

People are the only creatures that can make the world worse or better. Devon could see why animals make a deliberate choice to run into traffic or fly into an airplane engine.

To pass even more time Devon took to reading short stories, stage plays, scripts and novels like Heat of Darkness, The Brothers Karamazov, The Metamorphosis, Anna Karenina, Atlas Shrugged. These were all novels that Devon once found incomprehensible but were now easy reads.

He saw how people had become so numb that being belligerent was a crime, not following directions was executable, and having a bad day was something to be incarcerated for. The media and the government made great storytellers.

He watched those in positions of power tell the masses that something is against the law, it's illegal. He watched those same people in positions of power breaking the law a hundred times a day.

He listened to the mothers who spent their lives crying because their children kill in spectacularly mundane ways. He saw people fighting the peace. They aren't lifeless, they are lifeless.

Devon trained where no one else would train, he fought battles in cars, elevators, mountain trails. To avoid the lines of connections between people, he wore dark sunglasses at night, but there was nothing he could do about the rift. Each time he looked into rifts, a chill went up to his spine.

Devon watched otherworlders cause accidents and natural disasters and then he would try to save people. Devon intervened with the females by merely flashing his blue-ribbon smile.

He would perch on tops of buildings and stare at them in an acknowledgment that he could see them. The female otherworlders weren't as tall as the males. They each had a tattoo of light emblazoned on their right shoulder, and they wore a variety of elegant garb.

Their hair moved as if it had been painted in a fresco. They moved almost as if floating. Their light gowns flickered randomly with soft light. The brightness of their dress color intensified based on their contact with a subject.

At their most intense, they were glimpsed from the corner of an eye, but the human brain always discarded their appearance as too much information and relegated them as merely a figment of the imagination.

Years before Devon was changed, there were moments in his life where his anger had got the better of him. In the heat of the moment, he would make up his mind to go somewhere or to do something, but a misplaced key or missing wallet deterred these impulses. These are the kind of questions the search for answers brought about.

The Earth, this Earth, wasn't broken as far as Devon could tell; it moved along without a hitch. It was something that was bought into, something that was propped up, something which one died for. It allowed one's mind and ego to be stroked. It allowed for one person to place themselves over another. It was pure, no-hope-Americana.

People, these people were byproducts of someone taking advantage. They didn't know that their arrests, life, and sicknesses were blue chip commodities.

Children, above all others, were the most manipulated. Innocence in a young child is rudeness in an older one, but here there is a pill for that.

Parents prostituted children for causes. These pimps placed their children in pageants, sports, and shows. Some of these parents are in the stands cheering about rabid in their behavior.

Others allowed their children to be coddled and molested by the state. Still more have sold their children to corporations, or placed them in front of a screen and didn't monitor what was on it. That way, the parents could claim they had no idea where any bad behaviors come from. The parents pretended they didn't know why the child had a tantrum in the store for the newly released, five times marked up, new product.

Advertisements are technological nursery rhymes to children. As Devon watched them, it seemed that parents hate their children, and their children grow up learning to hate their children. Mom and Dad had been replaced by a screen, and to them, this was normalcy, and here, there is a pill for that.

Parents want the children educated just enough to pass muster, but not enough to excel beyond them. This is why they have long go-nowhere debates about education. These parents never told their children that they were conceived for loyalty, not love. Consumption drove everything, and here, there is a pill for that.

Devon was growing more cynical by the day because the average person seemed to have a greed gene that reared its head at the most peculiar moments. Food was everywhere; there were people who gouged themselves. All around him, people regularly tossed food on the street as if it were filth. There were other people who allowed fruit and juices to run into the gutters.

People smiled as corporations had them eating term papers. Corporations couldn't resist adding the unique formula to tomatoes. This special formula made the vegetable grow faster, it made the tomato juicier, and it made the tomato insect free.

This formula also caused diseases and a craving in humans that could be best described as an addiction. This addiction made it easier for other formulas to enter into the human diet, and there is a pill for that.

Ten-minutes of observation is all Devon required for a complete psychological analysis. Where most people saw shame and disrespect, others see an opportunity to play the victim, as if bad things only happen to those that speak out on them. Social change for economic profit isn't social change.

He was part of an industry of allegation and each allegation requires an industry to report and defend. He promoted the social contagion, politically correct, disingenuous partisan discussion to create a perception above facts. He had applauded those that said feelings are more important than reality. Now all he had was.

Nightmares.

Four walls.

A small window.

Devon consumed all of the darkness. He woke up from these twisted imaged. Otherworlders don't just exist in darkness; they aren't just blurring the lines between real and illusion.

Every minute they are judging each other on folds of skin; equality takes away your choice. They believe that beauty requires suffering and that these ideas only exist to us, to society. It exists nowhere else; and everyone is in a universal delirium a mixed state of being. None of this is a malfunction.

He existed above the dolcid scream from thouse focused on hats. In this open-air petri dish most watched screens and those that weren't were blinded by denture cream and bullshit. On those screen "This product contains nicotine," becomes an advertisement.

Devon replaced the tattered heavy bag that hung from the ceiling beam. He wrapped his hands and wondered what would have happed if Sarah had received the glasses instead of him. Perhaps this was the only way things could happen.

To people a thing is only sad if the masses say it is. A think is only tragic if the masses say it is tragic. They were ruled by emotion, fueled by media.

They were medicated just enough to hold a job, just enough to have a relationship, just enough to consume. Moments that they think are organic, or viral are really well orchestrated marketing plans. There was no moderation here, people want spectacle. They should be ashamed, but they weren't.

He again thought of the generations raised in fear of being told no. The look of irritation lain on his face. Devon was constantly in a peacefully rage. He was unentertained by frauds before they reveal themselves. He wasn't interested in people who were respected for who they've married or for what family they were born into.

"People like to look busy as they implement pointless programs, while struggling to justify the existence of their job," Devon thought as repeatedly hit the bag.

"They casually dismiss any evidence that doesn't align with their thoughts. This bias is weaponized, and becomes an echo chamber. In this chamber competing lies stare tensely at one another.

"It's easy to accept someone when they reflect your morals and values. These being are unaware that their actions seem to summon the otherworlders," Devon growled.

For Devon, each city was a new possibility of a different adventure into insanity. He was nameless, faceless, no matches on fingerprints, no hits on DNA. He wore various personas, each having their own origin. He shoved dozens of aliases into a well worn mental box. These instances of pretense required Devon to be allergic to honesty. Devon spread out his abilities liberally here.

He watched the amniotic fluid of capitalism flow through their veins as their outrage was monetized and they are grouped into outrage cliques. He struck the heavy bag a few more time as he silenlty wept for those that derived ethics from social media.

None of them wanted to be accused of thinking. Intellectually they know their separateness and isolation are an illusion. We know that we are all made of the same thing—the blown-out pieces of matter formed in the fires of dead stars.

People once experienced the same movies and shows this created a universal attitude, a common ritual. Society makes sure there are shared ideas and beliefs. Now the proliferation of technology erased the ritual that was watching movies. Using technology to redefining life and existence.

One service, two services and all of it used to decentralize age old morals, causing a splintering. This social splintering leaves room for undesirable and unique things to enter. People are shaping their own rituals and beliefs and this spreads the human conscious into many areas.

Free-range humans thrived on a planet made more hostile by otherworld scum. Devon could now see what was occurring, why it is occurring and how people are being manipulated to think in a certain way, but what could he do about it.

All of Devon's observations registered as complaints from the powerless. This was the last act of 'Di quella pira l'orrendo foco tutte le fibre m'arse, avvampò!' It was a struggle watching all of this play out, yet he still found room to pity himself. Devon stood on a corner and looked at himself in a curbside puddle.

From twenty stories up, he could still hear the cries from the streets of more blood…more blood—more blood. He told himself that this city will be different, that these people won't be vile. He thought that this time he wouldn't have to endure the lies, that he wouldn't have to hold the secrets.

Centuries of agenda fulled conflict and politics had devalued human life. The excitement he felt after saving the first person was erased by the chore of saving others. Devon was losing faith. Every city caused a sadness inside of Devon but he search for the answers would not stop.

He told himself these things, but yet his nightmares were once again realized. He wasn't confortable with any of it. He couldn't run fast enough or far enough away from the memories. The memory of loss had been etched onto his psyche as if it were an ancient hieroglyph?

*Everyday people look up and pray, 'Save us!'*

Devon shuffled his feet as the pigeons cooed and looked at him.

*I shouldn't...*

The nearest pigeon gave its approval by providing a timely coo. Yet, night after night, Devon donned a long black trench coat, boots, a beanie or hoodie, and black gloves, and he saved them. The dark streets and shadows hide him.

He rescued the young, the old, the men, the women, and children. He escorted them through violent neighborhoods, barking dogs, and intermitted illuminating yellow street lights. He rescued them from water, fires, and from their own creations. He was neck deep in the global industry of outrage and discontent.

There was no limit to the ways a person can be categorized. Gender and races are the most obvious groups but cognitive ability is a bigger factor. The world was slowly being destroyed. It was being fundamentally changed mentally as well as physically. Humans and otherworlders were tearing the planet apart.

It wasn't all the otherworlders; people were authors of a particular insanity, a delusion. People wanted a reward for not being a stereotype. Mixed into everyday average people were senders. These senders, influencers really, control the decisions of an individual...through media, entertainment, digitally.

People no longer claim to hear the voice of the gods; it's the voice of the popular. The popular can affect anything with the right sales pitch. The otherworlders operate outside the perimeters of human consciousness, but the popular have a sort of omnipresence not entirely residing in the mind.

Rights are only rights as far as you extend them to those you disagree with the most. For all of their big talk and summit meetings, people couldn't tell the difference between tolerating bad words and tolerating actions. Every single transition from democracy to authoritarian began with laudable goals. The means justifies the ends, because winning is more important than rights.

People will give up their rights for security and once people gave up their rights they discover that they weren't going to be winners after all. You could call this ignorance, but the problem is isn't ignorance; it's knowledge added to ignorance which produces fear. Fear is the weapon of authoritarianism.

So fear becomes a commodity. The more people push fear, the more they justify the ugliest of actions in the name of the cause. The goal of political speech is to enact political policy, without legislation. They won't do the dirty work themselves.

When fear is used, pointing and calling them the scary word is all that's needed. Humans use this method on each other because it works. They believe in guilt after exoneration and they have no problem repeating allegations. If they knew their rights, they wouldn't know when to use them.

Devon's existence was more than hits that couldn't be blocked and punches bones couldn't take. He was saddened by happening he couldn't prevent and each horrific incident a monument to tragedy.

Devon presided over a pop culture apocalypse, stuck between real and unreal, seen and unseen. He was squarely in the middle of a reality beyond anything he could have ever imagined. He was always amazed at people's bottomless causal cruelty in a delusional society.

Those that walked below him found purpose by manufacturing conflict and chaos. They copied those more interesting, until none of them are who they think they are. They'll hide in cover before ever admitting fault.

They make the rules of engagement. They dole out punishment for being a stereotype, or they'll single you out for not being one. Devon walked among saints and demons, there was no room for anything in between. Every mistake lends to a stereotype.

Devon's stay in another casually bigoted city awash with dull primary colors was at an end. He welcomed the journey from the hordes marveling at their own magnificence. On his rides to other cities he'd appreciated James Hatwick's cubicle complaining.

The evil of the world couldn't hide from him. What would people do if the unseen became visible in all the horrifying ways? What would he do if other knew what he knew? Devon didn't know where to be or when to be there. Devon was alone, outnumbered, but there had to be a purpose for all of this…right.

Devon looked into familiar faces that could no longer recognize him, and he saved them from their terror. The fantastic view from an overpass or a bridge spurred the thought of jumping off. Would killing himself end his torment?

There was also a long list of untrue things that Devon had been taught, things he had repeated continuously. The opposite of fire is water; the opposite of air is earth. The opposite of salt is pepper. Salt and pepper go together to create; they are not opposites. Fire is simply an expression of energy, the opposite of which is nothing.

The opposite of water is earth; they do not mingle but have a symbiotic relationship, where they seem, for a time, to overpower each other. Devon couldn't have been uncertain but as the Greek philosopher, Heraclitus, said, the road up is the same as the road down.

When snowflakes pile up making the street impassable, Devon walked on top of buildings. He frequented places where the only sound was of him moving quickly past buzzing neon signs. He watched over the seedy bars, thieves, smoke filled nightclubs, cartellions, black-marketers and those having mind bending drugs rages.

At night, among the sounds and flashing turn signals; Devon was just another shadow. He explored cellars, vaults, and poured over financial records, criminal cases. In the daylight, he would send the files to the authorities and media outlets, leaving them to expose the ponzi schemes, fraud, and prosecutorial misconduct.

He could see computer codes and do all of these things, but intervening in physical altercations made him feel more, human and here, there is a pill for that.

# CHAPTER 13

Devon routinely walked among the masses toward work. On this particular Wednesday morning, he felt especially optimistic as he left his hotel room.

There was a little girl sitting with her mother on a bus bench, waiting on the number sixteen redline. The little girl had the cutest brown eyes. She reminded him of someone. She wore white shorts, a distressed gray and blue school uniform, and her backpack was pink with little tassels.

The yellow tassels did not come with the backpack; it was an undeniable attempt for her to retain her individuality. In a city filled with millions of people, this little girl was the only individual.

She quietly sat with her hair in small pigtails, signs of an older parent. This little girl's face was stoic, too serious to be so young. She couldn't have been more than five years old. She looked sad as if she had lost something. Devon reached into his backpack, and he quickly threw a stone sixty feet to hit a trash can. The noise it made sounded like a gunshot.

With everyone's eyes looked in the direction of the rolling garbage can, Devon placed a small stuffed deer, on the dingy blue bus bench and kept walking. He looked over his shoulder and saw the little girl smile as she picked up the deer. She looked around, but Devon's smile disappeared into a sea of faces.

At night, Devon watched the mating rituals of the human animal, most of which lasted no longer than the time it took for them to take off their clothes. They did this in a vain attempt to burn their desires out before those desires burned them out. To them, it was just sex, and they used it to keep their lives simple, controllable. They don't even speak to one another when they do it.

Devon watched people go off to their daily grinds, spurred on by numbers and statistics. The elite sanctioned those numbers because their fortunes depended on the labor of others. Other numbers told people they were less valuable if they didn't give forty hours a week to a corporation. Somehow, giving less meant the country was in economic freefall, and their life was a total mess.

People completed the eight hour days pushed on by politic, not a necessity. They clocked in, and they clocked out. They counted hours, minutes, and seconds, eagerly waiting on mid-week to plan their weekend freedom.

The elites pushed the consumption of devices that track, locate, and controlled the purchaser. The purchase of these devices forced the masses to shuffle off dutifully to their daily grind. On their way to these forty hours, they were assaulted by every psychological ploy ever devised.

The law allows businesses to discriminate on the basis of behaviors, behaviors that are tied to hanicapes, religions affiliations, ethnicities, race and gender. This practice isn't called discrimation but it is.

Behind plain looking doors is the legal address of hundreds of thousands of separate businesses. Its occupants, on paper, are global corporate giants. Nevada, Wyoming, Delaware, South Dakota are safe havens for money that needed to be unnoticed, but Devon noticed.

Citizens pay the government to fight corruption, while the government supports it. The government prosecutes businesses for paying bribes to nation states, but the government bribes those same nation states. Anti corruption policies are just tools to keep those that do not make the rules from the benefits of why they were created.

The truth was that world peace would immediately bankrupt a quarter of world nations. The nation had become a post traumatic society that would forever be at odds with its leadership. From the inside, society seemed successful.

Devon had conversations with total strangers; most of them talked to him for the sake of talking. On the street, a large unclean man was holding a sign. The man's face was in a constant slump as if he was waiting to tell you he isn't angry, just disappointed. He wasn't begging, passing out something, or preaching...he was just there.

His head gently bobbed above the perspiration and high fashion; his sign cut a path through dreams and dashed hopes. The sign read "Today is a lie, Tomorrow is another," on the back side "The End" was printed.

For three days, the man stood there just holding that sign, not saying a word. Everyone walked by him as if he wasn't there; even Devon walked by him. But today, for some reason, Devon approached the man, sat down on a nearby planter, and spoke to him.

"Who are you?" asked Devon. "What day is it?" was the response.

"Wednesday... My name is Devon. Who are you?" Devon repeated.

"John Doe."

"Nice to meet you, John..."

"Three days, I have seen you standing here, holding this sign...
why?"

"Because."

"What does it mean?"

"The End."

"The End of what?"

"Everything..." John said as he slowly put the sign down. "What happens at the end?" asked Devon.

"A new world is formed from the old," John began. "Slaves to s system created by law but is no longer governed by any law. A system that will absorb anything and everything it comes in contact with." John spoke as if he had been preparing for this moment.

"See them," John said, pointing to people in the square. "Consciousness viewing itself creates this illusion. For them, the reality is only a group illusion that is manipulated, morphed to fill mental crevices with messages to confuse and separate class from race and race from class.

"Freedoms, if there were any, were the first to be devoured. Hail could fall from the sky, explode on impact with the ground turn into molten lava, and it would not restore faith. Indoctrination has replaced education..."

"What do you know about me?"

"That you lost someone; you lost your heart that helped you understand."

Devon became increasingly uncomfortable as John spoke. He looked at John, and John looked at him with a pained expression on his face. John's eyes shifted as he stared through Devon. John's baritone voice became almost deafening to Devon.

Devon swallowed hard and said, "Can you see Them?"

"…I see everything. I see the sky laid to waste by men unable to fly. I see war waged by savages, kings, priests, soldiers, scientists, businessmen, and media. I see their self evident bumper stickers, broken campaign promises, and nude photos to protest animal cruelty.

"I see the snide comments, the rolling of eyes, and all day shopping. I see them choosing one group of people over another. I see them with their wild caught, naturally resourced, hydrogen powered badges. People have been given all the tools needed to destroy themselves.

"You see what's in front of you. Life doesn't have edits…agendas do. Nothing outside exist, everything exists inside." John said.

"You and I are travelers on a cosmic journey, just swirling stardust dancing in the whirlpools of infinity. You and I have stopped spinning, only for a moment, this moment to encounter each other, making us the co-authors of our history. Because of us, everything exists…" Devon added.

"Fear is the demand, and violence is the supply. In the hands of broken democracies, self provoked terror is the best weapon for control, and people are collaborators with this system…."

"The System…" Devon stated.

John continued, "It assimilates people, cultures, and minds. Look at them hurrying to their places of importance. The only enemies they have are the ones given to them. The barrier where reason and common sense once stood has been supplanted by irrationality and fear.

"The right to remain silent is death. Three things are needed to motivate people: economics, psychological, and military. Facts are shaped by those in authority into what they call truth.

"They will accept any official conclusion; they will accept any future, any statement of fact, any patriot act. A complete coup d'état organized by the omnipresent services of a secret. People live in a subtle world of terror…I, we, are free."

"Perhaps the time is only limited to what consciousness can perceive, maybe time doesn't exist at all. We just gave a name to something we never truly understood. Time is just a measure of change."

"…Change provides time the illusion; change makes each moment an individual whole moment, complete and existing in its own right, this is what people interpret…The Now…."

"Arranging nows into an order gives it structure," Devon said warming to John's conversation. "Every possible location of every atom throughout all of creation, every moment exists simultaneously. The only evidence of last week is the memory of it, in the form of a stable structure of neurons in your brain now. The only proof of Earth's past is the rocks and fossils we see now.

"Everything is a point linked to other points as they all exist simultaneously, but there is no actual record of time flowing from one moment to the next. John, what do you remember?"

"I remember the past, the future…I…I remember this." John smiled as he spoke. "The now is the only thing that matters," John patted his torn clothes, checking each of his pockets, even the ones with holes in them.

John quickly looked around as if someone had called his name. He produced two dozen lottery tickets neatly wrapped with a rubber band. He breathed a sigh of relief and put the tickets back into his pocket and continued to speak.

"I am alive, so I have a purpose. You are alive, so you have purpose… Undermine, undermind…the whole world is a sitcom designed to make people sit calm for profit, change… profit, change, profit, prophet… change." John said as he picked up his sign and held out a cup.

John smiled and didn't say another word; he didn't answer any more questions. He looked right through Devon dropped some coins into the cup and walked away. Over the next few days, Devon walked the same route but never saw John again.

These conversations let Devon that he was still human. Everything had just become so tragic. The truth was that Devon had seen these things before; they just didn't resonate with his privileged life. His mind glossed over the reports, discussions, and fifteen second news blurbs. His mind saw the wrongness but never acknowledged it.

The timeline of humanity is filled with marvelous revelations and adaptations, which allowed mankind to descend from the branches, create tools, walk upright, invent philosophy, and walk on the moon. As we evolved, we developed language, which, in turn, birthed lit- erature and numerics.

Quite often, during these developments, mutations were based on need. Mankind is an exemplary product of Evolution Theory but is that all there was to it…humans got lucky. A human can reason, anticipate consequence and devise plans without knowing they are doing so.

The human being by design and function is magnificent and the crown of creation. A being that if solely evolved from primate makes everyone just a bit more comfortable. If people evolved, then other animals are certainly capable of following the same path.

It is the similarities that draw people toward one another. It is the similarities that make them accept that their existence is due to the work of one designer, yet, it is the minuscule diversities that make life difficult to explain by naturalistic processes. The difficulty is not in getting a person to believe something that has never been witnessed; it is in getting them not to challenge their own good sense.

Devon was losing his mind among these speculations, but even the most mundane speculation turned into full blown moments of pure clarity. The pain of memory caused Devon to clench his fists. 'Normal' was nothing more than a faded memory. Devon was daily deluged with emotions that he was far too angry to weep about.

*People do bad things, so they must be scumbags or sick, maybe it is merely mankind expressing its inner psychopath. There is no support group for the resurrected, no twelve-step program. There is no Frankenstein, only the monster..."*

He had been back for a month home and already regretted it. All of the fun places he frequented as a kid were now pharmacies. Buildings interrupted skylines, the noise was unending, the beauty manufactured, the smell unnatural. Everything was congested, motorize, and blighted. Again, they are calling to be saved.

Some people don't fear ghosts or knives thrown from a distance. They don't give respect to those that deserve it. They don't welcome the sun. They don't value brotherhood or principles. People couldn't help themselves, the more they tried not to do harm, the more harm they did.

Devon's efforts to blend in led him to be a ghost, the shadow, the rumor many claimed to have seen. Nobody really believed the rumors; rumors were all the hope some had.

The poor were legal prey, body count; numbers on a report, society won't miss them. Prosecutors don't mind charging the wrong person. The state didn't mind that the wrong person is serving time. Communities became progressively worse because those who commit crimes sometimes got away, and those who deserved to be freed were not.

The law is society's way of patting itself on the back. Freedom, life, and death were being monetized. The prison sentence you get is often the sentence you can afford.

Devon got systems to recognize him temporarily; no one would know that he had been there...he was a glitch. There were millions of documents of corporate hush money that circumvented indictments.

Devon cracked safes and easily logged in. Not that logging into security companies was difficult. This was made more accessible by those companies occasionally wanting their networks to be breached in order to sell more services, according to the deleted internal memos Devon recovered.

The government publicly prosecutes one bad pharmaceutical actor so a hundred others can privately go about doing the same thing. People who got coupons for free prescription drugs never think that they are part of the drug trial, but none of them were ever deceived.

Devon had seen people treat others, even themselves like garbage. The elderly were treated the worst of all as if a background check would stop someone from being mistreated…their backgrounds had been checked.

He was only outside of the assisted living complex for two hours before he noticed the difference between how people mistreat children and how they mistreat elders. The elders see the pattern of abuse, the thefts, and the hits coming. This made him vomit.

Sex trafficking is an equal opportunity crime, women and men had twelve, thirteen, fourteen-year-old boys and girls walking the streets and performing in basements. This is an endeavor that is defended by deadly means if necessary. What is a teenager to do without a home, education, or money?

Laura Washington ran away from home seven years ago; she was fourteen at the time. By the time she was seventeen, she was headlining small strip clubs to survive. The following year was a blur of alcohol and drugs. She needed a protector. Her protector's attacks for disobedience were brutal.

Her look wasn't ideal for gaining media attention, and now she was too old for the police to actively get involved. She had no choice in the hours she worked, the people she had sex with or her fee. She showed younger ones the ropes while they were both being sold.

Devon rescued her two weeks ago from a well-known sex trafficker. Within two weeks, she opened her own an illegal endeavor and had gone from victim to oppressor.

Devon had gone over hundreds of records, years of files, and decades of invoices…most of which lead a trail to someone other than the accused. How could anyone's sanity not be in question when exposed to all of this misery?

Saving people brought Devon worship or vilification. In developing nations, violence was perpetrated predominately by males. In privileged nations like this one, violence looked like it had a gender, but it didn't.

Stopping crime was a low priority for the police; politics and industry dictate that they needed it. The inmates built this city; the inmates are the guards. They have pride in what they've built…they cannot see it as a prison.

From the documents, Devon read the village, where the drone attacked, was tagged to be a future military base for the United States. The problem was that the landowners wanted their home free from outside influences. According to these documents, that position was unacceptable. The village victims were unaware that they sat atop eight billion barrels of oil and a billion cubic feet of natural gas.

Devon went down one concrete section to other connectors with adjacent conduits; eroded shards of rebar and metal lined his path. The sewers were a patchwork of underground tunnels, vaults, rocks, and a poll of briskly moving foul smelling water.

He could disappear into the unlit bowels of the sewer at any given time, and he could emerge anywhere in the city. He watched affluent children sneak into poor neighbors to set fires and cause mayhem. Everywhere he went, in every city, every town, they called him Hero.

"Where are you, Hero?" they whispered. "Save us, Hero," they pleaded.

I am no hero.

# CHAPTER 14

Winter came, Devon's mother and father were gone. He buried them on that long highway, on that payphone, months ago.

Devon mourned his family in silence on the tallest building he could find. It was there that his thoughts of language, bio-frequencies, nucleon disparity, the drunks outside of pharmacies, other world forces, manufactured champions, and unindicted criminals stopped.

He remembered how his father said that he was strong willed. He recalled that no matter how well he planned, he still got caught with his hand in the cookie jar. He remembered how his gestures were never grand enough.

Devon's thoughts were shattered by the voice on a screen that was attached to a nearby building. Devon growled because right now there are scientists hard at work, thinking they have it all figured out because they can carry the one. All day, every day, people's minds were filled with illusions. To pack humans, the truth didn't matter, right didn't matter...all that mattered was the pack.

Truth is where Devon consistently found these otherworlders. He admired their no conscience, no delusions, no confusion purity. They were not ready made clichés to be slotted in anywhere.

Devon was amazed at how free time caused already dangerous people to become even more hazardous. They unavoidably committed dark acts of violence. Yesterday, no one knew them, today they are national news.

These people have created a violence horrible mark upon society. This mark will be etched onto the psyche of humankind. This mark could have never been made working nine to five. Acts of fear and anxiety push humans forward, faster than technology did. Acts of violence are more effective than any legislation.

*I have gained an appreciation of angles, circles, turns, and jumps. I see x-ray, hear beta rays, feel solar winds, and experience dark matter. Right now, I'm listening to butterflies in the field next to the bodega flap their wings. I hear the mice scurrying in the walls. I hear the footsteps in the hallways that nightly stop at my door.*

Devon grinned as he sat on top of a warehouse feeding seagulls. Six months had gone by since his last pleasant dream.

*With my normal vision, I see as people do, in this physical reality. If I really concentrate, I can enhance these senses; I call this tuning. I still see what I saw before, only now I can see through it.*

Daily, Devon got better at separating between frequencies. He found himself tuning into people without using his eyes.

*I see the full structure of the human body; how internal organs are positioned and how they function. I can tune into different properties, density, or flows. People are made up of atoms, and those atoms are made up of small subatomic particles, and those particles are not material things. They are merely minute energy fluctuations, information that flickers in and out of an infinite void at the speed of light.*

*The human body creates a new stomach lining every three days, a new liver every six days, a new skin every five days, new DNA material every six weeks, and a new skeleton every three months. The human body is the place memories, and dreams call home for the time being. If that is true, then the disease could be a disordered dream state in consciousness that is manifesting in our body?*

Touching connectors and tuning into frequencies was emotionally and physically draining. The more he looked into people, the more his disenchantment grew. At night, the red lights on the freeway curved like a deformed spine. Pigeons, crows, and hawks scurried out of his way as he walked rooftops and scaled buildings.

Devon quickly scrambled up one building and down another. The building's scaffolding, water tanks, tops of elevator shafts, pipes, risers, and skylights cities were his gymnasiums. The noise of people was intrusive to him. Human beings are surrounded by energy, and this energy was indeed transferrable through biological, emotional, and spiritual means. This was more than enough reason for Devon to stay away from bad energy.

In these concrete pastures, he felt the pull, the eyes, and the desires of multiple forces as if he would split apart at any given moment. He had spent too much time around the sheep. The self hypnosis and endless braying were disgusting. The skyscraping perches made him keenly aware that he was no longer a full card carrying part of humanity.

Devon got people wheelchairs that needed them. He bought school clothes and books for class. He bailed people out of jail. He found himself at charity functions, stage plays, museums, and watching special military operations that weren't so special. He did these things because he believed Sarah may be watching him.

This week he read Invisible Man, Outliers, Little Green, Mystic River, Medical Apartheid, Death from the Skies, Lighted Crosses and On the Road.

There was something about reading and learning that made him feel closer to Sarah. There is something about turning the pages of a good book that unlocks the crevices. Reading a book reminded him of spooning with Sarah in the dark.

High above littered streets, everything looks peaceful. He peered down a darkened street that was an obstacle course of turned over trash cans where he saw a disheveled, despondent man gently placed an empty liquor bottle on the ground. The man was eagerly rooting through a nearby dumpster.

This man was in the same dirty, torn clothes and he was less than two blocks away from where Devon had stopped a local street gang from beating him up four nights ago.

"Another quantum instrument wasted," Devon remarked to himself.

He had watched the uniformed authorities kill, but not because of bias, inadequate training or being trigger happy. They killed because it was cleaner, neater, and economical. If unjustified, the backlash from erasing another person was always less than the possibility of lawsuits and prolonged hospitals stays. If justified, the erasure is celebrated, even if in silence. It was less paperwork.

On the streets of benign neglect, Devon quickly found people through pattern recognition. He didn't need to go looking for trouble; he could smell it, sense it. The authorities didn't raid formal events, they attend them.

He followed the people who paid premium rent for obstructed views. It was his duty to follow the men and women who by virtue of birth wore privilege like twenty-year union seniority. They attended their secret meetings and were places they shouldn't be.

For some time now, Devon had been using violence for justice. He helped people by hurting someone else. He was balancing the equation, and carving 'AM' into walls.

He subdued the petty dealers and the thugs that took money from small business owners. He learned that anything could be used as a weapon, a shield, or to extend his reach.

Devon applied bandages and winced from painful shots to his ribs. He mixed in an elbow into an abdomen here and a suplex there. In rhythm bodies jerked from one punch to the other. There were those that were unable to answer his sternum splitting rebuttals. In these encounter he could have lostr control and rained 10 millimeter Westside horderves on flunky after flunky but he didn't. Because he didn't The Rumor grew, and so did the skill of the bodyguards.

Low grade vigilantes, poorly paid assassins…many were professional…government trained…tough…rugged…they never stay down, and they always talk. Their investment in top of the line, customized, night scope, triple barrel, semi-automatic, gas propelled projectiles, multi-clip, military-grade people killers was wasted. Devon had seen worse…much worse. Their stash of weapons and tools would be used against them.

Through muffled screams and labored breathing, they offered him money to look the other way. It would be those that he would bash with couches or slam into pianos.

The Rumor had them shaking every time a loud noise was heard. Bullet shell casings hit the ground followed by broken bones, man-sized holes in walls, twisted appendages. Their confidence was turned into tears in a room lit by shotgun blasts.

How someone steps reveal weak points. Devon attacked weak points. Devon made copious use of home and garden depots for creating concussion bombs, grappling hooks, stun guns, safety lines, and dart guns. If you smash ahead into windshields or break a leg, they'll whimper, but they'll talk. This talking led Devon to another scheme, a bigger fish.

The first time he knocked a door off its hinges, he miscounted the number of assailants in the room and was hit by a television and kicked in the face. The fifth time, one culprit had to be chased down and kicked through a window. Devon thought a young woman was being held against her will, but she stabbed and burned him.

Devon jumped on and ran on top of five moving cars and a van before being hit by one while trying to stop a kidnapping. By his tenth outing, he was gracefully avoiding haymakers in close quarters. His goal was not to be cruel or heavy handed. Most people were unconscious before they hit the ground, and sometimes he fell short of this not being a cruel goal.

Hitting Devon only made him angry. Devon made contact with this guy's cheekbone, and his head whipped around. Devon usually stopped when he saw blood, on his twentieth time, this time, he didn't stop.

He was comfortable among the innocent victims and malevolent forces that haunted streets. Devon didn't mind getting hit, but he couldn't allow himself to be shot, he wasn't bulletproof. Hitting Devon's body felt like it did when Devon hit Me and Ask, it wasn't good. Anyone with a knife only succeeded in slicing through raindrops.

Now he ran his hand along walls to determine if he should just charge into the room or reach through it to exact justice. His senses helped him draw pictures where his eyes couldn't see. Startled occupants jumped to fight and one by one he laid them out.

Devon kicked through thin doors and tossed assailants down corridors. They weren't all guilty, but they aren't innocent either. With calm fury, he disarmed one man to beat another with the disarmed man's weapon.

Unconscious bodies piled up higher than a stack of hundred dollar bills. Devon moved as if he were somewhere in between floating and lurching. He took on entire housing projects and made it into the sewer as bullets whizzed by him.

Devon reached out from the shadows to adjust attitudes. He hurt people; he didn't want to he had to. They needed to be hurt because hurt is all some people respond to.

Devon went from saving those who were ill, weak and crawling through war zones to rescuing people from lies. Devon wasn't getting worse; he was getting better. Those he saved asked, 'Are you an angel?' Devon would disappear into the shadows before giving an answer.

"It was dark. I really don't know what happened. I just know that someone rescued me. The Rumor..." they'd tell authorities.

"I was grabbed, hit in the face, kicked and thrown through a wall. Then he pulled out some kind of sword or dagger and suggested that I change my life."

Through sobs, vague reports he exacted vengeance upon those that deserved it. Devon tried not to take pleasure in the breaking of jaws and the shattering of teeth.

The Rumor— word was getting around. Because of Devon's pigment change, there were many rumors.

*The streets are filled with strangers that I used to know. Ninety-nine percent of the body is empty space and that one percent that's left you would think that it is substance, but, that too is also empty space—lives filled with nothing. Perhaps gravity is nothing more than a deformation in the structure of the mass.*

*Look at them grazing, thinking that life isn't worth living unless it is dressed up in pixels. They are taught what to feel, taught what beauty is—the truth is strange to them. They are baptized in consumerism. I watch them feed; they feed on each other.*

*Nations prey on nations, groups prey on groups, people prey on people, and in the middle of it all, I sit, and I watch; all of it be tied together by genealogy, by crime, and by acts of kindness. They are one and not one. They have the luxury of not knowing.*

Blood from an earlier cut dripped to the asphalt below. From Devon's perch, the repeated wail of night sirens sounds like crying. In front of him, people happily consume lines of code and algorithmic cruelties with each image and sound, this made him want to vomit.

He sat motionless atop the tallest building in the city, yet he was hurtling through space at a million miles per hour, launching thoughts into the vast continuum just as fast.

The partitions within Devon's mind returned accompanied by the noise of a nearby maternity room filled with small mouths that cried solely due to the horror of being born here. Three gunshots rang out; a distant scream captured his attention. He ran in that direction. Down one building, up another, he leaped two rooftops and was there in seconds.

He arrived, and there on the ground was a young, casually dressed man. Blood was oozing from the wounds in his side. Devon could hear the assailants' shoes scrape the pavement as they ran away. Devon and he backed away from the man's accusing stare. Devon could see life leaving the man's body; he applied pressure as the world poured out of the young man.

*We don't exist in the world; the world exists in us. We curve back within ourselves to create the mind, the body, and the physical world. We manifest it. It is us, we manufacturing everything, the mind, the body, the universe...*

Devon's thoughts trailed off as he hopelessly did what he could to save the young man. He couldn't be everywhere...the ambulance would arrive too late.

The sickness, the pain, and the violence were taking a toll on Devon. The moaning, tears, and splattered blood had become common. He had a special place in his heart for human traffickers; they got the worst of his actions. They would not be able to produce children... let alone walk again.

They would live with an 'AM' cut into their skin. Those were the moments his anger and rage got the better of him. He was afraid of everything and nothing. Very few people had met the whirlwind and lived to speak about it.

Bad actors always had a support system, they are never alone. They sold as long as others bought. He walked through dimly lit hallways, listening. He could tell where the gun was by the sound. He could tell where people were by the noise their shoes made. He could have shot through the walls with deadly accuracy, but that wouldn't be personal, even the worst of the worst are afraid of the dark.

Everything Devon had seen told him that all of this went more in-depth than third-party candidates in cahoots with the major party ones and governance by polls. It was deeper than one group accusing the other of offenses, while they too offended.

Devon stood up in the midst of a crowd and yelled: "I am here!" The people didn't look up long enough to take notice. He was just another face in a sea of faces. People made idle chatter. 'Hello,' 'Good Morning,' and the like, but they didn't pay much attention to him; they didn't pay much attention to anything.

Even with all the information coming from willow glass screens, body computers, and vidstrips, he still had no answers. While running on top of a museum, he could no longer block out the noise. He fell to his knees as the pain in his mind increased. Devon's thoughts reached out.

Devon missed things like home cooked meals and listening to Sarah. He never knew any of the answers, so he looked to Sarah, understanding was another matter. It didn't matter to Sarah that he didn't understand it; all that mattered was that he was there for her.

He imagined the sad faces of friends and relatives that must have been present at their funeral. He imagined the music, the ceremony, and the weeping that was done in the aisles. He grieved when he ran pass water tanks, air conditions, and pigeon coops. He mourned his family as he passed by rooftop gardens, skylights, and rooftop observation decks.

Not a night went by without the death of his family haunting him. Alone on the rooftops; the only distraction was gentle noise from slowly spinning vents. A scream that had been trapped inside of him was set free, and he could be heard for blocks yelling like a madman.

There was a hole inside of him.

# CHAPTER 15

Devon couldn't be a passenger on a train for the same reason he preferred to work in the open spaces. Working around large groups of people could mean his death and the death of dozens, possibly hundreds of others.

Devon made his way through the airport terminal by slightly modulating his electrical current to produce an opposing magnetic field to avoid the metal detectors. He boarded the airplane, took his seat, and buckled himself in, and that's when the buzzing began. He quickly unbuckled himself and got up.

"Sir, we are getting ready to take off, you need to take your seat," the flight attendant said.

"I, I, I can't...I'm hyper, hyperventilating...I am having a panic attack! Let me off, let me off this plane!"

They reopened the cabin door and let him off, the attack never occurred. As he ran across the tarmac, he imaged what the evening headline would have been, "Taxing Airplane Hit by Freak Tornado."

It was in everyone's best interest that he found other methods of travel. Riding on top of a train was easy, and he could get on and off quickly. Trying to ride on an airplane was another matter. He couldn't just run up and grab hold of a plane without thinking long and hard about it first. He had to understand the pressures and how to minimize drag.

Devon frequented airfields and began by riding on crop dusters. He did look foolish chasing crop dusters before they took off. His stealth technique needed work. The crop dusters he damaged he secretly paid for.

The dismount from the crop duster was not the problem; at twenty miles per hour, the drop from forty feet was the problem. A drop in which he traveled about twenty-nine feet per second, took one point six seconds from the time he let go until the time he actually hit the ground. The slightest miscalculation meant disaster.

Knowing the math of a thing and working the calculation of a problem were far different from putting a plan into action. Miscalculations caused him to roll into and damage a pig pen, two shacks, and a number of garages before he gauged it properly. He chipped away at fractions of seconds until timing it right, enough for him to skid to a stop.

Breathing wasn't a problem, reducing his air resistance was. From crop dusters, he managed to hold on to two hundred miles per hour small piston powered airplanes. Devon's experience with the pressures in the ocean prepared him to deal with the low air pressures of high altitudes.

He uses goggles with an altitude sensor and accelerometers to shield his face from high wind speeds. These goggles weren't as light or as sleek as Whitman's glasses, but they did the job. His biometric shirt and clothes fed wind speed, GPS information, heart rate, temperature, and biometric data into the display of the goggles.

Once while descending he was sent spinning out of control, ripping his parachute, he recovered and received a few bumps and bruises for his efforts. He still needed to get from place to place quickly. Because of Operation Dominic and other atmospheric nuclear tests, the otherworlders could attack him in the air.

Devon saw Turbulence grab hold of an airplane at thirty-two thousand feet. This slender agent usually rattled nerves, spilled coffee, and tossed luggage around. This time, the pilots saw the altimeter twitch, and the airplane dropped three thousand feet in thirty seconds. The falling aircraft zipped by the plane Devon was on; Turbulence growling as he pried the tail section open.

The airplane was like a helpless dinghy in a stormy sea. It was in free fall for one terrifying minute before Turbulence released the aircraft. The plane had to make an emergency landing.

For humans, the gifts of speech and reason just aren't enough. Humans envied the flying squirrels, flying lemurs, flying possums, and flying foxes which are really bats.

Those animals don't actually fly, they have thin layers of skin stretching from their front paw to their back paw, and when they jump off of something and stretched out their paws, it creates a wing of sorts. This produced tension, together with manipulating their body shape produced lift and thus a glide.

Pushing off of a microjet going three hundred miles per hour was dangerous, even for Devon. To accomplish this, he wore a wingsuit. The wingsuit was constricting, and it magnified the slightest movement. His body position was crucial, so he had to relax and focus. Wingsuits come standard with a safety parachute.

Devon rode on the outside of airplanes. Arrogance, coupled with Devon's thoughts of being able to conquer anything made him elevate slightly higher than the aircraft. The smile on his face quickly disappeared when he realized this produced an air pocket; he fell hard on top of the airplane.

Devon panicked as he bounced into the sky. Devon was disoriented, twisting, and falling out of control. He didn't recover until he was a few hundred feet from the ground.

The wingsuit took a lot of time to put on, and often, the speed of the airplane would rip the material. The wingsuit was too bulky to wear it under his clothes. Devon needed something custom.

His goal in this regard: infiltrate, don't look suspicious, don't act suspicious, and don't look suspicious. Just get what you need and get out. Look for "Authorized Personnel Only," "Restricted," and "Security Clearance Required Beyond This Point" signs. Follow those with "No Escort" on their lanyards.

He didn't need to crawl through air ducts and tunnels. He didn't need stopwatches, masks, or remote controlled robots. He could alter his appearance enough to fool the facial recognition software of defense companies. The doors that were locked to him always seemed to malfunction.

He pushed pencils, pretended to be a lawyer, a doctor, or an auto worker. He never stayed on a job for more than a week. All of the money he donated to the fourteen member families, living in two bedroom apartments.

He created from what he took from various off-the-book experiments. Contractors couldn't make too much of a stink about things they weren't supposed to have. They couldn't complain about missing technology that is not supposed to exist. Devon gave a new meaning to the phrase off-the-rack.

Devon had a particular interest in surveillance dust, thermite bombs and the tip of the bullet computers. He took other things like the soda can size MRI device and the polymer replicator. This replicator was about the size of a holiday tin of caramel popcorn. This device caused molecules to bond with one another. This created polymers.

Encrusted with barnacles, sea stars, urchins, crabs, and other creatures the docks had front row seats to Devon's creations. He spent his time taking up temporary residence inside of shipping containers, reading research papers, and building computers.

When he wasn't exacting his brand of justice, he gathered the materials he needed to perform better. He sewed two layers of fabric together, making sure that the pieces were symmetrical shapes. Those pieces became the right wing, left wing, and body sections. Each section had airfoil and ribs.

He added temperature proofing, reinforced zippers, and double coated nylon. When he ran an electric current through his creation, the wings and airfoils would take its full shape. His finished creation was light and could be worn underneath his clothes.

Using his new creation, his glide ratio became more efficient, and longer with each customization. Devon used the polymer replicator to create R.E.A.P., a ReActive Electro polymer; this was used to weatherize his flying suit. R.E.A.P. was flexible and extremely strong, and it could become translucent when an electric current passed through it. He completed his silver lined blue and white outfit with a customized helmet.

Because he could conceal or deploy the wings at will, his creation was more suit than wing. He thought he would never have the soaring feeling he had at La Casa del Arbol, the famed "Treehouse at the End of The World," …until now.

Devon also created sunglasses with embedded infrared lights; this generated noise around his eyes and nose. He added a retro-reflective coating to the tactical goggles to interfere with camera images, so his face would appear distorted. An umbrella with LED lights that when twirled confused even the most advanced surveillance object tracking algorithms. He created stealthwear that shielded him from thermal imaging.

Only red-throated loons and brown pelicans knew what Devon up to. The seclusion of waterfront and ports allowed him to work on a small propulsion unit he could stand on and fly. It was a turbine propelled magic carpet, which could be powered by his body. It was steered by weight and attitude. He was working on voice control, flexibility ratio, the interface, and increasing its maneuverability by altering the rigidity.

He coated the surface with a liquid that made it stronger. Its wafer thin wings were coated with solar power receptors that converted sunlight into electricity. This powered the miniature high-speed turbine fans.

This magic carpet could reach heights of fifteen thousand feet and speed of a hundred and twenty miles per hour, getting the turbines to register as a low hum was taking some time. It was made mostly of synthetic stretch fabric lined with steel alloy mesh. The craft was light, durable, but it wasn't ready for primetime, its six turbines created a lot of noise…a lot.

Many things were disposed of at the docks. People were trafficked, smuggled, hoarded and bodies were dumped…not on Devon's watch. There was so much going on at a shipyard that it was easy to disappear among the rows of containers. The docks were his workshop. It was a place where he could jump off of piers, fish and come and go as he pleased. The Shoremen near the docks ignored him as if he were a shadow.

He approached the warehouse by stealth, entering or leaving by windows or loose planks. The only evidence of Devon's presence in these warehouses were the vases, teapots, laptops, chairs, rocks, anchors and washing machines balancing on each other.

Social media platforms created biometric profiles from everyone, so he stayed away from using social media and the always tracking smartphone. Devon spent so much time in the air he saw air currents like winged raptors did. He used natural thermals in the atmosphere and used updrafts to dynamically soar.

The more Devon glided, the more natural it became; altering his approach angle determined how far, how fast, or how long he was airborne. Off he went downwind in a decent, then turned quickly into a gust and started to climb. From twenty thousand feet, the view of mountain ranges, metropolitan cities at night, and Lenticular cloud formations were amazing.

Devon used the slight diving position when flying for distance, the flat flying, or vertical position to keep flying as long as possible. His goal was not for him to stay in the air for long periods of time. The goal was to get from place to place as quickly as possible and land on target without being detected.

Devon could sustain glides for miles, or for a few hundred feet, before deciding to land. To save time, he dove steeply and quickly flattened out to slow his speed as if he were swooping down out of the sky. Most thrill seekers could slow down to about forty miles per hour; even the experts dreamed of landing speeds of thirty miles per hour or below.

Devon could slow down out of a dive to ten miles per hour, hit the ground running and disappear into a row of trees before the parachute touched the ground. By the time he graduated to riding five hundred miles per hour commercial airplanes, he often achieved a landing speed of zero.

He would glide from one plane to cling to another. He would fly in one direction, then another. He would cling onto a small plane, then a larger one, a slower one, then a faster one. He could drop down a thousand feet or simply move over ten miles on these atmospheric lily pads.

On the way back down to Earth, Devon listened to the classical styling of Steve Reich. The subtle acoustics relaxed him. It was this kind of music that opening the condensed space music usually forced him into. He got rid of the parachute. He no longer needed it for landing and it was too obvious.

Inevitably when the grit, grime, layers of filth and the stink of a city got to be too much for him; he would leave. However, Devon wouldn't move on until he had at least helped one person. He found that clinging on trains and airplanes effective, but primitive.

He toyed with electric propulsion, but the increased travel distance, caused the electric bike lose its earth moving ferocity. He settled on twenty inches, three-hundred-millimeter front and rear tires, water cooled, supercharged V-twin engine, geared toward the lower end for faster acceleration and no exhaust pipes. The exhaust was routed through the hollow aluminum/magnesium tubing in the bike's frame.

This bike covered considerable distances and handled off road as efficiently as it did the street. A flip of a switch converted it into feet- forward, knees-in-the-breeze cruiser. This became Devon's preferred method of travel. It was a titanium, carbon fiber, aerospace grade steel, one-fourth ton, fuel injected, rolling vibration. Devon called it the Soul Stirrer.

No helmet, no speed limit, and no cooling it down on curves. He donned his sleek, jet black outfit, no auto drive, and no networked computer on this Kevlar yellow and ballistic black motorcycle. Devon traveled with a no drag backpack complete with everything he needed, water, food, serrated blades, sharp sticks.

*I have to keep moving and stay away from the suburbs. That's where some of the most unspeakable acts occur... There were no antigens in my blood. I am just an uncategorized cellular anomaly. Tonight, there will be no more confessions, no last rites. From a distance, these huge things are just rocks; it is up close when you realize that they are history.*

Somehow the isolation and the beauty during rides removed clutter from his mind. Devon rode anywhere and nowhere. There he was bent over danger curves and rolling hills of hope, and all of it—breathtaking.

The engine roared deep into the night. The bike allowed him not only to see and experience nature but to also experience just how shoddy the road patchwork is—a complete waste of taxpayers' monies.

Devon rode towards the endless horizon, through the valleys, and around farm country. He explored places where the road rose through unpopulated woodlands and down through the gaps in the hills. Somewhere along the streets that flanked the mountains or where the rivers crept alongside canyons, his memory faded.

Narrow sections of road were the most dangerous in America. Every other bend was littered with small white crosses. White crosses pop up as often as carelessness drifts a person into oncoming traffic. Long, rural roads of quiet were where clarity occurred. Devon could travel from Los Angeles to New York in twenty four hours.

*There is nothing like the sun at my back and the wind in my face; it's just a few dozen corn snakes and me. On the desert roads, the dunes are flatter, on windy days sand blows across the highways, appearing as drifts as thick as any oil slick.*

*The needle leans towards one twenty, one forty, one fifty. At this speed, I can only hear the dull roar floating back from the mufflers. My eyes strained to see the centerline. I am always trying to provide a margin for my new reflexes.*

*These aren't roads; they were escape routes. I stay off highways; they may be God's waiting room, but those big slabs are always too congested. I can weave through traffic quickly enough, but what if otherworlders were to locate me during rush hour?*

Out here, there were no rooftops to run along, no homes to destroy and no people to be harmed. If otherworlders were to give chase through the numerous entry points, they were nowhere near as fast as his motorcycle, and they were far too heavy to ride one. Of course, there was always the occasional sandstorm he had to outrun.

At night when things got hairy on the road, his body created a small current to activate the bike's electroluminescent yellow pinstriping. Deserted intersections of streets that he tore down reminded him of those subtle lines that connected people.

*Déjà vu occurs when the path that our probable selves have chosen crosses paths with our present self....*

These connections people had were the results of action and inaction. Each connection, a decision, and each decision a different path. Each path existing simultaneously; it was the choice that created probable futures. Moments in the past existed as likely events and probable futures.

This explains why humans practiced prayer for millennia, prayer was a tool. Prayer could be what focuses our collective energy in cooperative ways to create an alternative reality. Devon saw more lines of connection when there was compatibility, agreement. People ignored these connections as if something prevented them from realizing these connections.

The nightmares brought by these connections gave him pause when it came to interacting with these connections between people.

Time's order has a way of making you think a certain point is the beginning. A person doesn't have a beginning or an ending; they just have moments where their body happens to be. Viewing these connections revealed a different way of understanding time. Accessing memories is downhill while attaining future points more an uphill process.

Memories take the self back in time; Dreams can take the self forward in time. Déjà vu is a simple skip ahead, yet all of these moments exist simultaneously. The self must have the ability to exist outside of time.

As Devon thought about déjà vu, he was reminded of the lightning in the ocean. From one source, other small diverging paths of differing intensities branched off and took on lives of their own.

*Déjà vu occurred when the branching paths intersected again. That crossing of paths created a widening. This merging was the only perceptual indicator that humans could sense of their other selves. The presence of self was the only thing that was real about people. Déjà vu is universes resyncing with each other.*

Devon was starting to sound like Sarah.

# CHAPTER 16

Under the hum of green exit signs Devon wandered down dimly lit yellow and brown hallways with sticky tan floors. He exacted justice from the Five Boroughs to South Central to West Englewood. These were moments where he decided to either shove well laid plans up well laid asses or sip on cheap wine with expensive labels.

Devon busted through a door and punched a 6'3" thug, and then he slid across the table to drop another bodyguard with a body spear. Devon flipped off the downed man's head to round house kick their boss through a wall. It was ten seconds before he landed on his feet.

Three people were laid out on the floor. Devon spun in the center of the room and unsheathed his dagger and cut off the lights. With his alloy reinforced tactical gloves, he tripped circuit breakers and emerged from dark corners to bust up drug houses.

Devon didn't just dispatch housing projects full of thugs; he caused power outages at social parties, made the well dressed vomit on polished shoes, fought inside cars, elevators, on rooftops and fire escapes. Devon eventually had enough courage to visit his old house.

Everything they owned had been destroyed. The home was leveled; even the trees hadn't grown back. It looked like a bomb had been dropped on it. The trees along the road were old and gray—worn.

"No clothes, hair ribbons, pictures, no video; they had been erased from history ... I can't accept their murders." Devon said out loud as the images from that night replayed in his head.

"I should have died with them." He said as he slowly walked through the garden of rubble and weeds. "The drapes, the crib, our home…everything is gone!"

Devon crouched down among the debris. Underneath the wood and stucco was Brianna's butterfly. Devon gently picked up the stuffed animal and held it in the palm of his hand. The colorful butterfly was dirty and burnt. His stomach tightened with the thought that this was all he had of her.

He held that butterfly and remembered that his mother and father always expected more from him. He could see his parents' faces; he remembered how he would always try harder after a big disappointment.

He remembered how his Nana would watch nightly newscasts and inexplicably remark, "Look at them," "Look at what they are doing now," or "It's always them." She would use copiousphrased versions containing the words "them" and "they."

He remembered a very young Devon asking, "Nana, Them who?"

His Nana looked at him, smiled, and said, "I don't need to tell you who they are. You have to go out in the world and find out for yourself."

"She wasn't as crazy as I thought," Devon remarked as his flashback ended.

*Our family was coming together nicely. At breakfast, she would tell me the remarkable goings-on of the world, and I would read about sports. Every time I looked up from the screen, she was reading a new study or looking at some chart.*

*Brianna changed us both. Having a child calmed me down. Sarah was the perfect mother. Brianna was so cute when she slept. She was beautiful, like her mother. She had just started walking. I recorded her first steps. Her first word was "no." Sarah thought she got that from me, she didn't. I think she got her stubbornness from her mother.*

*For Brianna's only birthday, she had cupcakes, cartoon videos, and a colorful stuffed butterfly. That day we all danced in the living room for an hour. When I came home from work, she'd jump up and down, wanting daddy to give her a kiss, and toss her in the air and I did.*

*She was a simple child; she held this butterfly and lay on my stomach. She didn't fuss much, but she got into everything. When we weren't looking, she put her mother's shoes on. Her laugh brightened up my worst days. And now she's gone, they're both gone.*

Devon brushed off the butterfly and attached it to his backpack. He sat on his bike and put on his black shades. He throttled the engine and tore down that familiar road for the last time. The warm weather caused Sarah's scents to fill his mind.

Sarah was always better than he was at figuring out things, she would have had answers to all of this by now. When Brianna was born, Sarah spent more time at home. She was smarter than Devon, too bright to marry an underachiever, but she saw something in him.

*She saw things in me. I didn't see in myself. I didn't deserve her. I only dated two women in college, that lying, soul sucking, psychotic, sex kitten, meat grinder in a poodle skirt Brandie Randolph, and Sarah Macintosh. I dated more than two women, but no one else is worth mentioning. Sarah was the best instinct I have ever had in my whole life. Sarah...*

Tears were blown diagonally down his face as he shifted gears.

*We met during her guest lecture on Pyrosequencing for my biochemistry class, a class I accidentally enrolled in. After the lecture, I introduced myself to her. Our first date was a gloomy day picnic at Summerville Park, where I promptly spilled wine on my shirt. I didn't think I had a chance after that.*

They walked in the park on the make up date. Devon spread out a blanket on the ground, picked her up, and put her down on it. He had brought a potato Gnocchi, with delicate little pillows of potato topped with sauce and silky mozzarella. Glazed honey fig salad with feta, pistachio, and mizuna. Chocolate covered strawberries and wine. They sat by the trees overlooking the lake wrapped in a blanket.

The moonlight allowed him to correctly make out her face. His arrogance melted away as she lay there as if she were floating in a stream, comfortable without a care in the world. He would say that he fell in love with her right then. She fell asleep with her head, nestled against his shoulder.

Sarah found it hard to meet men that weren't arrogant jerks or intimidated by her. Devon wasn't the chiseled jaw, stone-hewn alpha male she usually attracted. Six months after they met Devon proposing to her on the beach, it took ten agonizing minutes for her to accept his proposal.

*Sarah's head was usually buried in a book, but she made time for me. She improved my gene pool. Sex is the concrete expression of human value; the highest form of this value being love. Those that lack purpose find little meaning in human interaction, especially sex, although; they usually do it quite often. It has been months, but it seems like only this morning I promised to trim the hedges when I got home from work.*

Three years of marriage is a lifetime. Devon had earned a spousal master's degree in between, "I Do," and "Honey, when are you going to paint the nursery?" Working together took a lot of getting used to, but there is something about two people who were never supposed to get together, being together.

*She understood and encouraged me. She was the only grain of truth in my life. My wife was gone and in her place was this fiery pit in my stomach that returned every night. I should have finished school. I should have spent more time with my family. Even with these abilities, there is one thing I could never gain—time.*

As much as Devon didn't like visits with the in-laws, he contemplated visiting them now. "I love you," were the words women said to him, but he could never make his brain, get his mouth to say those words to them. He had no problem saying those words to Sarah.

*Regardless of her charity work and research, she always had time for us—she really lucked down. I wish I had paid more attention to her work.*

*When I first met Sarah, I felt something that made me clumsy. I felt awkward around her. I wasn't sure exactly what it was until our second date. From then on, she had me. She gave me every opportunity to slow down, every chance, every off-ramp to take. She didn't immediately let on that she felt something as well.*

*I was in the boat, rowing all by myself. Sarah left me in the deep end by myself for quite a while without acknowledging the shared feelings. She was good at remembering the past, but she was better at calculating. She calculated that the feelings for me would subside or that I would eventually crash the relationship car into a tree.*

*I had my plans, no family, no kids, and no suit to wear to a corporate job. I didn't want involvements, attachments. I wasn't the only one that forgot how to breathe around her. Sarah wanted to build a life, with me…me.*

*We were compelled to contact each other every five hours. I was doing things I had never done, like being honest. I was even respectful and considerate. I wasn't doing those things because that's what she wanted. I was doing those things because that's what I wanted.*

*What we felt turned into something we both thought was impossible—love. That mythical beast that everyone knows about but only a few have ever really seen. I saw it on that third date as we walked inside the theater, waiting for the film to start. I saw it in her eyes. That was the moment my life changed forever, my new goal was to change hers.*

*Even now, random thoughts of her excite me. She was my winning lottery ticket, and I wasn't just going to throw it away.*

*We moved fast, faster than our bodies wanted, faster than our minds thought possible. Her hugs slowed time. Her kisses were the stuff of legends; they lingered on my lips for hours. Villains from my past tried to ruin our burgeoning happiness.*

*Sarah was the kind of person that would fill an empty space that didn't need words, with hers. She was simple; she didn't have a bathroom full of sprays and washes. She had a unique scent that wasn't caused by perfumes, body sprays, or oils… I couldn't get enough of it.*

*She would quietly get out of bed to check on Brianna before going to her basement office. Each time I was near her, I made sure I got a nose full of Sarah. Maybe that's strange.*

*The rhythmic way she breathed in and out was musical. Sarah once told me that after fifteen minutes, a female has often made up her mind whether or not to have sex with a person. She said it wasn't like that with me. There was no overwhelming, undeniable pull to jump on me.*

*I took the job to move us forward. She didn't see our relationship as a goal, a set of talking points, or some problem to solve. We were from different worlds, but anyone around us for more than ten minutes could see our connection. Perhaps they caught me taking a moment to look at her lips. Maybe they saw the way she stared back at me.*

*They might have seen the nature in the way she placed her head on my shoulder. Maybe they saw the ways she would take her time to put lotion on my hands or the way I massaged her back, played in her hair or managed to say the right thing to lift her spirits.*

*Talking about work was the only time she didn't use tact; equations were extensions of her mind. I knew not to disturb her when she's calculating. I lived for the times when equations and philosophies were replaced by primal connections that periodically reached magical proportions.*

*Her trips and lectures produced a subtle sickness within me that was only curable by the sound of her voice. She made me want to be a better man; she gave me the opportunity to be a great father.*

*When she was pregnant, she was more focused than ever, she found things quicker, she solved problems faster, as if she and the baby were working on the problem together. It was like motherhood came with superpowers.*

*She held my hand; I rubbed her leg. She would put down a book just to pay attention to me. For me, sleep was the result of our intimate discourse; our intimacy spurred her imagination and pushed through blocked ideas. You could see the residual climax in her eyes, firing up synapses in areas of her brain.*

*Her figure was enhanced by every single piece of clothing she wore. Sweat suits clung to her like a second skin. In the bedroom, she took what she wanted from me, simultaneously giving me what I needed from her.*

*I respected her mind, and had a healthy respect for her in the bedroom, respect bordering on fear. It wasn't just in the bedroom; it was whenever the mood struck her. My life was great because every morning I woke up with her looking back at me.*

*Now, I am left with mornings and nights that are without color or brightness. In my dreams, The artful way her shoulder length hair lay on the pillow was a sight to behold and I can feel her lips on mine. I see her face. I always picture her lying on.... No, she's rolling across our bed in that sexy red dress of hers.*

*The red little number clung to her sides with the dangerously high slit; it freed her legs when she walked. I think she only wore that dress because she knew I liked seeing her in it. Red wasn't even her favorite color.*

*I remember her walk, her insatiable post orgasm itch, the slope of her neck—I see—I see—*

With a face full of hot tears, Devon quickly applied the brakes, and the bike came to a screeching halt.

"Wait, Sarah was working with a Noah Whitman, the package wasn't mistakenly delivered. The glasses were for her!"

The thought had been there all along, yet he hadn't noticed it. Of all the days, of all the packages he had to open, why did it have to be that one? The revelation lit a fire inside of Devon. He wiped his eyes and throttled the engine once more.

"Them will pay!"

Devon looked for natural disasters that broke the rule of the seasons. Eight out of season tornados, a reservoir unexpectedly cresting, Hurricane Season starting early these are the places Devon looked for them.

He combed through victim profiles of those killed or injured by natural disasters to see who the target was. His night activities now included tedious research.

Each otherworlder wore a weathered but natural unicoat. When the lights weren't moving on these coats, you could still tell which ability each possessed by the way their garments were adorned.

Each coat had armbands, breastplates, or a cape. Their coat's subtle black plate armor was a more flexible metal that looked as though it was forged by lightning. The designs seem to be influenced by a history that values the old ways and maintains cultural traditions.

Earthquake's coat showed a broken earth. The Earth's twenty tectonic plates squeeze, shift, or stretch, huge rocks form at their edges with great force. The plates all move in different directions and at different speeds. The plates crash into, pull apart, or sideswipe each other; this causes the ground to rumble.

Tornadoes are six times more energy dense than a hurricane. The average tornado contains the power of three hundred gallons of jet fuel.

Hurricanes are giant, spiraling tropical storms with wind speeds of over one hundred eighty miles an hour and unleash more than two trillion gallons of rain a day. Hurricane appeared anywhere along the path of a tropical disturbance. The warmer the sea, the more energy a hurricane has.

Hurricanes spin around a low pressure center known as the "eye." The eye of a hurricane is an area of sinking air. This area is noted for being calm. In this vortex is where Them are. The eye is surrounded by a circular wall of strong winds and rain. When a hurricane makes landfall, it produces water surges that can extend a hundred miles inland.

Devon was in a hurricane right now, avoiding flying debris. These otherworlders snarled, tossed one person, and violently shook another one to pieces.

Devon repurposed his pain. He used his abilities not to hide, but to hunt. Devon watched people as much as he did flocks of birds, but these otherworlders had his full attention now. Devon looked for those lights, those glowing eyes. He leveled his sights at any agent that was unlucky enough to cross his path.

On video, it would appear that someone was engulfed by a wall of mud, rocks, and debris, and then the wall stopped.

To observers, it looked as if a madman ran into the storm, while everyone else ran away. That madman was Devon. Devon stopped one happening after another.

Humans are too busy running and yelling to see if someone didn't evacuate. They aren't checking to see if another anomaly changed a tornado's velocity before the wind returned to normal. To humans, he was unknown, and they were comfortable not knowing him. Devon didn't want anything from humans; all of his answers would come from Them.

Devon made it his mission to stop, hurt, and prevent Them from completing their tasks. Landslide was surprised when Devon rounded the building. Devon grabbed Landslide before he could disappear into the void.

*I read about this in a book, but nothing compares to the actual killing of another being. Watching the life slowly leave a body stirred something within me. I tighten my grip as repeated waves of conflict, sympathy, and anger all crashed inside of me. This was not as I had imagined it to be.*

*It seemed so easy to kill from a distance. Killing from behind ma- chines took the humanity out of the thing. It took the feelings of loss, remorse, righteousness, and the finality of the action out of the act. To kill with your hands, up close takes something from you. Before tonight, I might have helped this being; not today.*

*My heart is knocking my ribs. I can feel his pain as my hands dig into his flesh. I wasn't prepared for how bones gave way under the right amount of pressure or the way the larynx collapses.*

Landslide struggled but didn't beg for mercy. He made no effort to cry out. With of Devon's hands around Landslide's throat and the other about to snap his vertebrate; Landslide's heartbeat grew louder until it stopped. Devon wondered if Landslide had offspring, a family and then—Snap.

Landslide's lifeless body laid there in the mud as Devon climbed out of it. Landslide offered no answers, no reasons; he never let out a sound other than the groan as his spine snapped. Devon killed, but there were two victims, Devon and the one he killed. Each time he killed, something inside of him died.

Landslide was silent in battle; others weren't so quiet. Others let out screeches as they succumbed; this unnerved Devon. In one battle, a tornado appeared to reverse its spin; this was caught on video.

These otherworlders were all in supreme physical condition, and they weren't accustomed to being challenged. They seemed confused when Devon attacked them. The whys and reasons no longer matter; the only rage remained.

These engagements caused Devon to be slammed into unoccupied homes, kicked into parked cars. These battles caused concrete to be ripped off the streets and chunks to be knocked off buildings. Devon's rage only grew with each storefront he was hurled through.

In these engagements, Devon's strength increased, his senses were heightened, and his eyes gave off a golden glow. Devon was able to harness bits of the black energy because his engagements created a subflux variance.

Subflux waves caused digital devices to malfunction. This variance allowed him to carry what he wore into the subflux. This variance caused Devon not to sink into the ground or be swept up by whirlwinds. It allowed Devon to be on an equal playing field with Them.

A violent encounter with Them often resulted in wounds and exhaustion. Some otherworlder's escaped his clutches and made it back to the rift. Devon's mind was full of anger and the distinct smell of sulfur.

The realization that the glasses were intended for Sarah occurred before Devon learned to master his rage The loss of control scared Devon. It was times like these when he did not wonder if Brianna would look up to him now.

The first time he killed, he was disturbed. He washed his hands for days. He couldn't sleep. He trembled for what seemed like a week. All the soap and hot water in the world couldn't wash away the grime. The next time he killed, it was easier, and he felt a little better.

When Devon engaged with these otherworlders, he was able to express himself. He didn't have to hide or hold back. His anger became hand strikes and kicks. His hate became dodges.

Devon was now six feet tall. His forays in battle were art. He computed how to defend and calculated his responses. He was a one hundred ninety-pound acrobatic fusion of martial art and violence.

The most talented otherworlder was Extraction. Other agents would come and destroy, then crowds of people would come to help or be spectators, and then the agent would retreat into the void. That was how things were between humans and this otherworld scum.

When otherworlders expended too much energy and were unable to return, Extraction was dispatched. Extraction was a large imposing figure. His black coat had red light hand and fist patterns. He had a unique skill set, mimicry being one of them. Extraction worked alone. Extraction carried away and rescued those Devon could not kill.

*I will not kill Extraction; it is doubtful that I even could.*

Through these encounters, Devon discovered more about the otherworlders. The blue coat lights showed that you were a commander of some sort. Yellow meant the wearer was in training. Those wearing red were grunts and enforcers and green were usual operatives.

# CHAPTER 17

Companionship was the one thing Devon lacked. He didn't have the passion of a kiss or lovemaking. The intensity of an embrace, the emotion in a conversation, the passion in a thought. The kind of passion that drives you; the kind of passion that inspires ... Devon missed that passion.

Devon watched the flow of human attraction and affinity be altered by these otherworlders. Devon saw how these interactions, in some ways, benefitted people. It was almost comical to see humans go one way, and then another at the urging of Sway.

He also saw humans fighting their influence. Those that fought these invaders woke up shaken. Their only options were to stay up until they couldn't stay up any longer, or they would attempt to remain asleep. If you were their mission, they would keep trying.

Devon was in Louisville, Kentucky. He was there to watch the Kentucky Derby, but that's where he saw her. She was in a condo, in the kitchen rearranging food in the refrigerator. His presence usually caused someone like this to return to the rift, but not this time. In this two bedroom brownstone, she caught Devon's attention like a hairline crack in reality.

She wore a dress that looked like aged white leather, painted with gold. It had a platinum colored neck holder, accented with golden metal. The tight fitting, contoured dress lovingly hugged her curves. It appeared to be made from snakeskin, but it wasn't.

Devon approached her. She looked into Devon's eyes and smiled as if his intrusion was welcome. She gently touched his shoulder; the muted voices calmed within Devon. She touched him, and a current ran through his body.

He was strangely comforted by her touch, and he felt lighter. In the distance, he could see his dreams forming.

In these visions he was cold and alone, his childhood replayed against the night sky. He shut his eyes as he fought these feelings even though the physical contact was needed, even if not human.

"Your energy signature is odd for a human," she said in a soft, whispery tone.

"Yours is odd for an otherworlders."

"I am Influence. Many things I have heard about you." Influence had a softer inflection in her voice than Devon anticipated.

"You have?" Devon said.

"We all have," said Influence as her long, slender fingers broke contact with Devon. "This is my first time, touching a human."

Devon grabbed her hand and said, "I hope it was all you expected. If you have heard about me, then you know you should've run." "Some of our legends have not returned."

"Legends...."

"Every citizen that goes through the rift is a hero, a legend...."

"I don't know anything about legends. I only killed those who murder innocent people!"

"Are you going to kill me as well?" Influence questioned, freeing herself and facing Devon.

"I kill out of necessity," replied Devon.

"We see what we do as necessary. An event happens in your city, and the next day across the world, a similar event happens. This divides the human's attention.

"Yet, you are the ones hiding in shadows, dark corners, and lurk- ing in nightmares."

"You sapiens are so shortsighted. When unconscious, your kind is more receptive to us. Humans fear hurricanes but have yet to cool the ocean to dissipate approaching ones. They are governed by fear.

"Fear that others recognize as opportunity, an opportunity for profit and control."

"That may be, but it seems rather mundane to be moving around a carton of eggs," Devon smirked as Influence led him to the bedroom.

"Look at her, sleeping so peacefully. When she wakes, she'll notice something wrong; she will feel something strange about her surroundings. Her energy will change, and that is when our influence is the strongest. In moments of emotion, outrage, and confusion, I altered minds. What I do today is as important as the others I do tomorrow."

"People don't need the anti-hydrogen crowd destroying what we can destroy ourselves. You are not needed here," said Devon as they walked out of the bedroom and into the living room.

"I will be back tomorrow or the next day," said Influence. Her response was quick and to the point. "If I don't return, another will. Instead of governance, your kind is tyranny. Instead of justice, your kind is oppression and bias. Instead of hope, your kind is proudly launching missiles against the innocent. Is this what my mate, Ailden gave his life for?" Influence said.

"Look at what you've become...a purposeless killer bent on revenge," Influence continued. "How do you feel knowing that you are the reason families are without fathers? My offspring are without their father, and I am without a mate. You dishonor my mate's memory."

Devon was dumbfounded at Influence's remarks. Guilt climbed into his psyche. Influence's words topped Devon cold. Her mate had revived Devon. He had spoken of his family, his mate, and his offspring while he operated on Devon.

"You are just trying to save yourself...," Devon responded.

"You have become a shining example of why we do what we do. Some say what my mate did was an attempt at peace; others say he had to correct his errors. No one really knows, and you were the last to see him," Influence said, walking toward the front door.

"Why don't you just stop all this and tell your elders to talk to our leaders? I am sure we work all of this out..."

"I am not on the council and from what you have shown us, it wouldn't change their decision. You're asking for my help...I thought you had everything figured out...."

"Not everything. So, I may as well just kill all of you egg rearrangers as fast as I can."

"My whispers have moved debates. It is no small task for someone to have an idea here and for others on the other side of the world to have the exact same idea and to have all of it written off as coincidence. We have a purpose, even if you don't understand it."

"I understand wrong!"

"Is it wrong for stadiums full of people to raise their hands to form the same sign?" Influence said, staring at Devon. "Is wrong for crowds of people to move in unison with a song? Is it wrong for musical notes to get stuck inside a composer's head?

"You pretend that you don't need anyone. You have hidden in places where no one thinks to look. You have ruled over the cities when they are the quietest. You didn't feel human until someone else's blood ran down your face."

Devon could only look at her face as her silver eyes pushed right through him. A single, black tear left the corner of her eyes and cut a path down her cheek.

"I have caused the day and night business professional to suddenly quit their job and pick up a surfboard. I have caused people to look where they otherwise would not to find discoveries they never would have

"You think it mundane. Is it mundane to rearrange smaller thoughts into bigger ones? Is it mundane to cause a person to change their vote?" Influence said. "It is mundane to cause a frat boy to take a class he never wanted, to get a job on Wall Street, and to marry the woman of his dreams?" Influence said as she walked out the door.

The curtains inside the house flapped. Her words had convicted Devon. The truth was laid bare at his feet. The gentle sound of the door closing snapped him out of his trance. When Devon opened the door, Influence was gone as if she had never been there.

Because of his worldwide travels, the world was smaller, more manageable. Devon presently resided in redlined areas, buildings under construction, and dark spaces. He was in no man's land. He no longer followed directions, and he no longer did what he was told. He ran through hick towns, snow covered plains and evergreen forests.

In cities like Chicago, Philadelphia, Washington and especially New York, hid his night prowling went unnoticed. Devon sat next to the sparrows on the rooftops of homes where bedtime stories were still told to children. Right now he's hanging off the side of this forty-five stories building, wondered if things would ever be normal.

*There is no such thing as a credible source…*

Devon often found himself cloning Sarah's walk, superimposing her smile on the face of another. Influence could bat her eyelashes and change the will of people. Influence had awakened something inside of Devon.

As he wandered the streets near a theater, a pair of jade tipped hair sticks intrigued Devon. She stood underneath the tattered blue and white theater awning. He watched the rain lightly fall at her feet.

As he came closer, he could smell the faint hint of butterscotch. He was uneasy, but he approached her, introduced himself. They spoke, but she didn't reveal how old she was. Her name was Gina. She was a purchaser for a clothing manufacturer. She had been stood up by her date.

Her makeup was modest, devoid of the 'look at me' bells and whistles. She was slender, and her hips were shapely, as for the guy who stood her up, it was his loss. Her face was filled with the same old regrets that every broken heart knows.

She assumed Devon had seen the same movie she had. He had seen the film, but not that night. It wasn't her beauty that attracted Devon, it was the way she carried herself. She had beautifully sad, light brown eyes.

Tomorrow, she wouldn't be able to pick him out of a crowd of the thousand faces hurrying to work. He decided to not look deeply into her for fear of eventually loathing her. An introduction, a shout of laughter, and the uneasiness was gone. The two shared an umbrella as they walked four blocks to a coffee shop.

The coffee shop was small, quaint even. It had red walls, a rustic brown floor, and those chestnut colored tables that all coffee shops seemed to have. Wooden holders of magazines, newspapers, and books of poetry were in the back. They sat by the window as a dozen conversations mixed together.

The only thing Devon could pick out from the noise was the constant grinding of coffee beans. There was something about Gina's voice that helped him remember. The smell of vanilla made its way to their table.

"I'll have that," Gina said, pointing at the special. Devon had his usual.

"You're beautiful," Devon said, breaking the awkward moment of silence.

Her carefully tousled ends couldn't hide her blushing face. She paused for a second when she started talking again, her tone had changed. Devon's body didn't crave the caffeinated concoction, but he did have a few scones. As he listened to her, his thumb moved to support his chin; his fingers partially covered his mouth.

Gina is 5'5", slim, altheltic and her voice was airy. It was at least forty degrees out. She was not dressed for the cold. Perhaps, she was trying to reveal a little more of herself than her original date was worth.

"So what do you want to know about me?"

"Everything…"

Devon increased his body temperature, which slightly elevated the ambient temperature around them as they sat in the small booth. She wore a very short green knit skirt and stockings, a white pleated blouse, and a shoulder jacket emblazoned with a corporate logo. She was drawn to his smile, his thoughtfulness, and how he didn't seem to be in a rush.

"Do you want to go back to my place for something a little heavier?" Gina softly said.

Devon put the carrot cake in a to-go box, and they took the short drive to her apartment. Her one bedroom apartment was midway down Cypress Street, just a few blocks away from downtown.

Her apartment was wedged between a market and a flower shop. She held his hand as they went up the stairs to her apartment. Her hands were warm, and her legs were like young apple trees. Gina thought Devon's nervousness was cute.

They entered her dark apartment. Gina turned on a light and felt Devon's muscles as she helped him out of his coat. She put his hat and coat on the coat rack. Devon walked around the living room before planting himself on the couch. Pillows were everywhere, but her apartment was warm and contemporary.

The living room was filled with picture frames. On top of the entertainment center was a large vase with three old roses in it, surrounded by dead petals. There was a small table in the corner that had some type of needlepoint on it. On the wall, were two pictures, maybe they were of family members, perhaps those photos came with the frame. The apartment was as unassuming as Gina was.

Gina dimmed the lights and pressed a few buttons. Something soft and slow came out of the entertainment speakers as she poured herself a shot of something.

"I have been in these heels a lot longer than I should have," she said, tossing her white heels in the corner. "I am going to change into something a little bit more comfortable, don't leave."

"I won't."

Devon took off his shoes, put them back on, and then took them off again. He squirmed on the small couch. He thought that coming back to her apartment may have been a mistake. Devon had practiced, he had evolved, but what was before him frightened him.

Gina emerged from the room wearing a blue eyelash lace teddy. She slowly walked around the living room, arraigning this and that. She touched

Devon's shoulder every time she walked by him. She sat down next to him. She gulped down another drink. She slowly licked her lips, smiled, and said

"So, what should we do now?" she said, looking him his eyes.

"You tell me," Devon said.

A small smile played at the edge of her mouth as she grabbed De-von's collar and kissed him. Her lips were warm and soft. She leaned in and kissed him as if she couldn't get enough of him. Her breath was heavy; her kisses were passionate, long, and wet.

She moved her hand underneath his shirt, and she whispered in his ear. Devon forgot what it felt like to touch another person; her soft, delicate touch reminded him. The scent of her perfume was more apparent as her body temperature rose.

Devon slowly navigated her body. She felt soft in his large hands. Hands that should have been rougher for someone that worked with engines dug through dirt and climbed buildings all night but they weren't.

Devon stood up and took off his shirt. He slowly allowed his pants to fall to the floor. He stood in front of her in all of his naked glory.

"Oh my," she said. He was bigger than she expected. His length and girth intimidated her. Gina was never one to back away from a challenge.

Devon took a step back, "No...come closer," she said. Gina tossed her usual caution aside and wrapped her hands around his erect member. Her touch was firm but soft and he grew in her hand and her breath was hot on him. As she put her mouth on him, his mind traveled back to his climb of Mount Roraima. A black mountain summit he feared, a summit thought unreachable as clouds hid the peak.

Her legs parted slightly as he moved up inside them. The closer Devon came the father apart the legs moved. Her moans were angelic, her nipples rose to meet his hot tongue. He turned her around a smacked her on her ass. A sweet spasm ran through her body.

She would have been happy to continue to believe that her body didn't need this, that her mind didn't need this. Parts of her body that she didn't know she had were igniting. A fever ran through her, then delight followed by the blush of embarrassed intrusion that showed on her cheek next to the subtle smile that only appears when taboo present.

He slowly ran his fingers from her purple lips to her stomach. He put his hand underneath here and lifted her up. Her feet no longer touched the floor. He kissed her flower and licked its swollen petals leading to tight a head. His tongue moved with purpose. His lips glistened with her juices as he began slowly take apples from her tree.

He took his time as he could see parts of Gina that should have been touched, but had not been; those were the places he would go. Sweat ran down her legs as her body spasmed. He had never brought someone to orasan that quickly.

She felt a warm sensation in the center of her body and a spark of pleasure was set off. This spark sent pleasure waves through her body. She pushed him from between her legs and looked as if she were injured, until she giggled. She looked him in the eyes and straddled him. After an hour, her purple lips quivered, "I can't...I can't take any more."

"You will," replied Devon. Gina locked her arms around Devon's neck. Urged on by her passionate declarations Devon's limb showed no sympathy for the object of its fury. Her inner achrtechure altered by each stroke. There was something about her movements, there was something about her warmth, something about the give and take of their union.

Moans escaped Gina's mouth as tiny little fireworks made her muscles contracted, subsided and contracted. Devon's chest heaves as he grunts; his mind had reached summit, his muscles tensed, and he exploded from his very core.

Devon slowly lowered himself to the ground; he was at peace. She curled up next to him. They breathed in each other's warmth as his hand gently rubbed her shaking legs.

Everything hurt and everything tingled. "Stay with me," she whispered in his ear. Devon kissed her forehead. "I don't even know your last name..." was the last thing that fell from her lips before she slept. He didn't know hers, either.

As Gina slept, Devon grabbed his clothes in the dark and quietly left, leaving only his hat. Without knowing it, Gina rescused Devon, if only for a little while. He rode with his firarm hanging weaking at his side, he'd never use the AM moniker again.

# CHAPTER 18

The past was like a stream creeping up a mirror, just to cover what's in front of you. Everywhere Devon went people said the bad actors were the Americans, the Chinese, the Russians, the Iranians, the Canadians, but never the otherworlders.

The fire had burned ten acres before Devon arrived. Devon helped the evacuees. They needed water and blankets. Things were missing… pets… medication… people… There were already ten fire crews on the scene. The blaze created its own wind.

The humidity dropped, and the winds increased, and that's when bad things started to happen. Wildfire landed, waved his cape and turned air into flame. Wildfire burned over him.

Wildfire reduced several towns to ash. Hundreds of homes and other structures were lost. Everything was blanketed in ash. In eight hours, 20,000 acres had been scorched. Devon clothes had burned off, and he had wounds that would take a week to heal.

Devon led six groups of people out of the fire to safety. He had no time to investigate exactly what was Wildfire's mission because that's when Commotion was sent after him. Commotion, like Extraction, had greater sustained energy. Commotion's coat had red lights, he was an enforcer.

Commotion tracked Devon all night through the Florida swamp. Running in knee high water was no easy task, even for Devon. In the swamp, Commotion caught up to him, his coat ablaze with symbols.

"I knew they'd send someone. Your first mistake was taking the assignment." Devon said as the two faced off in the water.

"And the second?" retorted Commotion. Commotion seemed young, he spoke quicker than Devon expected, and he did not waste words.

"…Facing me."

A nearby lightning strike set fire to a tree line as the two jumped towards each other. The growing flames provided warnings to alligators and water moccasins to leave the area. The two sizably different shadows fought and splashed in the cold water.

Commotion's answers to Devon's questions came in the form of blows. Devon responded with a loud groan as he scrambled to his feet. Devon sidestepped his silver eyed opponent. The larger Commotion hit Devon with kicks, elbows, and punches.

A blow glanced off Devon's ribcage; the sharp sting faded fast. Their breath rose in a vapor before them. Commotion grinned as Devon quickly jabbed against his abdomen. Commotion pivoted and struck Devon harder than he had ever been hit before.

Again, Lightning struck as Carpophorus and Crixus faced each other in the center of the Colosseum. A thousand leaves blocked the moonlight. Devon went on the offensive.

Devon lashed out, aiming for his opponent's gut. Commotion proved equally effective at defense, as Devon's fist met a meaty forearm. Devon tried again, and this time he connected. Devon connected with a flying double kick and landed an elbow in the middle of Commotion's back. Commotion dropped to his knees.

Commotion elbowed upward into Devon's abdomen and rolled into a palm strike to the groin. Commotion's arms coiled around Devon's midsection like a living vice grip.

Commotion tossed Devon against a large white pine, which split his head open. Devon landed on an underwater tree root. Devon howled like a wounded coyote as blood ran down his side. The trickle of blood from his head started to gush. Water, branches, and leaves splashed about them as each drip of blood sounded like a dull thud as it hit the water.

Devon swept Commotion's leg, and while Commotion was falling, Devon punched him with all of his might. Commotion was hurled through the air, knocking down several trees before he landed face first in the almost knee deep water. Devon leaped into the air and landed with his knee squarely in between Commotion's shoulder blades; this produced a loud, dull roar from Commotion.

The silver in Commotion's eyes dimmed. Devon dug his fingers into the bicep of Commotion's swinging arm and ripped at the muscle while striking the forearm on the same side.

Devon was a golden eyed whirlwind of motion as he hit Commotion from multiple directions. A spinning back kick from Devon doubled Commotion over. Then he dug his fingers into his throat, grabbing the windpipe as he wrestled his opponent to the ground. He grabbed Commotion's arms and quickly swung his leg over his face.

Commotion took several deep breaths and let out an unearthly bellow that only called attention to his labored breathing. The moonlight shifted briefly. Commotion's submerged face looked even more hideous underneath the duckweed covered water. Commotion's arm should have broken, but it didn't.

Devon mounted Commotions as he gasped for air. With one hand around his throat, Devon drew his fist back for a blow; lightning flashed as Devon rained strikes down into the water as Commotions arms impotently flailed.

Commotion's eyes closed and he made a gurgling sound as he choked on the cold water. Commotion never screamed, but that was the first time Devon saw it—fear. In that fleeting moment, Commotion tossed Devon off of him. Devon slid twenty-feet on top of the water before coming to a stop.

Devon refocused and ran toward Commotion. A kneeling Com- motion held up his hand; the fight was over. Commotion surrendered to him under a lightning filled sky. A bleeding Commotion righted himself as the noise of the swamp quieted.

"The group wants to meet with you." Commotion slowly said.

Devon had three days to arrive at the coordinates Commotion gave him. Commotion slowly inhaled, turned, and ran off into the horizon as mist settled over the water. All that was left was the crackling of flames and the coordinates.

This was the meeting Devon had been waiting for. Devon's clothes were ripped and wet with blood. The fact that his backpack was no worse for wear made him smile.

Devon had been dispatching foes in increasingly creative ways, so there was equity in taking this meeting. In the days that followed Devon prepared winter camouflage as his body healed.

The coordinates that were given to Devon were 66°48′ 48″N 150°38′ 38″W The location was just above the Arctic Circle. Two days after his battle with Commotion, Devon was completely healed.

Devon headed to the nearest airport he could find, jumped a fence, and grabbed a flight. Devon hopped a dozen flights; the closest he could get to those coordinates was prospect Creek, Alaska.

The nearest airport was sixty-three miles away. He could have glided in, but he stayed on top of the aircraft throughout the descent and disembarked before the craft touched the runway. He made his way across the tarmac and over the rusty old chain linked fence. He quickly disappeared into a line of trees and bushes; he would have to hike the rest of the journey.

Most of Alaska's glaciers sit on top of mountains ranges, of which there were many. Glaciers were also present at ocean inlets, popular tourist attractions such as Glacier Bay and Icy Bay were created by the recession of a glacier. Devon and his white camouflage disembarked near the Endicott Mountains.

These mountains are one of the biggest terrestrial ecosystems in the world. It is one of the few places in the world that is largely free of roads and industrial development. This area is characterized by severe winters that often lasted six months, and a continuous belt of coniferous trees overlaid glaciated areas.

"Good thing I dressed for the cold," Devon said to no one as he ran toward his destination, his backpack bouncing awkwardly on his back. Dwarfed by icy mountainscapes and gorgeous vistas, he may as well have been the moon.

Alaska's red earth was covered by so much snow that certain regions are only accessible by specially outfitted helicopters. Vehicles that drove through seemed to fishtail around every turn. Single lane roads crossed through deserted landscapes as rugged snowcapped peaks rose in the distance. He made it to the highway, which was thirty miles away from the coordinates.

The river was crisp and clear, it was cold and flowed briskly. He knelt down to drink from it. As he did, he noticed that ten meters separated him from a huge brown bear. A brief moment of eye contact and the bear and Devon came to an understanding; he was just passing through.

These winding trails and winds would have pinned anyone up against the mountainside. He had a choice climb up the edge of the mountain or cross the river. Devon decided to cross the river. He scattered caribou, Dall sheep, harlequin ducks, and largemouth bass as he waded through the icy water.

*I should have climbed,* he thought as he changed out of his wet boots and socks.

Devon ran across this whiteness, trudged forward as high peaks, and his destination loomed in the distance. He jumped rhythmically from rock to rock. Devon's fast pace knocked snow from leaves and pounded down layers of packed snow. A bald eagle glided high above him as he quickly navigated the constantly shifting, jagged frozen lava.

Some of the huge ice sheets were flat and had trails that were easy to follow; the path to these coordinates had to be forged. He quickly moved through basins and rappelled down mountainsides. He found himself scaling the snow covered mountain peaks with black horns goats.

Some people would call this an adventure, but one wrong move could end tragically, even for the most experienced hiker. No one knew where Devon was; there would be no rescue, no search party, and no campsite. The cold fought him up one side of the mountain and chased him down the other.

He moved across the hard moss and the crust of frost along the muddy river banks. His trail took him between trees that pierced the heavens. It was ecstatic beauty and annihilating terror mixed with the cold.

There was an audible crunch as he stepped, which caused a large brown and white hawk owl and several white crowned sparrows to glance in his direction. The cliffs were behind him now; he was almost there.

These mountains covered the skyline as far as he could see. This was the great unknown, a land of frozen death. Black and gray bits of exposed granite sloped through the desolate summits. Rock and water had through centuries, cut lanes through the state.

The sound of the intermitting gust held vague, chaotic musical notes that suggested the landscape hated itself. The frosty nature of the state demanded the swirling winds displayed nothing but whiteness for miles.

Devon cautiously stepped between three adjacent peaks. A large blue glacial sheet had cut through the mountain range an era ago. These ice covered peaks rose hundreds of feet. Devon had expected a heavily guarded corridor, there was nothing but whiteness.

This glacial ice had tiny air bubbles embedded within the crystals. The denser the ice, the more air bubbles are forced out. Devon rested on an ice sheet that appeared almost turquoise. It appeared this way because the remaining ice absorbed all the colors of the spectrum, all except blue.

The clothes he created kept him dry and comfortable, but the instant the wind shifted, he felt the air's frigid finger touch the back of his neck. There between those three peaks, he fell to his knees before nature.

"Why are you hiding from me?" Devon yelled. His shouts echoed through the valley. The wind suddenly stopped, there was silence—everything was motionless.

"And, you are hiding in plain sight," echoed a booming voice.

Three hundred feet up, a hole slowly opened on the side of a glacier. Devon cautiously climbed the mountain's snow face with his heart in his mouth. The air around him thinned as he slowly entered the opening. He felt as alone as he did on his first day of school.

Devon followed a series of circular paths lined with ice columns which led to a large marble lined foyer with translucent wood pillars on either side. He ran his hand over the engraved white walls; his espression held the delight of a child at the moment of discovery.

The wood was soft but felt like steel. Over the door post "The Ones Who Came Before" was carved in a pen line wireframe font. The large Lignum Vitae double entry doors slowly opened, revealing a dark chamber.

Once inside the doors slowly closed behind him. Devon felt heavier. He was alone in the chamber. There were no banners, no adornment, and no light. The chamber was surprisingly warm. He no longer needed his jacket; he no longer saw the vapor of his breath.

The chamber was a dark celebration of life made of metal and stone. The monumental structure was a place to worship, something to salute. Vaulted walls and towering carvings had the purpose of intimidating all who enter. The fact that this space existed over three feet up in subzero temperature inside of a mountain on the threshold of a subflux, only added to the effect it of those allowed into its presence.

The huge crystal sculptures that decorated the walls were designed to make an unforgettable impression on all who looked upon them. This place was far larger than any cathedral he had seen. The intent of this place was to humble, to reduce in stature any who passed through. Here, space collapsed in on humanity.

After a moment of silence, Devon walked through the dimly lit chamber, noticing the streaks of gold in the silver granite floor.

The sixty-foot vaulted glass like ceiling shimmered the way ice does in low light. The near translucent walls looked out on the state. This was the most spectacular sight ever witnessed by man. Along the wall was a twisted designed that lead to an elevated enclosure.

In the middle of the large hall, the floor had a hexagon basket weave pattern made from bleached oak cross pieces, the end grain hexagons culminated in a large circular metal medallion. At the opposite end of the chamber was a single doorway.

Straight ahead of Devon in the center of the room was a widening beam of light that light cut through the silence. From that doorway, silhouette of a humanoid figure emerged. The figure walked towards Devon. The closer the figure came to Devon, the brighter the chamber became. The advancing being caused Devon's stomach to churn.

# CHAPTER 19

The whole of understanding was in question amidst the rising tension, the impossible choices and barely contained frustration.

As the being advanced toward him, he contemplated music. The music, the lyrics, the composition, is divine, eternal; it's something that lives in the collective unconsciousness of everyone.

It's was the same as a musical theme that repeats itself and pops up in unexpected places. Different people hear it and grab it out of the ether and write songs. It's a connection of the divine and the mortal, yet no one knows precisely how they composed it.

Outside was a world of justice, a world of rules, tattoos of light, symbols, corruption, devices, and generated fears. There was a song here, a song that tied together the eons, the stars, and the people.

"Who's there?"

The only answer Devon received was slow, deliberate footsteps. The figure's robe was a perfectly tailored layered piece of art that extended to his ankles; the fur at the top of it flowed with a sheen. Two black eyes peered beneath his helmet; the helmet hugged the side of his head. The figure had a robust and confident stride.

"It's not Olympus, but it will do," said the being dressed in gold and white trim, a sash extended diagonally from his shoulder to his hip. "Devon, welcome, the council has been expecting you," he said, removing his helmet.

"Is the council also expecting to get their ass kicked? Show yourselves, cowards!" this was Devon's clenched teeth response as his eyes panned the chamber.

"Would you have preferred to meet in the Icelandic Badlands?" said the figure. Devon responded with silence.

The figure waved his other hand, and a bright holographic universe engulfed them. What the holograph showed was so vast it could be called monstrous.

The giant star field moved like it was alive. It was an organism like nothing Devon had seen before. The hologram was not lit from the front or the rear; these light particles moved and weren't distorted by the presences of the two people within it.

This was a complete logarithmic map of the universe contained quark-gluon plasma and colliding pions and kaons particles. Neon RNA molecules, chemical graphs, symbols, and changing equations floated throughout the holograph.

"Look..." the graveled voice as it reverberated throughout the room.

The electric lettering drifted off into space and a craft left the planet. It was silent in space, floating against the backdrop of millions of shining stars.

The craft quickly made its way to the other side of the known universe past purple nebulas, moons circling moons, asteroids and asteroid belts, black holes, sun planets with hot looking tentacles as their core, and once beautiful planets broken into debris.

The ship corrected its course near silicone, glassy, water filled, filament laden, irregular, and fragmentary shaped planets. The craft's destination was a binary solar system. Twelve planets orbited a massive twinkling blue light star and a closer redder star.

"This beats bumping into people just to feel alive...doesn't it?" the figure stated.

Devon fell to his knees as emotion overcame him. Devon tearfully looked up at the floating elemental percentages before him. The silence in the chamber seemed to stretch on forever.

The figure waved his hand, and the edges of the elevated enclosure began to fill with faces. The faces appeared with their eyes closed as if in sleep, death, or a bit of both. The hall gradually came to life with this muted color audience.

The first face was oval, soft features, a female. More faces emerged from the darkness until a dozen faces floated in the elevated enclosure. Males and females; they moved into position.

Their pale, ghastly lips began to twitch. Their features, which had been expressionless, contorted and their mask like eyes opened, revealing sharp whiteness. Twelve faces in all, their bodies shrouded by the enclosure. They sat in uncomfortable darkness.

"I am Prime," said the person standing in front of Devon. Prime cradled a planet filled with life with both hands.

"What am I seeing?" said a tearful Devon, looking up.

"The future..." Prime smiled. "...please stand," he said, walking toward Devon. "We are honored you are here. I sit at the head of The Group." Prime said.

Prime was imposing. He was taller than Devon, but he was the smallest otherworlder he had encountered. His layered garb was topped with a breastplate. The deceptively lightweight of its internal bone plates were like armor shielding

Devon could tell that he was young, but his hair had grayed. The white streaks in his hair were testaments to his tenacity. Prime had a regal appearance. Through the darkness, Devon searched for the hidden throne.

Prime was an otherworlder, and this place existed on the outer edge of the subflux. Prime's eyes were sullen.

"Where you see conflict, others see control. What you view as Armageddon, we see as rebirth. What you call destruction, we call restructuring," smiled Prime.

Devon slowly stood up. "You call destroying the Earth restructuring?" said Devon.

"We are preserving. Devon, I know why you're here. I know what you've been doing, why you hardly sleep, and why, night after night, you walk rooftops and climb buildings. You're looking for a purpose. I know because I was once looking for the same thing..."

Prime moved and spoke in a measured, methodical, authoritative way. He spoke as if he was being scrutinized continuously.

"I am only here for answers," retorted Devon. "The Earth is in peril, and we do what we must,"

"We do what we must..." The Faces echoed.

Devon looked at the faces, at the hologram and then at Prime. The cradled planet had an atmosphere; it teamed with strange, different, indescribable vibrantly colorful life. The planet had sculpted canyon, land masses, bodies of water, and two bright stars.

Prime interacted with the hologram, carefully moving a mountain, altering the course of a river, and gently placing DNA strands as the planet slowly turned.

"Life will begin again," Prime said as he put the planet back into the hologram.

"And, what now?" said Devon, letting Prime know that he wouldn't blindly accept his word.

"You've beaten some of our best…"

"If you say so…" was Devon response to Prime's hostile compliment.

"He was one of our most decorated operatives. He carried out many successful missions. He was a valued operative, a legend, and a friend. He was caught and tortured for some time before I came to the rift edge. He told us nothing about you or what he had done to you, so agents were sent after you.

"As we learned more about you, we figured out that Whitman had sent out a package intended for your wife. Chasing after you distracted us from our mission, that's why we stopped coming after you."

"I never got to tell He thank you…"

"It was not easy to end He's life. It was with deep sadness that the removal of He was undertaken. When his energy was almost depleted, he groaned to be killed. In the end, Ailden begged to be put out of his misery."

"And what was his crime?" "Disbelief.…"

"Destroying is all you're doing, nothing more!"

"Unchecked, humanity wouldn't make it another hundred years. There is nothing deadlier than the human mind."

"If what you say is true through research, we would find a way to save the planet."

"Research is the culmination of past searches. Biases always creep in, leading to desired answers. A new search was needed. Such a search yielded a solar system, where we found the unfindable, a planet that could sustain for life. Planet F.

"Millions of models show this to be the place to begin. They will rise from the ground and from the waters. This search engine carries the most important payload. There is nothing more important than this mission. Their abilities, their training is all in service of this goal."

"Killing, driving people from their homes…You and this group of yours intend to change the destiny of the human race?"

"Mankind will end—here, another kind will rise there. We are the protectors, we are liberators…"

"You kill and destroy."

"What we do is out of necessity…"

"It's necessary to blow around papers, plant thoughts, and destroy trailer parks?"

"…actions to move the herd. No one gets to the top of the ladder without help."

"You help with the falling also."

"Exactly. You sapiens dream of integrating human and machine. You want the motors, the signals, and the blips. You are confident that if you give machines life, life will be given back. You are enthralled by decadence. Your anxiety is spurred by insecurity, synchronized by a rage that is not quelled by background checks and waiting periods.

"People harbor contempt and whims that can freeze your account and shut down your signal. They create DNA databases to implicate family members. They have created a legal demand for humans that run on a single charge. There is no firewall to the human mind; this is a preschool classroom, with a military."

As Prime spoke, Devon watched as interstellar dust, asteroids, gas storms, planets, and galaxies were briskly passed by the craft. The vehicle traveled in space through the turquoise of time and passed the yellows of history.

He also saw the craft moves pass fiery comets and the black ice of space. It shifted course around black holes and star belts…all in silence. The tapestry of stars stretches beyond what was known.

This small craft with strangely glowing exhaust sucked carried within it the genetic code for the change. A gently pulsating with a black light entered the front of the craft. It used dark matter particles like strings to pull it towards its destination.

"This is the solution," Prime said.

Prime's matter-of-factness caused Devon to stare off into the darkness, his mind bombarded with feeling loneliness, anger, confusion, and fear all at the same time. All of which were useless thoughts because he had no reason to believe anything Prime said.

"Before the nineteenth century…" Prime said waving his hand as the hologram changed to historical images, "we did not possess the technology to give the human conscious large amounts of creative fodder, except for the occasional dinosaur bones and projectile points.

"Over time, we allowed people to make more discoveries and larger finds of fossils. We planted specimens, millions of years old in the earth to draw out the curious ones. We left fossilized eggs here, a bone, a claw or something else there.

"All of this planted to keep the human mind guessing, wondering. We used thought capturing objects and lights in the sky and spurred rumors of alien beings. This engaged the toilers, cranks, and kooks, and then we mixed in bits and pieces of legend.

"When a war is being fought, and you are not a part of the war, the war is being fought over you." The images continued to play out the actions Prime spoke of.

"This isn't a war; it's a slaughter."

"If it is a slaughter, it is a necessary one. We use machines to give us disciplined micro-targeting of gene conflict, and we are preparing for the next leap, to save humanity...."

"How can people be destroyed, and humanity saved?"

"People have lost track of what humanity is. It is people that have perverted humanity."

"And, me, my wife...my child... Was that for the betterment of humanity?"

"We didn't know how much was known. It was necessary."

"Necessary! Look me, look at what I have become," Devon said.

He took a step towards Prime. Prime put out his hand in a pausing gesture to Devon.

"What you have become is magnificent," said Prime. "Magnificent..." The Faces echoed in unison.

"You developed outside of the structure. We watched you pushing, testing your limits. We watched you climb another story higher, run another minute faster, and think clearer. You have seen what no human has. You have seen us and humans all of it, naked.

"But...you still have some of their flaws," Prime offered. "Like humans, we had hopes and dreams. We searched for ways to make life better. Devon, seeking a better life is not an external activity. Surviving the impossible does not mean victory, it's merely a beginning."

"Your ancestors painstakingly crawled up out of a swamp, and now your petty jealousies rule you while you privately scorning each other. How you were upgraded doesn't matter now, they fact that you are here does.

"You have a front row seat to the decline of the man's empire. Saving man is good; saving humanity is the greater good. Are you ready to proceed?" Prime said, extending his hand.

Devon didn't answer but looked thoughtfully at Prime's hand, but didn't take it. Devon felt the eyes of the faces following them as they slowly walked out the chamber and down a long corridor.

# CHAPTER 20

Prime directed Devon's attention down the hall to a door. As they approached the door, it disappeared, and Devon was pulled inside. He was instantly suspended in midair. Prime, extended his hand and Devon grabbed it. Once Devon grabbed his hand he was once again in the long hallway alongside Prime.

Devon's eyes narrowed as the liquid wall panels seemed to exhale. The hallway seemed smaller from the outside. He thought the halls would be extravagant like the chamber, but they weren't. The various rooms and passages seemed endless.

"You must have a lot of questions for me." "I have only one..."

Prime waved his hand, and otherworld actions on different continents were projected onto the walls of the corridor.

"You have been granted legal protection here. No human has stood in these proceedings. All objections to you being here have been decided. Devon, you have made great strides," Prime continued to shower Devon with accolades. Prime turned and walked down a bright passage. Devon followed as Prime spoke.

"You see the truth is as time passed, people lost the ability to see and feel these other selves. They look puzzled when a child laughs randomly, stares off into the distance, or playa with no one. They lost this ability due to social assimilation and pollutants.

"However, there are times when you have been walking down the street and suddenly hear a conversation in your head or music playing that you have not heard before. You have had distinct dreams in which you return to the same places over and over. And, when you awake from these dreams, it is as if you had not slept. All the emotions are as if you just lived out this dream experience.

"There are many different ways to sense the Earth I am from, just as there are numerous ways to sense this current time and space. Beyond the speed of time is thought. For most people, the paths of time mix together and access to specifics is littered with obstacles, but for some, things are as clear as they are now for you.

"Most of the time, humans shrug off these feelings; choosing to remain disconnected from consciousness. The universe is composed of multiple dimensions. When our plane intrudes on the four-dimensional world of yours, we are seen as miraculous and dangerous, and we are always denied existence and thus viewed as the fantasies of disturbed minds."

"Do things seem to be out of balance? Yes, but to say it is over is a pretty big jump to make." Devon said.

"The Earth creates what you call natural disasters and extreme weather in an effort to balance itself; we assist in that balance."

The hallway was lined with rooms, rooms that were filled with activity. Halfway down the second passage, there was a door. The door had a small window. The closer Devon got to the door, the more transparent it became until it disappeared. The room was large, and a person was sitting at a plain looking desk.

"What's in there?" Devon asked.

"The Watcher…"

In what resembled a military Central Intelligence Center, Devon saw hundreds of floating screens, beneath the screens sat The Watcher. The room was dark, the only light coming screens.

On those screens were people and places around the world. These screens did not filter life with extra pixels or scaling; they were utilitarian, archaic, but beautiful without frames. On a screen in the background, a radar type screen illuminated. Devon watched as screens showed harvest moons, senators, food that made your mouth water, train wrecks, sunsets, TV shows.

The Watcher methodically called down a screen interacted with it and then placed the screen back above him. This was a process that was repeated several times. Some screens showed otherworlders, some showed places Devon had never seen before. One projection seemed to be monitoring something with various levels rising and falling on them. Another projection was of a darkened world with a blazing sun looming in the distance.

It was hard for Devon to look away from the clenched jawed jittery men, shrieking mothers, and distilled terror that was displayed on some of these screens. Devon took a step and was engulfed by the room.

Behind him, an ocean wave covered him and pounded a city. He reached out, and his hands felt the cold water. He turned his head, and there was fire, he smelled the burning flesh from wildfires.

The Watcher stopped what he was doing, pushed away from the desk, and turned towards Devon. The Watcher's face was obscured. The Watcher's glowing eyes slowly scanned Devon's face and that's when Devon's pounding heart stopped.

The Watcher grinned and mouthed the words, "I see you," pivoted in his chair, and continuing his tasks. The mouthed words shook Devon's focus, and with one step back, he was again in the passage next to Prime.

"What do you think?" Prime asked.

"Give me a minute…"

Devon looked down the corridor at the doors that lined it. The corridors were a single sprawling series of interconnected passages that were connected to the chamber. The sheer enormity of it made Devon wilt.

This discovered planet needed to be pondered and researched. All Devon thought about was how this new planet needed to be studied, photographed, and explored. This planet's fate has already been decided by these otherworlders.

"Yesterday it was energy blooms, today its cell towers, tomorrow every mobile device will allow us an entry point. Devon, would you like to continue?"

"Yes."

They continued walking down the passageway. "There are far more people that do good works. People that are worth saving," Devon said.

"If that is true, then where are these people when the evil ones carry out deeds? Why do they support half measures that do nothing but make them sleep easier at night? Why are they making donations, affixing stickers, and wearing shirts—is that what you call the good that people do?"

"Given time, we can come up with something other than the death of all humans."

"With the right leadership, the right information, right…," said Prime, laughing. "You had that, what have you done with it? You think that your leaders don't know what they are doing is immoral, that the lies are unsustainable?

"Which is it now…The free West struggles against the tyrannical axis and eastern powers, or is it the free East struggling against the tyrannical axis and western powers?

"Your kind has become deceitful enough to create want and use rules as shackles. Your violence is sanctioned by law and reason. They want to be admired for their clothes, not their deeds. They inhale fear and exhale anger, but in every hopelessly imaginable way, they believe in hope. They cheer the use of chemical, biological, nuclear weapons and call it war. What your kind has done cannot be mistaken for world building.

"Your kind will not choose what's right. They won't acknowledge what's wrong. They will choose what's popular. People are biologically outmoded, obscene, and nondescript."

Devon did not understand what Prime meant by that, only that Prime's tone had turned accusatory. Devon had spent dozens of nights lying under a myriad of stars, floating towards black horizons. Devon could see that the weight of the office was around Prime's shoulders. Prime's eyes were moist and heavily.

"The truth is something an individual has to accept. We present the truth, we cannot make a person see nor accept the truth, it is up to them to choose, and your kind has chosen.

"The more independent a leader appears, the better the following. People willingly collaborate with The System, bargaining for a better deal as The System extends its reach, increasing its power. They collaborate because they want to. They are on stage performing because they like it. This is how slaves are made."

"If what you have told me is true…then people on both sides have suffered enough," Devon offered.

"…Indeed, they have." Prime responded.

"I've lost my family, my wife, my daughter…I've lost everything, but I haven't lost hope. Hope is never so far from reach that it's worth losing altogether. We cannot sit on the sidelines mouthing pieties. This is the moment for our kinds to pull together, to become one."

"All of your tales of superior beings are based on Christ's conception, reception, trials, and resurrection. Your themes of heroism, a greater good, powers, are based on him, yet you shun his teachings. You dress up Christ stories as superhero tales because it provides distance. People have misplaced faith into machines.

"Are you are going to be the one to show them that they aren't alone in the universe? Here, politics are just humans pulling different ways, authoritarians rise, and leaders will be deposed. And, each tim, people error on the side of fear and bureaucratic function. They vote out the lawyers and the lawyers make life so unbearable that the people vote them back into office.

"Your leaders tell you that the old system will not protect you, and that giving up a little freedom comes with the new system. Then, you pride yourselves in trying to keep certain people from certain types of actives, and when all else fails, you'll create a list, a registry. People will spend their time wondering... Is my name on the list?

"They'll pay not to be on the list, they'll rally against their own best interest to support the list. The list keepers add more names to the list than they prune from it. The list that began with one name soon has thousands, and no one knows how to get off of these lists... because you can't.

"The list is just a fabrication, just another means of control. As long as you're not on the list, the process works just fine. Behind every human smile is dissatisfaction. The government is a special interest group, the only interest group. It is a self sustaining entity that inherently creates a demand for representation by those it alienates. No one's interests are secure and advocated in high places.

"For most, the appearance of free will is enough for compliance because they are afraid to admit that they are scared, that science has failed and that they don't know the answer. They are immoral, which makes what they do collectively moral. Indifference is your culture's illness.

"And what of me?"

"Well, you're something different..."

"I am no different."

"All of this works so well because people don't want to under- stand. The System is the process and the method."

"I am guilty of things people will never know about. The answer is not killing men, women, and children for no reason...."

"There is a reason! From terrible events newness springs; from the ashes, there is birth."

"What about Landslide, Flood, Hurricane, Earthquake... I have seen your kind kill rooms full of people, towns full of innocent, without any thought..."

"There is much thought put into these actions. Are not a few lives sacrificed to protect all life worth the cost? Nature doesn't feel bad be- cause your house was flattened, it doesn't care if your insurance won't cover the damage."

"We have had rebellions and revolutions throughout history; this could be our greatest triumph...."

"Yes, the rebels. Your media can divert the worldwide narrative from one reality to another, with a change of a channel. Each newscast shapes minds, thoughts are quelled within each twenty-two minute block, senses are muted with each song, and touch is dulled with each added chemical.

"Soon, the conflict between determinism and the faceless institutions will fade away. Then a deal is made, and instead of going on proudly to victory, the rebels stop at the gates and apologize for their rebellion. When you don't have any beliefs, it's easy to change them."

Devon looked around for the flashing applause box, there wasn't one. "You don't know what's going to happen, no one does," replied Devon. "It's the future; the future is in a constant state of flux."

"We cause systems to fail, and you people set about saving them. We tell you about equality, and you'd rather project power. Mankind is flimsy, selfish, broken, scheming.

"Even now, people are running around creating threats and conflicts only to profit from them later. At this very moment, people are calling out to be saved... can you hear them?"

***Save us, hero...save us, hero.***

"I can..." Devon sadly said. The hallway walls started showing the vilest and horrific scenes from human history. Somehow telling him about The System didn't have the same impact seeing The System in action did, and it was terrifying.

"This is all you." Prime unnecessarily added. "We are not without our sicknesses."

"People are the foulest creatures that walk this earth. They infest the darkest, filthiest places. They wallow in decay and despair. They drain peace, hope, and happiness out of everything around them.

"Mankind lost the pain of being a man and became monsters, and monsters breed. The inventors of murder have become experts in betrayal. Hope has killed more people than all of the wars combined."

"Not poetry, art, or literature...murder is mankind's heritage?" "Give them any reason, any excuse and they'll show you."

"You are talking about going to some planet in some far-off quadrant of the universe that hasn't been glimpsed, and that will somehow be the place for a new form of life—"

"There is already life on Planet F."

"Life?"

"There has been life there for millions of years…"

The hologram once again formed focused on one star, one planet. Underneath the veil of coulds that surrounded this planet, Devon saw what could be called plants but weren't. They were products of a different evolution.

"We are only taking from what is already created and making something new—the end result is birth. We are the salt of the Earth, they will be the salt of Planet F; we are merely provided the spark."

"Playing God, are we?"

"We are not like your kind. We are Them. We are not cutting and pasting DNA fragments into genomes or using de-extinction processes, we aren't making those mistakes."

"No, you're make new ones…"

"Them are taking sets of basic, perfect hominid DNA and relocating them, allowing them to bond naturally. DNA strains free from defect and weakness. These molecules will become one with their environment, their planet, their conditions. We are almost at the point where seeding Planet F is possible.

"The journey will take a year to complete. They will be created; birthed in weaker gravity and stronger magnetic field."

"Nature is unmatched and unpredictable."

"More perfect people create more perfect systems… This mad, random and pointless existence you call humanity will end and a more perfect version of humanity will rise elsewhere."

As they walked, the hologram materialized in front of them like pixels on a screen. The crafted pushed past planets where hot air falls, and cold air rises, it pushed beyond ionized gas giants where atmospheric waves travel vertically. They watched the wakes of waves of light bent by gravitational lensing as the vehicle quickly moved through the starscape.

Prime detailed an operating system beyond current DRADIS (Direction, RAnge, and DIStance systems). He spoke of quark scale computations and the perils in furthest reaches of the universe. These images caused Devon's thoughts to drift towards Sarah.

He tilted his head, and vivid memories of Sarah flooded in upon him. In his dreams, the only special ability he had was that he could touch her. He could feel the warmth of her hand. He could smell her jasmine perfume on his shirt. The thought of her body next to his was only possible in a dream.

"Neutrino and tackeyon emitters...restructure themselves in order to dissipate increasingly more energy. Matter inexorably acquires the key physical attribute associated with life...."

Devon had always been drawn to Sarah's navel; it was one of his favorite places. Her beautiful brown eyes revealed the deepest of blues. When he surprised her, she had this joyous low rumble; that's how he knew he did something good.

She never really wanted to be beautiful; she didn't want to look like a model or to be made up to look like a painting. She didn't want to have looks made people stop and stare.

Only now could Devon see the waste of time, money and effort spent in making a person look the way they wanted to look. What's inside of a person eventually spills out, yet they spend a lifetime covering up, while their insides rot away, and according to Prime, it delayed gene expression.

For all the confusion in the world, Devon was the person Sarah wanted to figure everything out with. Unlike most people stuck with the best of a limited option, he didn't settle. Sarah existed in the consciousness of his mind, his thoughts, and his memories. Even now Devon was seeing what wasn't really there, like magenta Sarah's favorite color.

"...Diffusion being limited to two dimensions increases evolutionary jumps in a species. When inevitable doubt creeps in, they will find common ancestors. The mate or die structure won't change...." Prime's voice intruded into Devon's illusion of Sarah.

Sarah gathered Devon's pieces and gave them back to him in the all the right order. Prime flicked a gold button, and new images appeared. Now Devon memories replay in slow motion in front of them. The images of his family were as if his wife and daughter were there with him.

Devon was again experiencing their first kiss, the moment they feel in love, the pressure of her hand, the way her hair felt on his shoulder, her after party smell. The smile on Brianna's face caused hot tears to run down his cheek. Devon's smile faded along with the images of his family.

"Why are you showing me this?" "For its probative value."

"You have this grand master plan, but you are hiding in a glacier. You can't get this accomplished without the help of people, so what if it all were to just stop!" Devon said.

Prime stopped walking, looked at Devon, and said, "Never dis- count fear, it works. When the waves throw them from their homes and their celebrated structures collapse like match sticks, they'll they respect it.

"When the water no longer quenches their thirst...they'll respect it. When power plants explode, and the only light is from the flames engulfing their home... they'll acknowledge it.

"When the thick dark mist suffocates, cities are destroyed, and the next disease is more brutal than the previous one...they'll understand it. If anyone ever needed to be smitten, it is your kind. Devon, you alone have exceeded expectations."

"How? There are no monuments dedicated to me. The only way a person could say that I have succeeded is that I've loved another with all my heart and soul. I learned the rules, I found my way. I learned to survive. I gathered the strength to go back home. My memories are broken, and I am as broken as any of them. I didn't choose any of this... This plan of yours isn't nearly as big as everything I've overcome."

"One misfortune after another was piled on your back and you survived. You look worried..."

"I am not worried," Devon said his voice a little stronger despite the gravity of the situation.

"You should be worried if you think you can just be honest with people...people will hate your honesty more than they will hate us."

Devon braced himself and said, "Why send for me if this is all predetermined? You wanted me here, and here I am!"

"Nothing ever just happens; not coming would have been viewed as failure to appear to court."

# CHAPTER 21

Devon and Prime turned down a smaller hallway. Looking be- hind him, it appeared to Devon that the hall extended forever. The floor was charged with electric particles. Devon reached out to the wall, but as his fingers approached the surface, the wall sensed him and blue ripples emanated from it.

The upstream and downstream face of one ripple collided with the holographic waves of another. Each collision brought a different color, a different wave frequency, a different action.

"This is your technology?" Devon said as he thought of the seriousness of the charges.

"It's the data stream networked our cognitive quantum processor. Think of each ripple as information," said Prime. "You know it as fluid dynamics. The progressions of the ripples affect each other. When we can, we guide the direction of the ripple.

"What if a random meeting wasn't so random, or if a strange twist of fate, wasn't so strange?" Prime used his hand to erase one ripple and move another. Prime moved his hands as if he had done this a thousand times before and by all accounts Prime had a flair for the dramatic.

The wall color changed each time Prime interacted with it. It turned green or red when a happening occurred on the other wall, yellow when he altered rift locations and blue when any action was on the other side of the rift. Red sparks slowly fell to the floor from Prime's contact. Light reflected off the walls like small dots in space.

As Prime poked and prodded the action on the wall changed, Devon's smile of wonderment faded. People would never embrace a collective consciousness, let alone be evolved into a singular one.

What Devon viewed as colorful ripples were lives. Prime had just changed the lives of hundreds, maybe thousands of people. Devon gathered himself, and he and Prime continue their walk.

As they walked, Prime spoke more of this thing he called The System. Devon knew that were no nations; just corporations. Corporations sponsored the propaganda which tied class to race and race to cultures of poverty. All of this was propelled by some unidentified sys- tem, unidentified because it prefers not to be.

Devon had seem many systems ,but he had no idea that there was one system above all others, a system that is woven into the lives of everyone. A System that were it a program could simply be unplugged but it was more than a program.

That this System has spent decades massaging agendas into malleable psyches. These psyches had their sexuality weaponized for a purpose even they didn't understand. He couldn't have imaged this, yet there was the truth, staring Devon in the face as it had always been. Indifference was an infection is spread from person to person, transmitted not by bite or cut, but by proximity to an action.

"The System has been keeping tabs on people for years," Prime said. "It rids the world of natural born leaders; this makes it easier to get masses to follow a perceived leader."

"The System's goal is executed by roads, rules, and limits. Eventually, a true leader would see the truth of The System and guide their followers to get rid of The System. The System doesn't just exist to survive; it wants to grow.

"The System uses shadow organizations to lend assistance to those who go along with the program. Corporations aren't doing anything wrong, because they have laws passed that say they did nothing wrong Notice how your leaders never admit that they knew, so in all cases they are right.

"Admitting an error is an indication of weakness, even if the path is the wrong one."

"What happens when those selected stop following The System?" "There is such a thing as outliving one's purpose. Slogan swallowers do what they are told. All the public needs are a few embarrassing, defamatory foibles, some timely revealed indiscretions, or one word to be rewritten and they will move on to who is in place next.

"Once a leader is on the wrong side of The System, they have flaws no one saw when they were in their position. They are dicredited before the notion to change The System can take hold within the minds of their followers. Those that can't be controlled in life, The System will control their legacy in death.

"You may know the particular mass, the density of the metal as well as any variations in density throughout the coin. You may know its precise coefficient of friction, its air resistance, and its rotational velocity. You understand everything about the chemistry and physics of the coin's flip. But, even with this comprehension, you still can not predict the outcome of a coin flip with absolute certainty. We herd the sheep.

"We move people in such a ways to slow The System down. We want the tired, the downtrodden, those that are holding on by a single thread. We want those souls that can't be easily led. We chose people with unique skills; they don't know that they have. They come in many forms, their brains capable of leading the brains of others. They are able to grab onto small patches of certainty, unaware of the contradictions in that certainty."

"People are stronger together. You've lost your humanity!"

"People have no duty, no service to owe, no commander, no regulations to follow."

"You are trying to convince me that what you and these hidden faces are doing is benefiting all life."

"Being a great artist doesn't mean you are a great human being. They worship people just as flawed as they are. Look at them, the finest among you is one or two psychotropic pills away from leading the nation.

"You think that if you dispense enough free sodas and snacks these malfunctioning machines of flesh will love you. They are sleep deprived, drugged and abused…tortures they've done to themselves.

Take it from us, they can't be set straight. You won't be sponsored by a shoe company. Their children won't be playing with action figures of you? No! Mankind is a gloriously failed experiment. If you had stayed in one place long enough, you would have seen people put on paths to enrich their lives."

"And the penalty for choosing another path is the loss of their life,"

"We guide, we help…" "You control."

"When there is no hope we are that hope. When there is no cure, we are the cure."

"You main, you destroy."

"We are fate. We wake people out of comas...." "Comas you probably put them in."

"Why won't you understand what I am telling you...?"

"That's just it Prime, I do understand. It's The System...a system created by the people for the people. This system now only serves itself. You talk about The System as if it is pure evil. There is only good or bad in how a thing is used. Humans maybe misguided, we make errors, and these are correctable.

"What I understand is that this Group of yours is just as bad as The System."

"Don't you see that we are affecting change to alter the destructive course that has ruined humanity here? Our purpose is greater."

"If it ends and begins with us, then it shouldn't it be our choice? If we thrive, that too should be our choice."

"You speak of choice as if the Earth belongs to humans, humans belong to the Earth. Everything is connected, we all surge with blood, and that should have been enough to unite us. This is a connection that travels beyond time and space. Whatever happens in the sky, the ocean, or in the soil carries a connection with it, and it is a reflection and projection of consciousness.

"We are all connected at the deepest levels of our beings, all of us. All things in the universe make up one organism, an organism we call life. We are simply droplets of water in a vast ocean. Man did not weave the web of life; he is merely a strand in it."

"I now realize that an oak tress is as important as a blade of grass. We can change, we must change," Devon spoke with force, but he felt empty inside.

"Change has many enemies. The government changes slowly, so those in power can hide their riches and continue their programs. The slow pace gives them the proper time to avoid the changes altogether.

"We have tried to change embedded brain patterns of people. I dare say that we have provided humanity's greatest service."

"What do you mean tried?"

"When people didn't listen, the happenings become louder. We sent messages through structures, Bimini Road, Egyptian Pyramids, Nazca Lines..."

"We buy organic, natural, free-range, Fair Trade, Alliance products...hell, we're recycling! Things aren't pitch-black, yet we are making progress..."

"It was we who led Niels Bohr, Galileo Galilei, Alan Turing. Them connected with George Anderson, James Van Praagh, Lisa Williams and Uri

Geller. Them showed Edgar Cayce, Jeane Dixon, and Nostradamus. Them pushed Alexi Ananenko, Valeri Bezpoalov and Boris Baronov, Valentina Tereshkova, Mary Wollstonecraft, Aung San Suu Kyi, Socrates, Edith Cavell and Joan of Arc…your progress… needs more progress."

Devon's mind silently darted with questions.

"God is infinite." Prime paused for a few seconds and continued. "You can't create infinity; it already exists outside of any concept of life. It has no beginning and no end. Eternal sources don't have creators. It can't have a beginning or an end and still be eternal. Only something that exists outside of time and space could pull it together and command it."

"So, you can read minds?" stared Devon.

Prime smiled. "No, but since you've been here, I am learning to read the human heart. Why would a supreme being choose such an undeserving creature?" said Prime, laughing.

"Out of love."

There was more laughter from Prime. "People are proof that intelligence isn't a prerequisite of a successful life. Humans think in straight lines, God does not. Without an order—a design—scientific laws couldn't exist. Having a title, a piece of paper on a wall or a large vocabulary does not mean God will perform for your amusement or provide you with answers you can't comprehend.

"God simply is. Beyond religion, beyond thought, God is a being that existed before light, before time. It is the creator who laid the cornerstone to all things. People think the universe is supposed to give them answers based on calculations…

"You revere the universe, but that's not God. You study it. You profess it. You teach it, but that's not God. You ponder its beginning and its conclusion, but that's not God. The universe created and is inside of each and every one of us. There are those moments when the universe reaches out through an individual, through the science of discovery, or words on a page, but that's not God."

"Science can't even tell you what a thought is beyond a series of electrical impulses, yet it is thought that drives them. That's faith, faith that they use every single day. Ironically, it is the faith of others they seem to have a problem with. "

"After years of neglect, the human spirit may be run down, but it is still there."

"With what you've been given, you should be living the lavish life, the life of a mogul; you could have just been happy that you're alive. But you wandered the globe, starting campfires in the wilderness, stalking college campuses and living in fleabag motels… alone."

In Prime, Devon finally found someone that he could talk to. It didn't matter that he was most likely insane.

"Humans have the ability to completely change their world. They already have changed it for the worst. They can change it for the better," Devon responded.

"No, they won't. This planetary movement, in our estimation, has occurred at least five times, thus the alphabetic marker F."

Devon wondered exactly where Planet F was. Devon's interest was given over to a thoughtful silence that was a befitting response to mankind's murderers. Then, Devon blurted out, "So, all of this has happened five times before, and now the plan is to genetically invade Planet F because the human race is to chicken shit to reboot!"

"We are sending the best of mankind to Planet F."

"The best of mankind? This is pure madness."

"In the meantime, people will search for reason and order, and we will give them that."

"Why have you told me all of this?" Devon asked, walking ahead of Prime.

"Your existence outside has been problematic," said Prime. "You are alone, and you are out of place, you don't have anyone to trust."

Devon lowered his eye to down at Brianna's butterfly; he was having a hard time letting go.

"Problematic to you and your jackbooted otherworlders," Devon added, though no explanation was necessary.

The glacier began to shake; the shockwave knocked Devon down to his knees. Thunder could be heard in the distance as the mountain rumbled. This shaking was followed by an uneasy silence.

"No pleasure, no enjoyment, just duty. Them only know their mission. You, on the other hand, need something more purposeful…"

"This can't be the solution!" Devon shouted at Prime.

"This is the only solution. You've seen the plan in the manner so prescribed here, and still, you want to go back?" Prime questioned. "Plant species have begun to disappear, the coral reefs, insects, and soon the reptiles, other animals, and then humans. Life will still hurl toward destruction, that won't change."

Devon didn't answer Prime and shook his head as he thought…

*Instead of tongue lashing Influence, I should have thanked her for her counsel.*

All of this talk of extinction made Devon uncomfortable. Prime threatened everyone and said it was it's in our best interest. Prime had lost pawns, a bishop and a rook, was he now looking for a counter play?

Prime turned down another passage. That passage was different, smaller, and less bright. Devon eagerly followed.

Devon couldn't sense anything beyond the door to his left. "I can just go into any room I choose?"

"Sure…"

"How about this one?"

"Which one…the one with the chair and small light on the wall." "The projection room pick another one."

"Why?"

"You don't want to go in that one…"

"That's a testing room to help us wade through the systems installed in humans."

"So why don't you want me to go in there? You said I could go into any room…and this is the room I want to go in."

Prime moved out of the way, and Devon entered the room. He sat in the chair and looked around. Devon initially felt nothing, but then his skin started to crawl. He couldn't move, as if gravity had increased fourfold. He could only look straight ahead as the walls rippled. A light engulfed him. He started to fragment. His conscious was pulled out of him.

His conscious drifted from the chair, out of the mountain and over several states, finally arriving in a small town where a young man was taking a nap. The man's conscious resisted the presence of Devon's. Devon's conscious melded with young man's.

The man's young son and daughter were with his new girlfriend shopping. The mother of his children was knocking on the front door. When the man opened it, she smiled at him and unloaded two bullets into his abdomen.

The bullets ripped through his shirt and pushed him halfway through the living room. He fell over the couch and hit his head on the floor. The man's heartbeat echoed loudly. His hands were full of blood. His son's mother came around the couch.

"No, no... don't!."

She fired two more bullets into his back. The heat seared his flesh and blood shoot out the man's mouth. The child's mother closed the front door and left. An uncontrollable wail left his mouth. Devon was bombarded with information...too much of it. Shot four times, close range...

"Help!"

*Is this all I can get his mouth to say?*

The man laid there as redness spilled onto the rug. The pain was unbearable. The bullets cooled, but the smell of burnt flesh remained. Devon's body jerked in the chair each time the trigger was pulled.

*Make this stop!*

Devon couldn't pull his conscience from the dying man.

*Move...move...* the man shuddered.

*Get up...get up...* the man slowly got to his feet.

*...ok...ok...now*

*One leg...the other... On to the porch...*

Where is the black Guzzi...there it is.

*...now...down the walkway...*

*Don't pay attention to the screams. Get out the keys.... which key is it?*

*Damn it...get off the ground...you can do it.*

*Up.*

*OK.*

*Get on the motorcycle. Turn the key...*

Where is the nearest hospital?

Nice bike...

*...it's on empty...*

*Pull off slowly...slowly...*

*Go straight...go straight.*

The man's heart raced as fast as the six-speed transmission shifted. Devon was guiding the man as best as he could.

Look at the gauges...

*Vision blurry...*

*...green lights...turn left...*

Two more miles to go.

*Feeling heavy...*

*Stop shaking...stop shaking! Drifting right...*

One more block.

*Slowing down...*

*Don't hit...don't hit the bus stop...*

*...too late...Sorry...*

Where is the hospital?

*Get up...you're in shock...you can make it...*

We're not going to make it.

*Stop crawling and stand up...Stand Up.*

The screaming woman had a chocolate mousse éclair...

*Step with the right leg...drag the left one...you can make it...*

There's the front/

"Help me." The man uttered

His pants were ripped.

*Please stop with the screaming... Arms numb...*

The sliding doors are open.

*...keep moving...extend your hand...*

"Stop right there!" the officer shouted.

*Put your hand back down...keep moving...*

Say something... "Help...help..."

"I said stop," barked the officer. Another officer came forward, and his eyes were full of adrenaline, and he had donut crumbs on his beard.

*The eyes won't stop darting... the body won't stop losing blood ...don't shoot...*

Too late, the taser prongs landed next to an entry wound.

*Collapse...*

*Can't see...can't feel...darkness...silence...*

Hello...hello...

*Wait...wait... I hear something...*

*I hear something rolling...something metal...it's getting closer. Open your eyes...open them!*

His ears filled with the piercing ring of charged defibrillation connectors.

"Clear!"

A jolt of electricity ran through me, through us.

*Open Your Eyes!...*

There are people in smocks...

*Eyes closed...*

*Open your eyes; show them you want to live.* Another jolt, but this came from Devon's conscious. *Eyes open...heartbeat in the distance.*

"Help me...help..."

"We're here to help you, sir. Try not to move." A nurse said.

An oxygen mask was placed on his face, and the man was lifted onto a gurney. Six people quickly pushed the man into the operating room...

*Heartbeat erratic but steady...*

The shadowy wisp of Devon conscious slowly... painfully... drifted from the man. The image becomes larger, widening, until finally it consumes everything, filling up the screen. Then it fades away, revealing that Devon had returned to the projection room and rejoined his physical body.

"He'll make it. In time, he'll recover. He'll be different. His children will still have a father, but now, they won't have a mother." Prime said.

"What was that?" Devon said, wiping the sweat from his head.

"This is the kind of confusion we have to go through when dealing with you humans. Your suggestions to the man saved his life..."

"So, all of that just happened?" Devon said still patting his body down to make sure he was all there.

"Yes. We've only had limited success in the projection room until now," Prime said, handing Devon a handkerchief for his bleeding nose. "What if a small push could have prevented all of that from happening? Wouldn't it be worth it?"

"What if the small push caused all of that to happen?" Devon said, coming out of the room. "This is a room of absolute horrors. It's absolutely terrifying."

"None of this is easy... Shall we continue down the hallways?"

"The hallways will do just fine," Devon said, his legs still shaking as he walked. It was four steps before he could breathe again.

As unnerved as Devon was about being forced out of his body, there was ingenuity to it. For a time, he was tied to the data stream of the mainframe.

The corridors seemed to go in circles. With each step, Devon believed more and more that he was somehow connected to this plan. His choice was between entities that leave violence and destruction in their wake and the humans that do the exact same thing.

The hallways were silent and well lit, all except for one. One had darkened corridors and was filled with wall banging and loud growling. There were also flashes of light reflected through the hall. Prime and Devon went in the opposite direction of this corridor. Devon stopped walking and deeply inhaled; he couldn't smell her anymore.

"Prime, her smell is gone."

"You're one step closer..."

"Closer to what."
"Redemption..."

# CHAPTER 22

The mountain shook again. This time it shook as if it were struck by a high magnitude earthquake. The shaking now occurred every ten minutes, followed by thunder.

Devon's boldness in accepting the invitation may have been a miscalculation, but it reminded him of being a child and thinking that he was invincible, but when he got older, he became scared of losing, scared of failing. But there is a part of people that believes they cannot fail.

"Yet, it does fail, it has failed, and each time it fails, it takes longer. Each time, every time a civilization reaches the pinnacle of decadence," said Prime, interrupting Devon's thoughts.

"So, you've done this before."[1]

"Not us, others. You had a moment of clarity in the town square. That moment was like when you realize that some kind of medication would be required for you to stop doing what you're doing. Unfortunately, people need something more substantial than a moment of clarity to deter them. They require something bigger... we are that something.

"We have seen the anger, the rage that drives you. The time for this world has come and gone, just like the other worlds before it. This is a lost world, a breeding ground for violence not worthy of saving. The Group functions to ensure that this world won't die in vain. We've been watching...waiting... If you had not come, we would have held an ex parte proceeding."

"He felt something in people—not what we are, but what we could become," Devon said. "You won't admit it, but maybe you have feelings just as humans do. Them believe in their mission, maybe some are just doing their job and want to go home. People need to be given the chance of saving ourselves from extinction."

"In our world, men and women are exceptional, not exceptions. Your kind doesn't help the needy and suffering because it's the right thing to do. They do it to feel good about themselves. If it were the right thing to do, there would be no need for charity.

"Your kind looks at themselves through broken mirrors. Your kind was given eyes to see and minds to question, but they choose to manifest unjustified paranoia. They allow a pervasive river of fear to run through them every hour of the day.

"Your kind refuses to accept responsibility for what they've done. With the fate of worlds hanging in the balance, their only concern will be how it affects them. We are all connected to each other biologically, to the earth chemically and to the rest of the universe atomically, yet people will say 'It's not really our fight.' To this end, we have been a check against man's corruption.

"Conflict gives your kind reason. We will take their reason prisoner. Your kind is beyond saving. This is for the greater good. Each time this relocation process occurs, it takes longer to reach mankind's demise. Your kind's existence here is the result of previous efforts."

Devon got a distinct impression that Prime was not used to having his edicts questioned. "If we had more time...more information..." Devon muttered.

A smaller sketchy slowly forming hologram played before them, but this time Devon noticed that the dying planet wasn't Earth. This time a craft journeyed across the heavens to Earth. This time Earth was the planet filled with life. The hologram played out the history of the human race on the floating blue sphere.

"The only alien on Earth is the man," Prime began speaking again. "Life, as you know it, was imported here and shortly it will be exported elsewhere."

"Earth is not man's home planet..."

"Did you really think man was a random outcropping of intelligent life? Long before man roamed the Earth, there were The Ones Who Came Before. They weren't like man, they were different. The Ones Who Came Before arrived when the mist of the Van Allen belts was much weaker.

"They saw their world coming to an end, and they were desperate to save what they were. They were in a hurry to create a life with fewer flaws."

"How do you even know about The Ones Who Came Before?"

"Not everything has been erased. The Ones Who Came Before caused the first scar...."

"Scar...."

"What we now call a rift. It was sheer luck that you feeble two legged animals even developed within this heliopause. They didn't know that normal matter lives inside of dark matter, but because of their efforts both your kind and my kind blossomed.

"They could only travel to planets that were sublight hours away; by comparison, Planet F is many parsecs away. Life on Planet F will have no labels, no psychosis. This time, there will be more connections to the whole. We will remain behind, and life will begin again, naked, simple."

"I don't believe..."

"You don't believe which part...the Earth dying...mankind's extinction?"

"I don't believe any of it. I can't believe that we were abandoned on this planet!"

"Abandoned...no. The Ones Who Came Before placed within us the genetic material necessary to create life. They had, after many trials and errors, created what they believed were perfect beings... humans. They left guardians to cultivate man, but those guardians were riddled with frailties.

"They were humanoid, but also something else. They fought among themselves over what they had created. They craved its attention, its love. In this war, sides were chosen, and while the new life grew, they battled one another. The perfection they sought was not within them. They developed a need to be worshiped—remembered.

"They revealed in their creations and fought over the direction this new life should take. They basked in what humans were capable of and horrified by the directed the life actually took. They left their world because they had to."

"Why didn't they come here and just start over?"

"They couldn't all sustain existence here. These beings knew their existence was coming to an end, and they wanted to save the best of them. Their nature caused them to destroy their world and each other. Their kind was different in many ways, but they were every bit as fragile as humans are.

"They brought their science, equipment, their trials, and errors. They also brought their pettiness, their anger, and they fought and plotted against one another. They were doomed by the very things they tried to escape from."

"What happened to the trial and errors they created?"

"Destroyed, died off, or your kind killed them like you do everything. The Ones Who Came Before eventually died off, but not before leaving simple guidelines for human survival—guidelines to be found, discovered, and pass down. The lore of this seeding is still with you today."

"You have all of this glorious knowledge, and you are proud of achieving this goal through deception. Wherever The Ones Who Came Before were from, they had their time of happiness and discovery. When they discovered it was coming to an end, they took from themselves and added it to this planet. They gave us a chance..."

"They couldn't have imagined the damage humans would do to this world.

"They probably hoped that it wouldn't get the better of us. They hoped the new would love more and fight less. They hoped that the ills that beset them, we would avoid. For us, they wanted a different outcome."

"It seems that deep within the human being is a self destruct button, a button that gets pressed every time people wake up. This time the choices will be different."

"You just said choices were different, and the existence here was longer."

"Yes, but the outcome is the same. Devon, we will succeed where The Ones Who Came Before failed. This time there will be no contingent accompanying this new life. There will be no desire to be worshiped. No hurried genetic relocation. This time they will have life and have it more abundantly. We thought of everything."

"I can't accept this!"

"How you feel is highly inflammatory and immaterial because you don't get to select the facts you like and those you don't. The new life will not need scriptures, constitutions and false narratives.

"The new life will evolve beyond the need to enslave, or the boredom that facilitates the need to create false lore. They will bond with and have passion for their world. It is our hope that they will never be forced to leave their world."

Devon felt like strangling Prime with his bare hands, but Prime's words that made the absurd seem possible. Prime's ideas were far stronger than any act of violence could ever be within Devon's mind.

"You won't be able to convince people to just give up their DNA...."

"They already have. Once the DNA was mapped and sequenced the outcome was an inevitable byproduct of time and legislation. We just needed to look in the right places to find what we needed and now our long journey in that process is nearing an end.

"Some of life's code was found by matters of happenstance and the rest by technology. The better technology has gotten, the quicker we have reached our goal. We have been surprised by how willing your legislators are to pass DNA gathering laws and the populace's acceptance of them."

"So, this system manipulates and kills, and you manipulate and kill. It is brilliant theater, the glacier, the sister Earth, tornadoes, floods, The Faces —all of this. I have to hand it to you, you put on a good show...all of you, but I don't see a shred of difference between what you are doing and what this system is doing!"

"The difference is that The System lacks imagination. The System runs down hope. The System enslaves, herds, and manipulates for the sake of itself."

"And you, watch over those enslaved looking for the perfect molecule that will give life to another planet."

"Basically..."

"Do you know how crazy that sounds? I said it, and it still sounds crazy. I mean...Planet F..."

"You can call it Eden. Now imagine how things would be if Them didn't exist, if there were no Group, if your kind had gone about uncheck. The System fosters unrest as better deals are made. The System is skilled at connecting what you love to what you hate, pitting immigrants against citizens. The System is watching your ideas form as you type."

"This all seems rushed, I… we have time to change this..."

"Time… How would you know that?"

"The sun isn't imploding; an asteroid isn't hurling towards us; the Earth isn't crumbling beneath our feet...."

"How would you know?

"How is this even possible?" said Devon, sensing that there were more questions than ever.

"There are data vaults around the globe that store information, where there is a virtual version of each person. The System runs tests to see the outcome of various scenarios.

"The discontent of people was pacified by the very remedy they created. You have created comforts like psychology to justify your actions and history to justify your existence, yet you have never learned the lessons from history or psychology.

"We had to act. Something of this size and scope cannot be politicked or left to those with clouded minds and little vision. We track those with weak sight and recessive genes. We monitored illness and the making of mental conditions with each pill consumed. We exclude those ruled by their heart, emotion, or addicted to electronic cocaine.

"Water is unique in its properties and functions. Carbon and hydrogen make up water, and both elements are abundant throughout the universe. Water and other complex molecules easily form and have been detected in the harshest environments of space. Your officials publicly they say they are searching for water, but they are searching for planets they can inhabit, and inhabitants they can dominate.

"We engineered Kennedy's reversal on the Space program and The System removed Kennedy from leadership. The System caused Khrushchev to blink, to be embarrassed and removed from office. We took it upon ourselves to slow your progress.

"It took us five years to get your kind's thoughts off the moon. For all of your efforts, The System left you with communication and weather satellites and of course weapon systems disguised as those same communication and weather satellites.

"We provided the motivation, and The Space Race provided the means. Wide Field Infrared Survey Telescopes, Hershel, Hubble, Spritzer, Kelper, James West, Corot, JWST, Gemini planet Imager, Starshades, and NExSS, all of were necessary in the identification of this new world. Finding Exoplanet F took millions of equations, numerous amounts of code, and many minds.

"This new world is not so far away, but further than the human imagination stretches. We are a stopgap to provide the time to gather what is needed."

"So splitting the atom sped this process along and human nature did the rest. There is no gene for the human spirit, and every step science takes forward isn't always a good step," chided Devon.

"But, they do make seductive smoke screens," retorted Prime.

"If what you say is true scientist would have said something."

"Would they? Science reveals as much as it hides. Before the brilliant tinkerers among you fall out of line an offer is made, and you are the struggling scientist no more."

"I supposed you are going to tell me that you put a stop to the return to the moon."

"We have slowed your pursuit to leave this solar system. Do you think we want humans to pollute another world?"

"We have the power to choose; we vote, and each vote is an expression of hope. Hope for humanity. Give humans hope, and they will walk toward it, embrace it. I have seen the good in humans, just as He had. You haven't seen the love in our hearts, felt our passion, or experienced our ingenuity." As Devon spoke, Prime interfaced with the wall, and then quickened his pace.

"Electronic devices allow The System to connect with all minds."

Prime noticed Devon was looking intently at the space vehicle as it sped towards its destination planet.

"You are wondering how? Shear waves, which move at the speed of light and ethereal pressure waves which are at twenty billion times faster."

"But mass can't travel at the speed of light…"

"Is that what they say…?" Prime said with a slight chuckle.

The ship was encircled by a blue glow as it was pulled forward by waves of dark energy. The exchange of momentum between waves, appear brighter and gave off a rainbow like appearance. This results in forces of repulsion or attraction between pairs.

"So space folds in front and expands behind it…" Devon said.

"Yes, its speed increases exponentially over time. See planets are like boats in a lake, they float on the ripples. The ripples cause them to bob up and down. This ship rides waves traveling faster than the trough, pushing space to the sides, creating a wake as it exceeds the cosmic speed limit.

"Its fusion reactor generates highly energized plasma, cycles linear arrays of twisted molecules, and zig-zags cyclohexane rings of carbon atoms which are held together with micro-lattice tungsten metal. Our DME (Dark Matter Engine) vehicle is a faster-than-light craft that shrinks space and time.

"If by chance a section of the ship becomes damaged, it can be jettisoned and the journey continued. We have witnessed that galaxies do not rotate as expected but we have not created mathematical entities such as black holes and voids to explain it. The universe doesn't rotate, it expands.

"That expansion is a combination of quantum forces and gravity. Slight differences in plasma currents create electricity. You see as a collective we embrace misconceptions.

"There are no missions to deposit supplies, no descent vehicles, and no landers. There is simply this craft. This craft will be energized by each passing sun star."

In a fiery ball of flame the craft crashed on a blue-green planet, with red soil and lush green grass. Parts of the planet had a frozen and wrinkled landscape, surrounding blue oceans and red hills. This planet was a baptized in watercolor and teamed with life. It was all amazing and none of it subscribed to theories or rules.

Devon was so awestruck by this interplanetary excursion he forgot the speech he had prepared.

"There will be no soft landing." Prime said. "Life doesn't grow out of want, it grows out of need. Sending the building blocks of life dark years into the cosmos is no easy feat. It's a delivery system, not a return one. Soon every gene here will be corrupted, except for the ones we've harvested."

"So, what do you want from me?"

"For you to listen…. What you call dark energy surrounds us, is infinitely abundant and barely detectable. This radiant energy will power the dark matter engines. It will shrink space-time ahead of it and expand it again behind it."

"…and this trip is only going to take a year…right."

"Give or take…."

"So, you get there and then what?" "Then we begin seeding."

"Seed the planet, just like that."

"Just like that…"

As Prime detailed this DNA sequencing, all Devon thought about was how much Sarah would have loved this. She had her own dire predictions of the world, would she have fought against this plan?

"Once this lifeform, this being is created, and we see that it is good. DNA will be taken from it to create a helpmate so that this life can replicate unassisted. They will naturally evolve at their own pace, and another kind will rise.

"When the numbers of this new life are sufficient, curiosity will lead them out of the safety of the lush areas to carry this genetic blueprint to every corner of the planet. They will shape their world, their reality; this is the beginning…"

"Prime, if things go wrong; migration could cause them to evolve into two separately distinct species. If things go right; over time genetic population echoes, genetic diversity, and adaptation will occur, causing a creative explosion followed by social formations, technological ingenuity and the ideological complexities needed to thrive."

"Yes... There, like here, the intellectual capacities of the peoples geographically separated in their evolution but will evolve identically in the beginning. So even if there are two species, one species will rise; as with humans did against other extinct species in the Homo genus. One became dominant, and the other extinct."

"You are saying that all this time people have been hard at work on a very large puzzle, never knowing where the pieces actually fit? People mark themselves unfit and their genes as undesirable. They fill DNA databases and social networks to aids your efforts? The System does this for control, but The Group hacks chromosomes and harvests the result for this purpose, unknown to The System..."

"We do what we must. Our mission control room isn't as fancy as NASA's, but it will get the job done. Our ship isn't as big as the SLS's, but it will get the job done. Humans didn't just show up one day and conquered everything..."

It was evident to Devon that corrections of history and edits to the present occurred periodically, daily. Lives had been referenced and cross referenced, edited and re-edited.

A movement was more than a slogan, a shirt, a rally. A movement takes time; a movement needs to be sustained. The world didn't need another movement. What the world needed was a revolution of the mind.

"What is truth?" Devon questioned.

"You came here for truth, truth comes from living. Humans only embrace the truths they can live with. For them, the truth has to be shaped and formed. This is why education has declined because it was unimportant. Humans don't require it. They don't care about fact, truth, or history. They get bored with thoughts that are too profound; it brings about unhappiness.

"Children are the summation of their parents, and their parents give them over to the sights and sounds of the world. To them, pixels are more real, than life.

Pixels connect with genes that make it possible for an individual to be disconnected. It is those genes and others like it that makes one undesirable for our purposes."

"The world has the smartest minds, the bravest and finest troops they will fight for our survival."

"Troops don't fight for a country; they fight for their lives and for their buddies who are beside them. They're not defending freedoms; they are tools for laying foundations, and are the basis for economic commerce."

Devon looked towards the chamber hall, he was already crafting his appeal.

Man had been indicted, and this was Exhibit A.

# CHAPTER 23

The walls still showed the space vehicle; it didn't appear as metal, and it was diamond shaped. The vehicle avoided evaporating primordial black holes and small spherical stationary storms.

It bent space, moved passed gravitational fields and neutron stars as this craft somehow sliced through space-time Prime talked about how sleep cycle changes, radiation assaults, calcium leeches from bones.

Destructive interference by humans has stunted the evolution of every living creature on the planet, including humans.

"You've seen the perversion of first world businessmen running rampant in obscure of countries. You've witnessed the street killings that fuel the international organ trade. You've seen the sadness in the eyes of parents that had to sell one mouth to feed other mouths.

"You were in the middle of the war for money enterprise. You see how immigration is used to tie nations to each other. You've publicly executed a president in front of the world to teach those that followed. You've dropped nuclear bombs as proof of your villainy. You've invaded and killed hundreds of thousands of people to save a nickel on a gallon of gas.

"You've have been witness to row boats filled with pirates taking over oil tankers and threatening the finest naval in the world. You've seen groups with no country and no military wreak international chaos.... You've seen all of this before you were changed, but you accepted it all as truth. You, of all people, should know that the smallest coffins are the heaviest..."

This meeting is the kind of thing you read about in text, something you might even hypothesize about, but when you were confronted with it, when you came face to face with it, you didn't recognize it.

Every answer Devon gave only further incriminated humans. In spite of all this before him the Earth was still his home. Devon reflected on what was presented to him as they made their way back to the main chamber.

"You are homosuperior but no better than the damned...." "I am better...."

"Tell the truth...tell the truth." The Faces chanted.

Devon thought for a moment as he and Prime traded glares and then he said: "O.K. I only helped Joshua with the application, but he gave me credit."

"That wasn't so hard, was it? You took that secret to the grave and back."

Them were more than form fitted exosuits and vengeance. They were more than dark matter and hoverbikes. They were more than superior physicality. All of Devon's questions had been answered, all except one. Devon had not asked the question he had traveled all this way to ask.

"I thought you were here for an answer." "I am."

"The answer you have spent all this time searching for, the one you've been desperately seeking...."

"Why me?"

"Because you survived."

"We have been watching you. Who is to say that we aren't scanning you, looking for a weakness?"

As they reentered, the chamber doubt had crept into Devon's mind. Maybe these humanoids wanted Earth for themselves? Why would The Group go to such lengths for a lie? Had the world gone mad, had it always been mad?

"Maybe I survived just to put a stop to this, this plan."

A projection showed a West/East hurricane hitting the west coast of North America and a tsunami pummeling Tanzania. Prime slowed his pace and shot a piercing looked at Devon.

"You can try." Prime's voice sounded grave, more than it had before. "We are too close; we will not go backward. You have pressed on the nerve of The Group. It would not please us to remove you.

"If we allow you to leave, for all of your remaining days you will never know peace, love, or friendship." Prime said the walls rotated with images. "You won't be able to hold conversations with others without us nearby. Your every move will be watched, scrutinized. In time your colliders and particle accelerators will become more efficient, more effective and smaller..."

"Our colliders and particle accelerators aren't dangerous..."

"That's what The System wants you to think... In the most indescribably and unlikely of scenarios black holes could be created. More importantly, stable rifts would be formed allowing us to bring our tools to this realm. Our weapons are deadlier than you could imagine. Our tools would make yours looks like bow and arrows."

"Did you think you changed one perception, one perspective? Do you think you saved one person?" Prime questioned. "You even took calling yourself...what was it... AM..."

"Don't call me that! The compassion of violence contradicts your divinity, Prime..."

"Maybe there is hope for you. By the time your kind turn their gaze toward this new planet, cataclysmic events will have begun that will render the Earth a non-life-supporting rock— insignificant, not remarkable, a memory. It will be as though your kind never existed at all."

"This new life would find evidence of some kind of craft, or transport that would tell them where and when they came." Devon said.

"What they will eventually find is a ten square mile impact crater that they will believe is responsible for a shift in the climate. They will believe that the crater's impact altered the course of life on the planet."

"So, you have it all figured out?" "Most of it."

"Why have people live in a constant state of fear. You and I could take that fear and turn it into hope..."

"A state they themselves have caused. The closeted insanity ends with this planet! Here there is a market for hate, a premium paid for ignorance. You have been apart for some time now; you must have seen this."

"I have, but...."

"There are no buts against the subtle edits, the rewrites that exist as fragments of truth. People are far too busy to entertain the question of why. As long as they can eat, drink, and have sex, they don't want to know. When, where, and how is all up to The System. You give humans far too much credit."

"Why don't you just write us off, write all of us off? If there is even is the slightest chance...you hope, and you keep on hoping."

"If it were that simple, it would have been already done. As long as humans have hope, The System will find ways to have them fund any conflict. The world is so much larger than this first world you've lived in and far older than the past few hundred years.

"Were it not, it wouldn't be possible to look at the broad sweep of human history across all continents, all nationalities, all ethnic groups, and draw conclusions about what cultural traits work well together and which ones do not. Which genes are good and which are not so good. We are a selection that is most unnatural. "

"You said there were other ways...."

"There were other ways. Beyond the typical brute force approaches, we favored this more symbolic, elegant plan."

"And the end will come in the form of plague, flu, virus, self-extermination?"

"All of it..."

Devon's mind rifled through thousands of possible responses, none of which he would utter. Prime continued speaking, "All the theories on matter cannot explain the conscious experience. Without cooperation with one's environment life cannot thrive. Life without balance will spiral downward. Assisted evolution explains the survival of life. This council, our council sets the arrival of life."

Devon thought about how humans never seem to really know who was at war with whom. Maybe perpetual war was just a state of mind, a state of being human; perhaps it is a matter of being frail, scared.

Perhaps humans were in a constant state of war because war was within them. Citizens in first world countries never seemed to have enough, no matter what or how much they had. First world charity was only equaled by its lack of empathy. War never feels like war, to them.

Devon could not remember a time in his life that did not contain some kind of war, for some kind of goal. He couldn't recall a period of time when troops and machines didn't engage other troops and machines, and yet somehow afterward, everything always seemed the same as if the loss life meant nothing.

Nothing in history, nothing in the present, nothing in the future indicated that this would, or could change. The intervals of peace could be measured in hours, not decades, and not once during any of these brief periods of peace did humans doubt their sanity. War is indeed, a human disaster, a human happening...perhaps there is a gene for that.

"Your kind is so unindividual that most have taken to identification with organizations and political parties to leech the power of those organizations, this too is a lie. For whatever reason, probably the same reasons as today, our kind was chosen to settle this planet. One lived in harmony with the planet; the other has become a plague upon it."

"Our history is filled with heroes, people who have done extraordinary things and uncommon acts."

"You cling to old heroes only because The System has gotten better at changing the course of the new ones. All who wear a uniform aren't heroes. They desire a paycheck, they want purpose, they want to belong and they kill for a scholarship…but heroes…not even close.

"Your kind is still buying pet rocks and don't even know it. They can sell and promote because just about everyone is addicted to something.

"You like everyone else was programmed through nature, nurture or both to be who you were. You alone survived the happenings and the darkened metropolitan streets and emerged a different being. You have been changed at a cellular level, but only you. The very leaders you would turn to can't accuse the other leaders without implicating themselves."

"I have been places where row upon row of trees shoot straight up towards the clouds," Devon said. Places where the winds made the leaves seem angry, where crackling fires lose battles to the cold. Places where a single flock of birds causes night, places where you can skydive into the mouth of caves, places where explosions of purples, blues, yellows, and greens are common. Places where expansive landscapes are devoid of human presence. Places well rusted, places ruined, eroded, and dusted over.

"And still humans are unique among Earth life. I have looked at everything with an unforgiving eye. I have looked on who we are as people without distance between abject truth and the narratives we construct around ourselves.

"I have confronted the fucked-up-itude of now, centuries-old resentments, and the process of using euphemism for unyielding bigotry—with fury and disgust. And here in the great wide open, I cannot claim distance.

"Humanity is fluid, imperfect patterns and chaos. You blame them for the accumulated external stimulus that's built up without them registering it. The System uses the minds of people against people."

"With our ascension protocol those negative energies will be left here. Humans are set for extinction."

"To the privileged, equality feels like oppression. All races, creed, nationalities…all victims. One group is pitted against the other by something they cannot control…The System. People are afraid of making mistakes, of looking stupid, or of being outside the timeline."

"The only thing consistent about people is their ability to hate. Human ability to destroy or assimilate anything they can not understand is unmatched."

"No one is free from the signs, symbols, and peer pressure. No human is free."

"Nations with little defense and unrecognized sovereignty make fertile testing grounds for drug companies, weapons testing, and human deviancy. Using charities to distract from real injustices is a mainstay of post constitutional North America.

"You've labeled a high school popularity contest The Senate... And for your children, you have crafted third rate schools and first rate high-tech prisons to incarcerating your most brilliant young minds. And you want our help...No...no....no...you are the man most unkind."

"It is our imperfections that make us perfect. It is our flaws that require us to need each other. We are perfect not because of what we have, but because of what we lack. We are perfect because of what we offer one another. We are perfect when we come together, work together and stand together. We had to be designed this way on purpose."

"Humans...want praise for everything, for just being human. You still defend them when you have seen all of the harm petty men and tyrannical women have done with their violence and morals..."

The light of the last passageway dimmed as the glacier shock. Each time the glacier shook the view screens briefly flickered. Devon stepped into the middle of the chamber. He felt different. He felt something true.

Devon waited until the shaking stopped and said, "Everywhere there is a dependence on oppression as economic support there is The System. I know that now. The System isolates and creates chaos.

"The System puts visuals in a box so that we can fight amongst ourselves over it. You say that The System won't allow people to hear my pleas or take note of my protest, but you can hear me, can't you?"

One by one The Faces, in the chamber, began to illuminate. Devon was resigned to be nothing more than what he was...undefined. Just then he figured out why he felt stronger when he sat atop places of worship. It was the power of being human. Not just the abilities, the skills, the knowledge, or even the power in life, but the power of life.

Life had a purpose, a reason. Life was not an accident. It was the overreaching motivation for humans. Connections drew people; it was the adhesive that bound people. Humans were not created to be slaves, not even the free-range kind.

It was not luck that causes a child to disobey; it is something that comes from within the child. Discipline, by way of a missile strike in a remote part of the world or by way of a hand pat to a child's bottom, was The System's attempt to incarcerate the human spirit.

Devon had witnessed how the use of colors, sounds, words activated bits of embedded programming; triggering a subconscious choice that the mind had been primed for, minutes, hours, weeks, sometimes years in advance.

He witnessed the systemic incarceration produced participants loyal to The System, but it also produced those broken within The System itself. For those that were broken, The System had codes and programs designed to remove them without killing, a removal that produced industry and sustained The System.

People protested but most were imperfectly happy without the truth, and Devon kept telling himself that there was a pill for it, but maybe there wasn't. In the halls of the elected, human's debate and talk about ending violence and protecting the helpless. Deep down at the core of humanity where no one sees—they liked it.

They liked the chaos. They put on a good show, but they like the violence, the depravity, and the trade of death for money, all of it. Words like hope and faith only amplified their well rehearsed narratives. They look the other way, desiring never to see what they've become. Each industry was an agent of The System, approving what information is known, by controlling what can and cannot be taught.

The thoughts and deeds of what made them stand apart would not be differentiated from the common criminal, but were they enlightened. They weren't really broken, but they didn't quite know enough or want to go along with The System. Prisons and mental intuitions were full of broken pieces so that even in the midst of rebellion The System could advance.

The System placed a value on, not just people, but cultural and social objects as well, whether they were pornography, religious, family,. or iconography. It subverted the mind and caused romanticized ideas about a place humans had never lived, the real world.

The System is a common denominator already contained in embryos. The scheming, cataloging and classification are in place to administer it. It crushes man's insubordination and makes them promote the formula, which replaces the work. It is inflicted on the whole and parts alike until the whole inevitably bears no relation to the details. There is no right, no wrong, not justice, no honor; there is only The System.

Humans are copies of each other, with slight differences the connections were inherent. They were a part of each other that was why they were compelled to huddle together, to seek out one another, to help each other, to create more humans. The power of the connection between humans was strength.

Devon had been forever changed. The alloy in his limbs, the molecules within his blood, and the thoughts within his head were evidence of this change. This change freed him from the falsity of perfection.

"Humans are so blindly convinced of their purpose and motivations that they have to be drugged to continue to exist. They help The System by being a part of it, operating within it.

"Once they began to accept the justice levied by it, it ceased being the justice system and became the legal system. The System uses each frailty, each vice as a point of coercion. And each point ties you more firmly to The System. People need The System, this system that tells them, guides them to its growth and their own demise.

"It uses your very nature to extend its reach, to tighten its control, to strip a human of humanity, to remove the very thing that makes them human. The System tells them what is important. People pick from what has already been picked for them.

"Once The System had incarcerated the human spirit…all was lost."

Devon's stomach couldn't tighten anymore. It took considerable focus to summon the will to continue.

"Were it up to me humanity would have already been eradicated for the seriousness of their crimes."

"And what of our children? They will be better than we are, they think differently than we did."

"Your children, they are better at destroying without thinking.

Even you have your doubts…."

"Because intelligent people have doubts, that's why there are questions. I needed certainty."

"Have you or have you not seen them battle their own extinction?" "I have."

"The people who hate, will hate you."

"I will let them know that we are just a piece of the universe expressing itself. And that the logic of desire means the end for us…all of us. With the right ideas in place, these ideas can expand exponentially. Our minds can affect reality today and tomorrow.

"It will be hard. It will take effort and the greatest of all will. We can choose to continue on this path, or we can choose to be better. We can't continue on like we have been. We can pay attention…we can learn how to think…we can be better…we will be better. This is the time when people need hope the most."

"You view free will as an agent of the rational, but free will is simply a course of action that humans select from among various alternatives. In this way, free will is a subset of willings. You believe people have the capacity to deliberate about possible actions in the light of one's conception of the good. True freedom of will is the liberation from the tyranny based desires and acquisition of desires for the good.

"Devon, there is one person you haven't forgiven…yourself. Let go of the pain, let go of the hurt, let go of the pain. Stop running from who you are. Stop being mad at yourself…forgive yourself," said Prime.

"The ultimate power is in being human, the connections, the focus, the motivation, that's power—real power!"

"The connection between Earths is absolute. We are not far from DNA perfection; once perfected we will launch. Remember the village outside of Temburong? The System assimilates what it needs, and then history is rewritten as if done by amnesia itself. The end result of The System is always to grow and sustain itself. The System doesn't need your consent, it doesn't warn you. It merely does what it needs to survive. For those people, it was just a matter of inconvenient timing."

"Inconvenient timing…." Devon said.

"That action was a small red pin on a very large map. Military actions divorced from consequences. Dropping bombs on people while they sleep, launching attacks on countries with no army. Deciding who lives and who dies by a button press, by pen stroke.

"Your leaders laugh about how the only way you'll see it coming is on video. It is in the best interest of the powerful within The System to keep countries poor and corrupt for the cheap goods they produce.

"There are no conspiracies, there is only The System reshuffling power bases. You stand steadfast before us with this hopelessly irrational hope, while lives lose value."

"Oh, God! Have we become a society of unattackable victims, an industry of defending villains, and bad logic boards? I am more than this body, more than this consciousness. There is something special about us, about this place. Super volcanoes, asteroid impacts, and naturally occurring pandemics—we survived them all!

"Mankind's track record of survival may be limited to just a few decades in the presence of nuclear weaponry. And we have no track record at all of surviving the radically novel technologies that are likely to arise, but we have always risen to any challenge.

"What you don't understand is that I am not something else. I am human. I know that there are others that will take on The System!"

"Is that so...."

"Just pull the plug...is it possible?"

"Such sentimentality, an insurrection! The System will launch worldwide conflicts on each continent. It will vilify everyone and indiscriminately kill billions of people. It won't ask questions. It won't wonder what you are thinking. It can't be reasoned with. There will be no trial, only justification. The System is not accountable."

"You could have just answered with a yes or no." "We are merely here to guide you."

"To what end?"

"To the end. It is not the end of men; it's the end of man. You talk this terrible privilege you have. The earth is older than the human imagination. Through the gulf of matter, we studied, we observed. For decades, centuries, millenniums, we listened to your prayers, your wishes, your hopes, and your dreams. We walked with you. We comforted you.

"We used energy to perform small happenings here to aid and assist humans. Happenings, you called randomness, coincidence, and accidents; sometimes you called it witchcraft other times you called them miracles. We were not aware that humans prayed, hoped, and wished for all the wrong things.

"When we nursed you through two evolutionary shifts, an ice age, and countless world wars, and here you are, special beings. We sharpened the human appetite to the point where it can split the atom with its desire and with that you built egos the size of this glacier.

"Digital signals fill every part of the world, and everyone's eager to dive into the dullest dreams with paper money, platinum plated fantasies until every human becomes a ruler of their own world until each becomes their own God and where can you go from there?"

Devon looked at the faces knowing that their deliberation would be swift and that there would be no appeal of this decision. Devon needed to ask for a continuance, but he knew one would not be granted.

# CHAPTER 24

Of course, Prime was right, people were not doing the best they could. Devon didn't need spiral halls to know that. There is no telling what this blessed petri dish of lost souls will do when confronted with this plan.

When people learn of Them, it will change everything, except their fear. People always had an excuse for the evils that they did. People called themselves special, so they could harm other animals as well as each other. They did bad things because it is a bad world, that's what they tell themselves.

"Once I awaken people to all of this, there will be no action. You need us," stated Devon. "If all of this is true, then we are at war, the biggest skirmishes taking place in the hearts and minds. The final battles for the future will not be fought in the future, it will be fought in the present, it will be fought now."

Prime turned and said, "If the humans knew of the sister world, our world would be in more peril than it is right now. It had been so long since we had a war, we didn't know we were already in one. Our last conflict lasted centuries…"

"…Centuries?"

"Our world war, your kind called that period the Dark Ages… Them fought each other; we had no time to indulge humans. The human heart can only find meaning in the small things it chooses to. There is nothing heroic or honorable about being killed in a global scheme to move a needle.

"We waited too long, made too many concessions…but you, humans, do have your causes and your peace prizes. You inform a human of this plan, and it will do nothing but tear at the very fabric of existence. Should we prepare for this metaphysical certainty, or do we tell everyone that the eighth day is destruction?"

"Tell a select few."

"We've tried to bring balance, money, protest, entertainment, causes, possessions, love, order, chaos, art, science, land, politics, drugs, intellect, fear, religion, economic, feast, and famine, but the world has been eviscerated by technology. Humans have never done well with moderation."

"Innovation with all the carrots and many sticks...."

"Yes," Prime said, knowing that his directives didn't need justification.

Prime had a look on his face that seemed to suggest that he contemplated ending Devon's existence, but he continued this journey to awareness with only a twinge of jealousy. Prime lifted his eyebrow and wrinkled his forehead, and for a brief second as if he thought Devon might be right.

And like Devon had before the universe started to collapse on Prime. A momentary speck of hope had touched Prime. Had he too been poisoned by human traits?

"The technology Whitman created is out there," Devon said. "People may be shocked, but they will have to believe, and they will react. And, when they do, all of this you've done will amount to nothing. We won't create; we won't build the technology needed to get to this far-off planet. We won't act in this stage play of yours."

"Tremendous amounts of effort and energies have been expended. The means of fulfilling this plan are closer than you know. The rudimentary and unreliable technology Whitman created has been patented, copied, and safely locked away on a shelf full of rumors.

"To reveal this plan would also mean revealing your abilities, you would be labeled a threat. Everything has its place; rulers of the jungle can only reach those of the jungle, lords of the street can only reach those of the street and kings of the world can reach those in charge of the world."

"Organizations don't have to be secret to manipulate. Governments create allies; they create foes. The System and our plans require the rise and fall of both. The System uses causes for the human psychosis to fit into for further control nicely, and uses access to celebrities and sex to distract."

"Causes?"

"Causes don't operate in a vacuum; they are tools that can be appealed to at any moment, tools to focus humans on notions of justice and rightness. They are platforms built from psychological tears. Every cause has a varying degree of psychosis—who exploits it first is what matters to The System.

"Each psychosis has a root, a stem, and a branch—the problem has always been the seed."

Devon presence was evidence that change was possible. The council could not deny that. They had to acknowledge the anomaly that was once Devon Heathrow. It was only fitting that he was here.

For months, anger and hate were sufficient motivators for Devon. He missed his family. His memories were broken, and he was as broken as any of them. Devon remembered his devolution and placed that indifference beside what he was feeling right now. For so long anger and rage were like old friends to him, comforting him. Those emotions were waning inside in him.

"Every time there is a chance to learn from history, you kind refuse. Every time there is a chance to retain your humanity, you prefer to lose it. Sooner or later, what is inside spills out. Not everyone can hear us, not everyone follows," said Prime.

"Why not?"

"Some people are simply driven by other forces. They work in the service of another power. The ones that just do things purely out of love we have no trouble with. The System has no problem anonymously vilifying, sickening, or causing people to disappear every day and no one notices. Even if it were reported, the incident would soon be erased from the memory of uncaring humans.

"Many times, what is perceived as racism is something much more complex, although racism makes it easier to define. Incarceration provides a sustainable industry while marking a certain individual. Today's thugs are yesterday's founding fathers; The System indoctrinates, enslaves, and eradicates all threats to it. Prisons are littered with leaders, enemies of The System.

"The System put in place false rules for partnership. It does not allow anyone to evolve beyond it, and any action against it was met with aggregated force, from the people within the system itself. Some people were aware enough to profit from it; others are completely oblivious to any overriding structure of control and are happy in their obliviousness.

"You have acknowledged that there are no good guys, no bad guys, just different brands. Every time you close your eyes, the nightmare is the same. And every time you open your eyes, as the screams and cries fade, you realize your family isn't coming back. The only way to be with them is to be tormented by the vision of their death…

"Your life will never be what it was. Don't for a moment think that we are the only ones in this room that know what it is like to be solely fueled by one moment!"

"Humans aren't perfect, we are perfectly human. We are always trying to fix the inequities for the benefit of all."

"The only thing you will do is have the masses hoping for a miracle when science has stolen all the miracles."

"We'll charge the finest minds; we'll come up with computer models. We can get everyone involved."

Perhaps, Devon's survival was the reaction of the collective human spirit, and it was that which allowed him to be revived. It was that spirit that sustained him, even now. The Faces now sat upright; as Devon saw the past, present, and the end of the future. His presence was the seed of the highest hope.

Perhaps, this plan was just one of many plans, one of many forces pulling and tugging at humanity. If people could not understand the present, what hope was there for the future? Even if humans were to change, Prime said it was too late.

"People are too busy going viral to understand that virility is our best indicators of defect," Prime said. "Computers don't calculate for human frailty. Your kind will celebrate as they gloriously waste their time creating computers that think. Technology only modernizes warfare; it does not end man's thirst for it.

"Your deadbeat cousins want to create machines that are substitutes of human interaction. In this way, human selfishness goes about unchecked. Why else would The System need petaflops, not for the people? For us, the benefit of technology is the access it provides; to The System, technology is the perfect Trojan horse.

"You have programmed devices to detect every pattern except your own. You want these devices to see what you cannot, to feel what you don't, and to hear what you've missed. How can you predict your own errors, your own frailties when the possibility is beyond you? Humans built it, programmed it, and humans thought it up, so it is perfectly flawed.

"They will continue to create. These creations provide them with a small doorway to look through until they can purchase the next product. Lights, sounds, styles, and multiple functionalities are nothing more than a mobile in the crib of a baby, a mobile that is replaced every so often.

"In the end, the baby is still in the crib with their diaper full. As the baby grows, they are mentally squeezed out empty like a tube of toothpaste. They were too young, too helpless to prevent it, and now their emptiness allows them to be filled with various indoctrinations."

"The System maybe indoctrinating people and manufacturing terror, but humans have done amazing things when we all pull together. You can help us pull together ideas and make real progress."

"How comforting first world self righteousness must be. The arrogance should sicken even you. If we all somehow banded together, how long would it be before humans eventually turn on Them?"

"In our space, materials are composed of molecules. Below the molecular level atoms, nuclei, protons, neutrons, electrons, quarks, and the smallest particles known to humans, neutrinos, which are still, far away from the smallest particles that exist. Isn't the scene of electrons rotating around the nucleus similar to that of the Earth rotating around the sun?

"On its own, that indicates an order, a structure on the most unseen level. Order and purpose exist even if they existed as only mathematical equations.

"We are more than amino acids clumped into proteins with DNA and RNA. In our bodies, there is an unfathomable distance between each atom. What is it that keeps us solid? Why don't we break apart?

"We don't break apart because we are special. We are beyond mathematical equations. I have seen the destruction you've sown. I have been a victim of it! You can't just launch things off into space as if no one will see."

"Arrows are shot into space all the time, and no one notices. Most planets have life on them. You couldn't detect our presence; how can you think of detecting the presence of life elsewhere. Your kind shuns the kinship of all living things; even your peacekeepers lead with violence. The continued existence of your kind is abuse.

"We don't view people as lines, targets, or blips on a timeline, we see all people as connected. Unlike humans, we value everyone and their contribution to this plan."

"A plan they know nothing of. A plan that they wouldn't agree with if they did know of it."

"You say that as if people are aware and agree with all of the plans around them now. Often, there are unintended consequences from what we do, your presence being one."

"You say that as if using natural catastrophes to kill people and being unseen tormentors to change thoughts is a noble endeavor."

"What you call torment is merely a sleepless dream, a gentle breeze that shuts a door, or rustled papers. Losing your keys is something humans forget two minutes after they are found, but that two minutes could mean the difference between having a date with destiny or a mundane day.

"The System's reach is beyond buttons on suit or stars on a shoulder The System is beyond countries and borders, beyond months on a calendar. It has no such notions as morning or night. Every now and then The System allows things to go haywire, just to remind people how much they need it.

"There are many systems, but only one System, and it doesn't deserve to be defended."

Heated whispers rose from The Faces. Prime's words hung in the air, thick and unyielding. It was a death sentence for this world, and Devon knew it. Prime knew it. The Faces knew it.

Devon's eyes followed Prime, noting the way he reacted. Prime wasn't sorry about any of it. Were it not for some kind of respect, Prime would have foregone this formal hearing and slit Devon's throat where he stood. If it wasn't clear before it was clear now that this was not a moot court, this was the real thing. Devon was brought here to defend humanity.

"Your attempt to make me feel ashamed for my actions is a useless one," Devon said.

Devon lowered his head as a hologram of various shootings, bombings, and uprisings played out in front of him.

"All of this is to fool the public…?" Devon wondered aloud.

"These things are done to manage perception. They are done to stunt logic and common sense. Often, reality and imagery are not the same. If the mind is blind, then so are the eyes. The longer you stayed away, the less The System had influence over you. The System uses control, and you were outside of that control."

"So complete control is the goal?

"No."

"What is the goal?"

"Chaos."

"Chaos. Why? For what purpose?"

"Because nothing motivates the human mind more pure than chaos. The human mind needs things to fix, so it creates problems where none may exist.

Without chaos, what would humans do? Humans cannot thrive without chaos; they cannot push themselves without chaos.

"What would people do without their vices? Humans, kill for sport, greed, envy, expansion, boredom."

"It is The System that consumes people."

"And who are the creators of that system. Layer upon layer, upon layer upon layer, upon layer, upon layer, upon layer, upon layer of blood is on human hands. Humans always talk of equality, but to humans, equality is another form of superiority. Inside of every man is the beast, the darkness of man. If given a choice, even a false choice, they would still choose The System.

"His kind has cut a blood path through this age with little effort and much joy. They have squandered billion of chances." Prime said as he waved his hand to the elevated enclosure.

"And you intend to cure the earth of humans?" Devon retorted. "I am not saying that I haven't wondered why we sacrifice our lives for lost causes, why we cheat our friends, why we reward our enemies, why we go to war, why we build machines in the hope of correcting our flaws, why we lie to those they love, why we forgive... This story-within-the-story is a brutal allegory about the worst natures of men..."

"Yes...and yours is a tale of terror, survival and revenge...right."

"Right..."

"You society is built on pushing...pushing victimization, pushing platforms, pushing powerlessness. People have turned themselves into legacy victims. They furiously live out their lives with the hope that the world would retain the smallest remembrance of their efforts.

"Meanwhile, we will continue to fight against The System here. We will prevent mankind's sickness from spreading. This sickness has done so much damage to our genes that our kind is unable to leave this planet."

"Them will die..."

"Yes... Soon there will be no elders, and we will die off. Therein is our sacrifice. You view free will as an agent of the rational, but free will is simply a course of action that humans select from among various alternatives. In this way, free will is a subset of willings.

"The System would have humans enslave the sister world and call it a partnership, so don't lecture us on the merits of what we have undertaken. The System makes deals in back alleys and breaks deals in public. The System cradles it's chosen, it supports them, it front- pages them.

"The System will hide every flaw, every weakness, and every vice until you are no longer needed. The System makes laws it knows will be broken by those it needs to break them.

"The System has people write reports against their neighbors and friends. The System directs actions against its own. The System uses industry against people. The System uses children against parents and brother against brother. The System uses electric waves to control your thoughts and actions. The System's only goal is survival.

"With growing power and no supervision, we will not allow you to walk out of here and to continue doing what you have been doing…"

All Devon really wanted to do was sleep and forget, but he could do neither. He knew a threat would come, but the threat that came only agitated. Devon's demise could have come from behind while walking the corridor, but it didn't. The pretense of civility that seemed necessary had now been erased.

"What would your wife and child have wanted?"

"They would have wanted to live!"

Prime made a gesture with his hand, and holographic images of Devon's wife and daughter appeared in front of him. Devon tried to touch Sarah, and her image turned into smoke. At his core, a deep sense of emotions ran through Devon.

Even when he could block out the dreams of his family, he could still see the bloody faces and hear the low screams of the people who have died because of him.

"Devon, you don't have to die," Prime said, and then he looked over his shoulder into the far corner of the chamber. In this corner, a dimly lit figure stood. This figure's coat had moving red lights, but the look on Devon's face was one of familiarity.

"You remember Him don't you…"

Devon quickly advanced towards Him, with anger in his heart. Him's silver eyes never left Devon. Devon abruptly stopped as he got close to Him. The tension in the room rose like a draft coming up from under a door. There was silence as Devon's eye pulsated golden.

"You're the guy who killed me…" Devon had killed Him a thousand times, in a thousand different ways in his mind. He had every intention of using his abilities to exact revenge.

"I saw love in my wife's eyes. I heard love in her voice when she laughed. I felt the love when my daughter called me daddy, and you took that from me! You took my family from me!"

"We were just following orders…"

Devon let out a yell that rattled the crystal ceiling. The durability of his cells, the pliability of his skin, the bubbling green liquid, whoever he may have been before… didn't matter… this is who he was now.

His life had been forever altered by people just following orders. It was because of Prime that Devon was other than human. It was because of Prime that Devon's wife and child were dead. It will be Prime's orders that will cause destruction to the world.

Devon wanted to rip this whole place apart because of Prime. It was because of Prime that Devon had died, it was also because of Prime that Devon lived.

"Prime, I am here now because of you! I know what you are trying to do, and it won't work." Devon slowly turned away from Him and walked back to the center of the chamber.

"Is that all you've got?"

"These aren't survivalist, contractors, or some extreme hikers. Are you so arrogant to think that you could fight Them along with your own fears and common sense?"

"I dispatched half a dozen of these weathermen of yours, it wasn't difficult. I'll fight them all if I have to!"

"Commotion and Destruction await you outside," said Prime as he flipped four golden seals no bigger than a quarter on his sash.

"As do Eruption, Lightning, Chaos, and Confusion?" Devon swallowed hard and said, "I'll do what I have to do."

"You've come all this way just to die…"

Prime waved his hand, and the walls of the glacier became transparent. Outside of the glacier electricity arced out of the largest rift Devon had seen. From this rift stepped the feet of Prime's best equipped acolytes, growling and stretching their bodies like long sleep beast. Each one larger than the next, Prime wasn't playing for a draw.

"I see Them," Devon said. Devon realized two things. One, humanity's survival required courage he did not know if he possessed, and two this was the longest conversation he had in a quite some time. The thought that taking on Them single handedly sounded like suicide.

Devon was close enough to make good use of his abilities to at least try to end Prime's life. The thought had entered his mind a half a million times. He was capable of many things, but would he be able to prevent the destruction of humanity. Instead he looked at Prime not sure of what to do next.

"You will also need to defeat the choices inside of people; the darkness that lives inside of people?" Prime said.

The strands, streams, and drops that made up the universe all struck Devon in the middle of the chamber, and he felt naked. He could see now that Diablo, the devil, Shaitan, Angra Mainyu, Baal Davar, The Tempter, The Wicked One— The System…was none other than human nature.

"What you are talking about isn't fate, or destiny…this is a choice. How can you have faith in a plan, when there are so many questions? People exert control over their own actions, even if that control is reasoned from a weakly reason-responsive mechanism.

"I believe that we view events through necessary outcomes. We draw from the events that have happened in the past. It is our introspective conviction that tells us that we are in control of our choices. We control our destiny; we are free to think and free to decide."

The Faces looked puzzled, and Prime's usual sneer was replaced by something that could be called a blank stare.

# CHAPTER 25

To Devon, the halcyon days were over as far as Them were concerned. Utopia by force was the plan. He stood there, here, in this chamber knowing that the judgment was theirs.

"You will always be presented with new information. You have seen that the foreign aid payments are really for permission to operate, by violent means if necessary, in that nation. You have seen nation leaders place its own citizens on a list for other nations to kill, only to stop the rise of challengers.

"In between your fits of crying, you've seen humanity's true face."

Given time, Prime might have admired people. Prime wasn't so much preaching to the choir as he was propagandizing to the captive. Devon would rather be listening to a raging river than Prime's sermon.

"Who decides? Who gets to choose? Who are you to alter our destiny?" Devon said.

"This is your destiny… cataclysm approaches."

"Accidents happen all the time. I think we'd be told if some catastrophe were going occur…"

"Why would they tell you?"

"You don't know what people are capable if left alone."

Devon didn't know how to state a case for humanity that even he could believe. If The Group expected for humans to give up quietly, without a whimper. They were sorely mistaken. The choice was to fight these invaders while trying to stop the world from being populated by all the horrors from the human psyche.

Prime was burdened with this purpose. Devon searched Prime for compassion, but he hadn't discovered any. Devon was the first human to set foot here. It should have been an honor, but it wasn't. Things were now worse than he imagined.

"Do you want to spend the rest of your days without love?"

Devon mistook the package, and he mistook otherworlders for humans. Errors had been made from that first encounter to perfecting his battle stance. This was really the only war, worth fighting. In the end, only choices remained, not answers.

He had been called there to account for human mistakes. He had no idea of how extensive all of this was. How long he had been gone? In all probability, his memory of Sarah was wrong.

"I was resurrected...." Devon asserted, knowing that even the best defense was but a feeble effort to prolong the evitable.

A new set of images populated the screens. On the screen, millions of people were huddled together in the midst of giant flames, explosions, ground shaking, swirling winds and lightning; the most terrible destruction imaginable. Them weren't whispering they were maiming, killing, and unleashing energy in the most exquisite fashion.

Devon had never seen this level of destruction. Planetary mistreatment, Genocide, unlawful colonization, mass murders, war crimes, the creation of abominations, scientific malfeasance... The human race had earned every horrific indictment. The screens faded, and Devon fell to his knees.

"I'm so sorry...I'm so sorry...I never agreed to this,"

"You agreed by remaining. The Faces will be fair and impartial in this proceeding."

"Am I being punished for something?"

"You are being rewarded."

"With what ... a pardon for my crimes...

"Opportunity..."

"Maybe people are all just poorly written characters."

"We are sending Genesis to furthest reaches of space because the point of restabilization was passed long ago. Wherever there is corruption, where there is despair, wherever there is strife, persecution...The System thrives. Sometimes appearing as a spectator, a face in the crowd...it is there...and it won't reboot itself.

"You are a witness that has been places no one has. A witness that has returned from places no others will. A witness that has seen and heard what no one has. A witness that has experience things no one else could. A witness that has felt things no one else could, a witness of unique value, an expert.

"And you would go back island massage parlors and a destroyed electoral process. Back to where madness and sanity are one."

Devon was now certain of Prime's madness, and there was no pill for it. Sarah's questioning of the universe began with "How is Santa going to get in without a chimney?" and it never stopped. Devon's questions only began a year ago. He always thought he didn't belong, but now through Prime's words, he believed more than ever that he did.

"Otherworlders roam our spaces, never once thinking to change minds and heart. We can do nothing about the past, but we can do something about the future. Maybe this time, this time we'll learn.

"And yes, I want to go back to neatly trimmed bushes along the driveway," Devon said carefully. "Back to a time before the panic produced by the humming, back before I had to brave air and ocean currents, back to a time before vengeance, before the unimaginable.

"Wherever there is intelligent life, there will be a system. And that system will survive by giving parishioners what they need, maybe even as far as tricking them into thinking that they need it."

"You with your life changing gifts would go back to lying in geothermal nodes, solving cold cases, and telling ghost stories at campfires?"

"I was a part of something meaningful; you took that away from me! You think you have taken all of the randomness out of existence, but you haven't..."

"Friday the 13th... Number 7 being lucky, beginner's luck...all us..." Prime said, moving closer to the screens. He made the images larger, then smaller by moving his hand. "In Hebrew, we were called Malakh. In Latin, Greek, Babylonian, and every one of your ancient cultures we are depicted as warriors and guardians...

"We are not something dogma invented. When humans needed hope, we give them that," he asserted. "When you lose your conscience, we became your conscience. We are your opportunity. We are your gentle and not so gentle, reminders and when the time calls for it—we are the fear."

A wave on nausea hit Devon. "There is no course on grace, no class on mercy, no Masters on being transformed. What are we to do with distorted hope?" Devon managed to say.

"It's only now that you truly understand that most of your friends silently prayed for your demise. The System specializes in discord, indecision, confusion, and fear. The System turns people and animals into commodities;

it is rigged against someone like you. The System is too brutal to feed it your ambitions of a global insurgency."

"Nevertheless, The System has helped build nations…making my kind as much victim as victimizer."

"You want to believe that regardless of their debilitating provincialism, that there is a deep quality in people capable of overriding their open act of profound selfishness, there isn't. We are the voice of reason. You won't be able to dance away from the edge of the abyss this time…" Prime said, shaking his finger at Devon.

Prime threatened no less than four checkmates, and there's no way Devon could sidestepped them all. It was Devon's move.

"I never set out to be this," Devon started. "Humanity is at our best when we throw ourselves passionately into the unknown. The System will run down hope, but still, we will preserve. I have been all over the Earth. I have seen human failure; I have seen human triumph. We can create a place where fantastic things occur, even as an imagined shared place that we can fill with other options…

"You see, saving humanity is a worthy cause, but the prospect of saving oneself is an idea humans can get behind. Called it an accident, fate, or dumb luck, but we are here, we are at this moment."

"The System will manufacture the flirtations between science and faith, the hand holding and the kissing. It will cause the dominant culture to view the minorities among them as insurgents. It will exhaust itself with manipulations of your iconography because it knows that your barbarity knows no end. And when your kind runs out of excuses for their behavior, they'll turn to guilt."

"You cannot chase me from continent to continent, maim, and murder without becoming something monstrous yourself. Them and The System are different sides of the same murderous coin…."

"How dare you!" Prime said his voice echoing the chamber. The silver in his eyes was showing. "We tried to keep you civilized for as long as we could…we slowed down the demise of man."

Devon felt some sense of responsibility and a sense of culpability. He was the proof of a flaw in the plan. Devon knew that whatever the plan was it could not have calculated for him. Devon was the X in the equation, the unknown.

A human walking this great hall, a human killing Them was a first. Any judgment that did not lend itself to leniency couldn't be just. As far as Devon was concerned, as long as he continued to fight for humanity, a part of him would always be human.

The why of it all entered his mind again, and a hot tear fell from his cheek. He had not been called here for this monster to monster talk. He was here to answer for man's crimes. He was summoned to answer one question: Were humans worthy of being saved?

"Here you are inoculated against compassion, showing me images and judging as if you had no hand in these fatalities…"

"Isn't judging others what your kind is best at…there is a jury selection taking place in every mind around the world."

"Who decides who lives and who dies… you Prime, these faces?

"We do more than make balls bounce on rims and bobble in hands. When decisions have to be made, we make them. When risks have to be weighted, we weight them. We make the choices, we do the guiding. You look at us on this side as a place. We are more than a place, we are a people, but we don't decide anything, people choose.

"Soon they will reap the pitfalls of what they have chosen. Hereto we are the executors of that fate."

"There's nothing redeemable about this…nothing! These people are dead!"

"Are humans redeemable?"

"I have to believe that we are. I have to believe that people can be convinced to change. We have to change the story we tell ourselves."

"And you want to go to this irrational, unprincipled, violent, tyrannical being that is foe to all dignified life and take down their church, their school; their pride; their commerce; their law; their arts and all of their work over something you will have no evidence and no proof of? "

"They won't be afraid of us, they'll fear you. You will be celebrated one day and considered a villain the next; if The System writes you that way…" As Prime spoke the screens filled with images of a darker world.

The surface of the world was largely covered by red earth and oceans of green water. Temples of light and large dendrite panels dominated the sprawling metropolises. On the clean streets, citizens went about their business of pushing forward in technology and culture. In the skies, were crafts of every description and size zooming along.

Inhabitants of this world peacefully lived their lives with a glowing ball of fire thundering in the distance. As Devon watched, yellow, rain like embers began falling on the populace and blackened pools formed on the ground…screams were everywhere.

"What about Themasarians?" Prime said. "What about the humans who have chosen to help us, do you loathe them as well? Your legislators have been bought, your electorate irrevocably divided. What of the wealthy that utilize awareness and knowledge of something as petty as money to control the populace? Where is your contempt for them? You curse me when you should be giving me a medal."

Yellow rain burned through dolls and toys were strewn about the black sand, plants disintegrated from view, never seen before sea creatures were in distress and small beings lay unmoving in pristine streets. Lightning rifled through the background…

The images showing on the walls were quite terrifying, Devon couldn't look away. Them had a legitimate gripe.

"I can't believe this!" Devon said, lowering his eyes.

"None of this is about what you believe. You chide us when humans right now are making efforts to isolate memories and thoughts in endeavors to change the valiance, to create human facsimiles, soulless beings, to create lifeless wombs as if life isn't already perfect… and they won't stop.

"You rally against us while watching humans day in and day out trying to convince each other that their deviancy is normal. You watch people digitally distribute their lives, pretending that they don't live in ruins…and you say that we have lost our humanity.

"Go ahead and tell them that the world is ending and watch them go about rooting out the undesirables. Shouldn't humanity strive for the best existence possible, not just this existence?"

The otherworlder called Thunder announced his arrival in a deafening fashion as the glacier violently shook again. The Faces flickered with the intensity of the shaking. Devon no longer held murderous thoughts in his head.

"When we are desperate, on the brink, that is when people find the will to change. Your agents once whispered in an ear, and a nation landed on the moon in fourteen years. If the public can be sold bottled water, they can be sold this." Devon said.

"We are not here to fight your battles. The System doesn't want peace or sanity? Conflict helps it grow. It doesn't want cures. It wants the growth of industry. While people are chasing the solution, The System will strengthen its weaknesses. That's what it does, that's all it does."

"At what point does reason override common sense? Can an experience be real without being provable?"

"Not to people. Artificial lines in society are the only form of human sympathy. There is no justice, only law. The System spreads the infection, the human infection. Whatever you're afraid of; The System will find a way to scare you with it. People are too frightened to leave their own thoughts, fearful to leave the comforts of The System.

"Once they see what you can do, you'll be the villain. The ones you think will assist you will become systemic agents that will have everyone convinced that you are an enemy of the state.

"Would you sacrifice yourself?"

"I have already died once, and the world needs to know," Devon said, remaining defiant.

"And you are going to be the one to tell them. You are going to be the one to lead them…you."

"…You're afraid of me, all of you. That's why I'm here. You are afraid that if one human can truly change they all can change."

Prime interrupted. "Now you want to be the savior? What are you going to do, who are you going to be when the whole world is watching?

"Devon, The System will not indict itself. You cannot expect different results from the same system.

The purpose behind what a person claims to be truth is to establish a relationship of control between the knowable and the unknowable. Reason and faith are complementary, maybe there is no truth, either in faith or reason maybe both are irrelevant once you have what you need.

"Even if people can't be saved, they have the right to know. You can't doubt the chambers of the human heart or the spirit within a being. All of this time, humans have been on trial, and I am the one charged to defend it…" Devon said, addressing The Faces.

"When our backs are against the wall, we are at our best. Our backs have never been against a wall like this! You can't doubt the human spirit, the human soul. I urge these face to look in Prime's eyes, he feels it too.

"You may have walked beside us, but without love for us, you were as distance as any universe. If you give us one last chance, I promise that you'll see something that no one has ever seen before—a United Mankind for all to see. The human heart wants to evolve, people are still good. We will do better. This is the only chance worth taking."

Around Devon, within the shadows, there was more mumbling.

"All of this is highly improper…," Prime stated.

These otherworlders had occupied large chunks of prime real estate in Devon's mind. His mind had suffocated all other thoughts, except rage. The charges spoke for themselves, and Devon knew there would be no petition, no motions, and no way to enjoin this ruling

Devon no longer felt small as he slowly paced. "We had to do certain things to thrive, to survive." Devon said as he addressed The Faces. "I was a helpless witness to murders, but no more. I have gone from being afraid to seeking revenge, to being called in front of you.

"We dance over bubbly drinks, and rock music blares when we grab steering wheels. We console ourselves with notions that our want to know supercedes individual privacy.

"Our entertainers sing happy songs and star in comedies, but their happiness came from what they drunk, snorted, injected. It was what they did outside of the studio, when the cameras were off that gave them the ability to entertain us in extraordinary ways.

"And we deride the special treatment these people received, even though we are the ones ho provided the special treatment. We demand that entertainers be held accountable by law enforcement and then we complain about the sober products that follow.

"Daily, we pray and reveal rumors and innuendoes about these people, and then we demand public apologies from people who have proven themselves to be only human. We never issues condolences, we just move on. We have wasted all of this time finding ways to hate…no more.

"I was one of those that wanted entertainers to be philosophical, genius, sober, a good parent, a leader, and moral. I was one who believed, who provided tax dollars and didn't care who got hurt.

"I made it through the grave treks and dark valleys. I have outlasted people. I have taken on Them. I have changed so much I don't know what I am anymore. I have forgotten much and learned little, but the one thing I have discovered is that vengeance destroys the avenger.

"I should know because I have spent this ghastly year with the fallen, the corrupt, the damaged and I still can't tell you: Why we cheat our friends, why we reward our enemies, why we sacrifice our lives and the lives of others for lost causes, why we build machines in the hope of correcting our flaws, why we forgive, why we defy logic and the laws of nature by our acts of compassion— We are flawed creatures.

"In an act of calculated desperation, you invited me here because you wanted to correct a mistake. The mistake is caused by the human brain being in conflict with a legal system that tries to coerce it into something it has not accepted or agreed to. The religion of psychiatry labels these actions, and The System sanctions fictitious diseases. Humans are pre-programmed with a form of mental illness from the moment we registered as citizens.

"Simply by being born, they have signed contracts with the nation state, The System. People and their attempts to fight or flee are viewed as illegitimate by their peers. My presence here, outside of the whole, shows that there is no consent, to begin with. It is nature that people try to escape or fight the constant coercion that they face as citizens under The System.

"Humans have not always lived under conditions where their peers were more loyal to a nation state than to each other. The word legal derives from the word loyal, and the human brain is designed to select peers loyal to them and not to this superorganism. The System forces a set of laws on everyone, removing the ability to question it.

"Humans are unique creatures; they don't care if the roads are fixed, if hospitals are good, if schools are teaching or if housing is adequate. They just want to know that their most base fears are shared and that they are right. They broadcast life with preconceived notions; they require permission to like a particular person and never run out of psychoses, but inside of every human is a spark.

"Prime has stated the truth, all of it. I don't deny any of it, but we are so much more...and that's what's scares you. You see what you could never be, human.

"Were it not for this spark I couldn't be standing here before you. It is this spark you have watched within me. We, humans, have made it a habit of defying the odds.

"Together, we can creates something stronger than right and wrong; stronger than belief; stronger than love, we can create hope. As such I request that you give me one final chance to create this hope..."

Devon stepped back, and Prime moved forward.

"Nineteen gunned down in thirty minutes," Prime started. "Mosques shot up, theaters shot up, daycares shot up, school children murdered, yet people went right on eating their cornflakes. If people were really concerned about eavesdropping they would be more careful about what comes out of their mouths.

"The witness has admitted that many times he loathed his kind. He stands there defending the strained idiocy of people tooth and nail, but there is a lack of conviction in his voice. Devon, you have put on a great show, a valiant effort, but the truth has provided you with no case.

"Your honors he said himself that people work hard to save themselves, but they won't do so to save the species. By his own admission, he has testified that his kind will cling to flawed constitutions and rights forged by compromise.

"Devon, you give people the benefit of the doubt, when all they deserve is doubt. People think they are smart because they know that the world is round, lightning is electricity, time and space are relative, and that atoms are composed of protons, neutrons, and electrons. The average human has only a vague notion; these things were even figured out.

"If people weren't taught these things by authority figures as a child and conditioned to accept them by their widespread use as facts in movies and television, they could have been easily led to believe something else entirely. The things they think are apparent are only obvious because of how they were taught. Your species intelligence is collective, not individualistic, and definitely not special.

"Ladies and gentlemen of the jury, Devon is an exception. He, by his own testimony, has witnessed man's crimes. Again, by his own admission, we have learned that humans do not want to wake up to the knowledge that they weren't what this planet intended or that they are not the center of all things. And now he wants to tell these beings our plan.

"These are the same beings that preemptively murdered and aborted the innovators, the curers, the leaders. These beings want; they crave the new and improved. They want death in the most horrible of fashions. Their appetite for violence knows no bounds. They kill not because of needs, they kill because of wants, and he thinks they'll feel safe knowing we exist.

"They allow The System to grab babies in their crib and assault them before they are born, with technology. The System has created beings with conformity coerced by corrupted consent. Beings that will only perceive the most literal, visible, surface qualities of a given thing.

"These people applaud their forefathers for crafting a society not for them to be adults in but for them to behave like infants in. Their society places people in positions of power, not in positions of control. It gives them only enough to do what The System needs to survive and spread.

"After appearing thirty thousand years ago, people are so intelligent, so enlightened that they consistently quote two-thousand-year-old dead people to justify their current mind state; and he is going to tell these killer apes, they are inferior.

"Humans apply their guilt and shame to one person, one organization hoping that will absolve them…but it never does. These sex-positive, sex-negative, shirtless beings don't know how good they had it.

"Esteemed Council, I have detailed mankind's crimes and charges through a thorough examination and numerous exhibits. Even our hostile eyewitness has testified that humans have been grossly negligent in its stewardship of this planet. I implore you to weigh the evidence before and see that man is not a victim. Man chose this path…"

As Prime spoke the light of hope dimmed in Devon's eyes. The only thought left to digest was—What if we are all wrong?

"These people spend everything they have, devote their entire existence to taking every cream, ointment, and pill trying to defeat father time. And, when they are on their deathbed, they can't even tell you why they did it.

"Look at how happy they are about their toothpaste choice, their fragrances, and cell phone plans— and he wants us to trust… these creatures… These are people that wear crosses to keep their demons internal. People can't be trusted. We can only trust in Them.

"I have seen the horrors people do," Devon said.

"Exactly and you have admitted to all of these things…"

"Yes."

"And you concede that if your kind where in our position they would respond with levels of skepticism and incredulity that would make ours pale by comparison…"

"Yes."

"So withdraw your plea that people can change…"

"I… I can't because I now know that we are a part of something that is greater than ourselves, that we are not now and have we ever been alone, that more than hope, people need faith and you all now know that people can change."

"You could reveal all of this to the sellers of sex, the liars, the thieves, the corrupt, the morally bankrupt, the diseased, the infected, the reapers. The good believe that they are good without ever considering the possibility of their goodness being just another kind of evil,"

As Prime spoke, terrifying displayed on the walls.

"I remember the first time the yellow rain hit my flesh." Prime said Walking towards the enclosure, "I remember the screams that rang out through the night. Do you remember it? Whether it was th rain, the skin peeling, the black pools, or the deaths... those that have gathered here have had similar experiences.

"We are a sisterhood, a brotherhood, a people, a mixture of backgrounds in solidarity, bonded by every nuclear detonation, by every act of human aggression. He dares to compare Them to people!

"We have fought our way through the darkness, with blood, sweat and radiation stripped down our faces. We go to bed knowing that today we made this world better than it was. Can his kind say the same?

"Listen to him. His love for those that would do us harm, drips from his every word. Human! Humans aren't even good at being human. Does he give us credit for their accidental discoveries, fortuitous bounces, lucky catches, near misses and close calls. No! Does he thank us for the millions of times people ran faster, jumped further, scored higher, and knew more? No!

"He doesn't acknowledge the occasions when people were shoved out of the way or were somehow saved from certain death. Nothing is said about the stopped incursions or protected artifacts...not one word... Yes, Devon may be an exception, but he is still human."

Prime spoke with a kind of corporate Kremlinology that would rightly take the place of criticism in assessing the substance and tone of any intention. His cape flapped behind him as he walked back and forth in front of The Faces.

Prime's closing argument continued, "Whether trenchcoats or battledresses our mindsets are in uniform. These horrors have brought us together. We are joined by our sacrifices and by our love for each other. We found purpose.

"We gather around the world, all that you see here was formed from the premise that humans won't stop their villainy. It's a shame because there are far too many of us who will never see the sun again.

"Instead of running from the rifts, we boldly entered them with the expectations that our offspring could be born without fear. This has been a lengthy trial that has painted the human race's villainy with ample strokes. We've invested too much time and effort into this project. We've come too far just to throw it all away.

"We have all seen the systemic denial of individual liberties, the forced abortions, the regimes of censorship, the thought controllers, the occupiers and incursioners, the sponsors of violence, the neighbor threateners, and those unable to see outside of their psychosis.

"We watched your cleavage bearing bodies bounce around the planet, destroying everything they touched like they were a child's building blocks. These digital human clones destroy like the next hundred years isn't right around the corner. Look at these sapiens as they scramble from one deal to the better deal, who has their eye on the planet? We do.

"It's buying futures, selling futures, when there is no future. All of them, with their eyes wide open; have run to this future. Everyone his kind thinks they can double penetrate this planet while using their virtual keyboard to post something they can't take back.

"When the air thickens, the water sours and honey takes on the metallic taste of radioactivity; that's when it will all hit home! To man, Mathematics is not the universal language, violence is. Why didn't minimum safe distance apply to our world? No...

"They haven't paid their dues; they lack respect, and now it's too late to cash out. Their stomachs are too full, their holes are too sore, their eyes are bloodshot, and they'll be crying out for someone to help...but guess what? No one will be there.

They'll be all alone. He thinks that these people are special... I can't feel for humans. God didn't let your kind down; it is your kind that let God down. This...this is the way the world ends." Prime said as he approached The Faces.

"All of human history has led us to this... I rest my case on behalf of the tens of millions intentionally murdered." The lights on Prime's coat flashed as if it were a gavel. He turned to The Faces and said "of lies...of murder...of malice... What say you all?"

Light expanded on each Face as they rendered an answer. "Guilty... Guilty... Guilty..." each shadowed voices rang out like a monstrous wind, with the roar of a long forgotten mighty beast.

Prime turned to Devon and said: "We find the human race...."

"Guilty," echoed the voices in unison.

"Humans have been judged and will be relieved of their stewardship over this planet!" Prime stated. Prime's eyes widened as a single line slowly extended from him and connected to Devon.

"You, and I, We ...are connected...this line can't be erased." Devon said as his face displayed multiple attitudes simultaneously.

"We have found humans to be unworthy. Your women, your men, your children, your kind, humans, the human race spends all of its time formulating solutions that hide problems and creating medications that work so well people think they no longer need them.

"Look at these humans celebrating their creation of punishment before the act. Humans live without believing the words they say. They can barely conceptualize ideas in a limited spoken language. Every purchase they make is pledging allegiance to The System.

"Buy, sell, consume, smoke, drink, sex, steal, lie, and watch mindless drivel because they are afraid. Infections, infestations, pollutants, riots, violent, and death all created problems. Problems created by decadence, dogma and ritualistic veneers.

"What The System is able to do is made possible because of humans with their insatiable appetites for deceptions. Freedom is whatever you are told it is, fear. Privacy is fiction. The powerless are easily demonized for effect. Poverty is man-made. People are manufactured into existence.

"And even after hundreds of centuries, you are still sacrificing your children to your various gods. Heaven, hell, good and evil... created by man and the only thing bigger than man's ego is man's capacity for self deception. And then when all of this is over nothing will be found in the ashes..."

Devon had no way to stop all of the many threatened mates against the world, and he only had one nonsensical looking queen move that simply gave her majesty away for nothing, a miracle strike against the white king.

"I get it," Devon said. "We are not what this planet intended but this right here, right now is all we have, and this is all I have. This is my home. The only home I know. It's all I have left. The System does do all of these things, for the world's most prize resource...the people. Prime you asked me a question before, and I didn't give you an answer.

"You asked me if anything I did made a difference... Devon closed his eyes, and the floating displays flickered, and the chamber shook. The shaking glacier wasn't why The Faces looked worried. They were concerned because Devon managed to remotely access their quantum computer and was now controlling the viewing screens.

Devon's eyes were golden; the eyes that followed him were wider than ever. One screen showed Laura Washington entering a rehab facility. Another projection showed little Fernando Perez. He was eagerly raising his hand and answering questions in class. A white elephant guarded the corner of his desk.

Another image was Sunita Singh in a hospital room. The surgeons were taking the bandages from around her head. "I can see you, mama…" Her parents embraced their daughter, giving her a brand new Lego set.

Another screen showed Influence on a mission. Influence stared intently at her subject as he tossed and turned in his bed. Unexplain-ably, Influence stopped her connection. Her lighted dress went dark. She just stood there and then she jumped out of the window.

There were hundreds of images displaying the people Devon had pulled from underneath rubble, those he had saved. They were living, lovin, and thriving.

"I have heard your plan, I have seen it, but you couldn't have counted on me. Your plan couldn't have factored me. You have taken everything from me! Hope is all I have left. This last second chance begins with me.

"Because even with all of your planning, all the protocols, there is nothing that can be done to prepare for this type of journey…"

Prime turned, looked Devon in the eyes and said, "That's why we are sending you…"

The sound of thunder pushed out the silence the moment demanded.